# The Spy Who Wants Me

# The Spy Who Wants Me

## LUCY MONROE

**BRAVA**

KENSINGTON PUBLISHING CORP.

www.kensingtonbooks.com

BRAVA BOOKS are published by

Kensington Publishing Corp.
850 Third Avenue
New York, NY 10022

All Kensington titles, imprints and distributed lines are available at special quantity discounts for bulk purchases for sales promotion, premiums, fund-raising, educational or institutional use.

Special book excerpts or customized printings can also be created to fit specific needs. For details, write or phone the office of the Kensington Special Sales Manager: Kensington Publishing Corp., 850 Third Avenue, New York, NY 10022. Attn. Special Sales Department. Phone: 1-800-221-2647.

Brava and the B logo Reg. U.S. Pat. & TM Off.

ISBN-13: 978-0-7582-2915-1
ISBN-10: 0-7582-2915-1

First Kensington Trade Paperback Printing: January 2009

10  9  8  7  6  5  4  3  2  1

Printed in the United States of America

# Prologue

Whit, affectionately known as The Old Man by the agents of The Goddard Project, frowned while scrolling through the employee file of one of his top operatives. Elle Gray looked like a supermodel but was as deadly as a scorpion and probably a hell of a lot faster.

Naturally, it wasn't her job performance that had him scowling. It was the fact that in the last four years, the only vacation time she'd requested for a period longer than forty-eight hours had been to attend extra training camps for either hand-to-hand combat or weaponry. The female agent had a serious obsession with guns.

Every agent—make that every person really—needed balance in his or her life. Whit might have discovered that great truth later rather than sooner, but he had no intention of allowing his agents to be as blind as he'd been.

And Elle was as tunnel-visioned as they came. She spent little time with her extended family even though he knew she loved them. She didn't have a pet or friends outside of TGP. She rarely dated. And yes, intrusive as some might find his practices, he kept an eye on every aspect of his agents' lives, including dating.

The problem was, Elle didn't *have* a life outside her job.

The assignment in California was perfect for her. In more ways than one. A woman with her intelligence quotient wasn't going to be attracted long term to a man who wasn't similarly gifted. Unfortunately, in her line of work, the brilliant men she met were usually working on the wrong side of the law. This assignment would change that.

It was an opportunity for her to meet several gifted and forward-thinking scientists operating on the *right* side of the law. Maybe the woman with a degree in chemical engineering as well as certifications in more types of weaponry than most military sharpshooters would make some friends as well as find a man or two to date amid the employees of ETRD.

It wouldn't hurt for her to be assigned so close to her hometown, where her parents and grandmother still lived. Whit had a feeling her Ukrainian mother and grandmother would be excellent if unknowing allies in the matchmaking game.

# Chapter 1

Spinning on her three-inch spiked heel, Elle Gray lifted her leg and kicked her perp solidly in the gut.

The stocky, overly tattooed man, who looked more like a thug than the mastermind in one of the biggest acts of technological piracy to hit the East Coast in a decade, flew backward. Elle dropped into a fighting stance as Harley hit the wall with a thud, but he just kept sliding until he was nothing but an unconscious heap of cheap leather and ratty blue jeans.

Man, you'd think with all the money he had made on his nefarious dealings, the man could afford a few nice additions to his wardrobe.

Hadn't that been easier than she'd thought it would be? Apparently, dressing like a biker didn't mean a man had the fighting skills to last fifteen minutes in a seedy bar much less in a physical confrontation against her.

With a cynical twist of her lips, she dusted her hands off, and then smoothed down the fabric of her short, black Vera Wang dress. The perfect designer for a woman in Elle's profession. *If only Madame Wang knew.* Elle had been happy to discover that several items in the sexy line had been designed in a way to give a girl maximum movement. In her opinion, being a federal agent didn't mean she had to run around looking like a female version of the Men in Black.

Besides, she'd learned early that a heightened fashion sense coupled with the looks she'd gotten from her mother encouraged others to underestimate both her intelligence and her lethalness. Just as Harley had done.

As she looked at the ungainly mound the insensate man made, satisfaction coursed through her. Sometimes, it was nice to be underestimated.

Flipping open her phone, she called in the cleanup crew. If she hurried on the paperwork, she'd have a full week to relax before starting her new assignment in California.

As she shut the phone, her gaze snagged on the hand holding the cell—more specifically on the middle finger of that hand. Amusement turned to irritation and she glared at Harley.

As if he could feel her ire, he groaned and tried to move.

Examining the damage with annoyance, she ignored him. She'd broken a nail. *Well, fudge.* She'd just gotten a manicure too. This case had been one irritation after another, but this really irked her. It belied the simplicity of the collar.

She hadn't even broken a sweat taking the guy down, but she had chipped her nail and that was almost as bad as getting a substandard haircut. Elle might be a federal agent with a bad attitude and more than one black belt—not of the accessory variety—but she had her little vanities like anyone else.

Worse, the broken nail meant she had misjudged a hit. And *that* really pissed her off. It wreaked havoc with her perfectionist tendencies, making her wonder if she was off her game.

Harley chose that moment to try to crawl away. Elle growled.

Harley froze and then looked up at her with eyes still unfocused from his blackout.

"Going somewhere?" she asked.

He told her to do something anatomically impossible, if slightly intriguing. But she wasn't in the mood to be intrigued. Or pushed.

Without another word, she stalked over to him, crouched down and flipped him on his stomach with one smooth move. To the accompaniment of another not even remotely sexy male groan, she brought his wrists together and secured them with a zip tie.

"Bitch," he said with venom.

She frowned, considered and then shook her head. "I've always considered myself more of a cat person."

He turned his head and spat at her. Spat. At. Her.

Disgusting.

And he'd barely missed the perfectly shined black patent leather boots that added such lovely height to her five feet, ten inches. She reined in the urge to smack his head into the floor. She was not an animal. And he was a lucky SOB, no doubt about it.

But at this rate? She was going to be in a bad mood until next month, which was really going to mess up that week of relaxation she had planned.

Maybe she *should* go ahead and spend it with her family.

Dr. Beau Ruston looked down at the pictures in the dossier open on his mentor's desk. "She looks like a Russian super-model."

Man, did she. *Attractive* was too tame a word for the beauty with chin-length straight black hair and eyes such a clear gray they could be silver in the photos. Stunning might work. Captivating. Sexy as hell.

He couldn't remember the last time he'd been so caught by a woman's appearance. Full lips set in a perfectly shaped face looked both kissable and ideal for giving a man's cock the ultimate pleasure. His own was hardening at the mental image. And wouldn't his granny have had his guts for garters for thinking like that?

Thoughts of how his deceased grandmother would have reacted helped to dispel his growing arousal, but nothing would diminish his sense of awe at Elle's appeal. Almond-shaped eyes looked flat and deadly in one picture and full of mischief in another. He wanted to know what they would look like in the heat of passion.

Good night! Did he have a one-track mind, or what? He'd been accused a time or two, but not about sex—about being able to think of nothing but his projects. He'd had two serious relationships in his life and a handful of girlfriends. Every single one of them had complained about how he got caught up in his work, even the ones he'd dated from the company.

He'd never fantasized the kinds of things rolling through his mind right now about any of them during work hours. Yet this woman had him by the balls and wasn't letting go and these were mere pictures.

How the hell would he handle her in person? Maybe she would disappoint his libido and be no more exciting than one of his female lab techs. He had this really bad suspicion it would be the full damn opposite though.

"Ukrainian."

"Uh . . . what?"

"She's not Russian," his boss, Frank Ingram, said. "She's Ukrainian. Or rather, her family hails from there. She was born a U.S. citizen."

"Whatever. She looks way too beautiful to be a secret agent under cover as a security consultant." On top of her classic beauty, she was tall and willowy, with an innate sensuality that piqued his desire even through pictures not intended for that purpose.

"And you look like a pro football player, but you are one of the finest minds of this century."

"I was a football player. The two are not mutually exclusive."

"Nor are beauty and deadliness. As history has shown time and time again."

*Deadly* was right. The dossier said that Elle Gray was not only trained in mortal hand-to-hand combat but also a weapons specialist who could throw a knife an impressive distance with an accuracy of centimeters. On top of that, she had an impressive university degree.

"She's not all brawn; she's got brains too," Beau mused.

And that made her all the more dangerous as far as he was concerned.

"Yes," the older man said with obvious approval. "A degree in chemical engineering is no small feat even for the most dedicated student."

"Which will make it that much easier for her to accurately identify our projects," Beau replied. Was he the only one who saw a problem with that?

"No doubt that's why she was assigned to this particular endeavor."

"So, why are *we* letting her come?" Beau asked.

"Mr. Smith believes it's the best course of action," Frank answered as if that was all that needed saying.

"Obviously, but why?" Was it a case of keeping their friends close and enemies even closer?

"Our security was compromised."

"I'm aware of that," Beau replied. After all, it had been on his project.

"Mr. Smith believes we need to take measures to be certain that doesn't happen again."

"By bringing a spook in to spy on the company?" Beau was really starting to feel like he was operating on a whole different plane from his boss and the mysterious man who had started and continued to fund Environmental Technology Research and Design.

"Cover for her real job as a TGP agent, or not, Ms. Gray is in the top of her field."

"Security was compromised by a dirty guard. How can she prevent that from happening again?" It was a question that had haunted Beau ever since plans for the antigravity project had made it into the wrong hands.

"I have no idea. Security isn't my area of expertise. However, Mr. Smith believes she will be able to do that and more. Whatever measures she deems appropriate will no doubt be an improvement on what we have now."

Beau's gaze again flicked to the pictures spread out on the desk. Was she really that good? "We had our security set up by one of the best companies in California," he felt compelled to point out, even if it made him sound a tad defensive.

"Ms. Gray is considered the best both nationally and internationally. We are lucky to get her."

"She's a federal agent."

"She's also the best of the best at security design and consultation."

Something about what Frank said before niggled at Beau until he asked, "Her agency has international jurisdiction?"

Frank steepled his fingers in a familiar gesture. "Let's just say the CIA isn't the only federal agency with their fingers in extranational pies."

Beau shook his head. "Amazing."

He wasn't surprised that the government had black ops that the average, or even not so average, citizen didn't know about. What stunned Beau was how calmly Frank and Mr. Smith apparently accepted not only their existence but also their interference at ETRD.

"Mr. Smith is quite pleased we've managed to procure Ms. Gray's services."

"So you have said, but I find that hard to believe. She's coming in to spy on us on behalf of the government." Didn't that bother Mr. Smith and/or Frank even a little?

"It's not as if she works for the FBI or the military," Frank said, with a small shudder. "She's under the aegis of The Goddard Project. Truthfully, Mr. Smith was surprised it took them this long to show a material interest in what we're doing here at ETRD."

"The Goddard Project?" What the heck was that anyway? "I've never heard of them."

"Very few have. I'm not convinced that even every president has known of their existence."

"But Mr. Smith does?"

"He knows a great deal the rest of the world is ignorant of."

"How?"

Frank shrugged. "I make it a practice not to ask that particular question and suggest you do the same."

Beau couldn't help his curiosity about the enigmatic benefactor who had started ETRD. Frank was the only employee of ETRD who had ever met with the man in person. Though Beau had spoken to Mr. Smith on the phone, even that kind of interaction was kept at a minimum.

"But you *do* know what The Goddard Project is?" Beau asked.

"It's a black-ops agency with a dual directive of protecting technology from falling into the wrong hands and making sure our own government does not overlook potentially beneficial scientific breakthroughs. It was started after Robert Goddard's rocketry technology was stolen by the Germans during World War Two. Technology our own government had not only ignored but dismissed as unimportant. It wasn't just the egg on our faces when we interrogated a German prisoner of war only to find out that the scientific discovery had been made initially on our own soil, but the very real threat of them utilizing it against us that convinced the powers that be at the time that we needed to take measures to make sure that kind of thing never happened again."

"As much as I may dislike it, I can understand that. But I still don't get why you and Mr. Smith see being spied on by this highly secret organization as an improvement over falling under the scrutiny of any other federal agency."

Frank straightened the papers and photos into a neat pile and closed the file. Beau had to stifle the urge to protest his loss of the sight of the supermodel-gorgeous agent.

Something must have shown on his face because Frank looked at him strangely.

"You were saying?" Beau prompted.

"TGP only steps in if it's absolutely necessary. According to Mr. Smith, they've done a lot for research and technological development over the decades since the war."

"If he's so enamored of them, why not just make a report of our projects and turn it in to TGP?" Beau asked. Then they wouldn't have to send a woman whose very picture knocked his libido right on its ass.

"If we did that, we wouldn't be getting the services of Elle Gray." Frank gave a faint smile. "And it's the principle of the thing. If they want information, they can work for it. We're not a government-funded facility, and on our side or not, we aren't giving tacit approval to their oversight by providing a work manifest."

Beau's lips twisted with distaste. "Politics."

"Unfortunately, they are a part of life."

"It's a good thing we've got you to handle them around here then. Left up to me, we'd probably end up in World War Three."

Frank chuckled. "It wouldn't be quite that bad, I'm sure."

"Don't bet on it."

The older man shook his head but said nothing.

"So, what makes me so special that I get to know the true nature of Ms. Gray's work and the other eggheads around here don't?" Beau asked.

Frank frowned, looking troubled. "We can't be sure the dirty guard was working alone."

Beau had been worried about that very thing—when he should have been sleeping. "The coincidental departure of Bigoley less than twenty-four hours after you announced a security consultant was being brought in implies he wasn't."

"Perhaps." Frank put the file away in the safe behind his desk and then locked it. "Gil Bigsley's disappearance is suspect, of course, but was it voluntary? And was it related to the leak on your project, or something else?"

"Presumably, this TGP agent will figure that out."

"I believe that is Mr. Smith's hope, yes."

"You still haven't explained why you told *me* the truth, only why you haven't told anyone else."

Frank's smile was warm, reflecting his role as both friend and mentor in Beau's life. "You're not under suspicion."

"But the others are?"

Frank didn't answer, but he didn't need to.

"Why aren't I?"

"I could say because you are as close to me as a son."

"Would that be the truth?"

"For me, yes."

"But it wouldn't be enough for Mr. Smith."

"No. However, the fact that if you had been conspiring with Eddie, he wouldn't have set up his partners in the north to sell plans that don't work is quite compelling."

"My honor saved by the incompetence of the criminal mind."

"Your honor was never in question with me."

"I appreciate that, Frank."

"You're a good man, Beau, and Mr. Smith knows that."

"I would have said the same for my coworkers."

"So would have I . . . before. Now, we can't afford not to be cautious. Some of our projects are far too close to positive resolution for us to risk them falling into greedy hands."

"It's why we work here."

"That's definitely true for you . . . and hopefully the others as well, but we have no guarantees."

"Right. So, I'm supposed to keep an eye on Elle Gray?"

"Nothing too cloak-and-dagger, but yes."

"You do realize this is all just a little more James Bond than I ever thought I'd get."

"We play the cards we are dealt."

Beau relaxed back into the plush leather chair facing his mentor's desk. "Why do I get the feeling that Mr. Smith is dealing from the bottom of the deck?"

"Do you?"

"On occasion. Speaking of cloak-and-dagger, the man keeps himself well hidden."

"And that worries you?"

"Maybe."

"Believe me when I say that if Mr. Smith is dealing from the bottom of the deck, he is only doing it for our best interests."

"Or so he says."

"He doesn't have to say it. I know it. And while you may not know Mr. Smith, you do know me. Do you trust me, Beau?"

Tension filled Beau. Trust wasn't something he easily extended to others. He'd learned that just because circumstances dictated you should be able to trust someone didn't mean you could. In fact, it was the people closest to you who were most likely to betray you. They were the ones in a position to get away with it.

Yet Frank Ingram had proven himself worthy of both Beau's respect and trust many times. The older man accepted Beau for who he was in a way Beau's own family and other important people in his life had refused to do. Frank had never let Beau down in the close to a decade that they'd known each other. Not once. Not in any way. There could be only be answer to his mentor's question.

"Yes."

"Thank you."

Beau shrugged, having no desire to even flirt with the edges of maudlin emotion. Now, or ever.

Elle opened the door of her Lamborghini Spider and swung her long legs out. She could feel someone watching her, which was nothing new and certainly not unexpected considering her choice of transportation. But something felt different. Whoever was watching her was doing so with a regard so intense, it was palpable.

Interesting.

She paused, knowing the metallic burgundy paint job on the sports car did a fantastic job of framing her. That wasn't why she'd taken her week off between assignments driving her baby across country rather than flying and renting a car for her assignment, but it didn't hurt.

She stood in one fluid movement, then straightened the jacket of her Akris suit and let her gaze meet that of a man watching her. He wasn't the only one doing so, but she sensed the dark-haired Adonis was the source of the concentrated scrutiny she had felt. Unmoving and apparently unconcerned with being caught staring, he stood in front of the huge, shiny, metal and glass building that housed Environmental Technology Research and Design. A backpack gripped in one hand and a leather jacket dangling over his shoulder off the finger of another, he looked more like a bad boy with attitude than second in command at one of the country's top research companies.

According to her files, the tall, muscular scientist was Frank Ingram's right-hand man as well as the project manager on the antigravity experiment that had been compromised, leading to TGP's interest in ETRD. Any other professional information regarding his role at ETRD was sketchy. TGP only knew what it did about his role on the antigravity project because his name had been on the intercepted plans. Frank had offered the information that Dr. Beau Ruston was his second in command when he hired Elle for the security consultation.

Other than that, she knew that the young PhD had begun working for the company as an intern while pursuing his doctorate. He'd been hired on in a full-time capacity even before he'd successfully defended his doctoral thesis. Other than the antigravity experiment and the projects that had gone public, TGP had no information regarding what the man did at ETRD.

The company was better at keeping secrets than the Pentagon. Much better. Hence the need for an agent on-site to determine the lay of the land.

She wasn't here to investigate Beau Ruston per se, but he was certainly someone she was interested in finding out more about.

She turned and leaned back into the car to grab her briefcase, giving the staring man a view of her toned backside in the tailored slacks. Being a good agent meant using all assets at her disposal to do her job. If that included flustering a man by exposing a little thigh, then she did it. If it meant bending over to offer a glimpse of a body she used as a tool for her job, she did it.

And her instincts told her that she wanted this particular man as off-kilter as she could get him.

She locked the car and headed toward him, noticing that he had not moved from his spot in front of the building. So, he knew who she was too and he was waiting for her.

As personal greeters went, she'd take him.

His expression neutral, he put his hand out when she was within reaching distance. "Ms. Gray? I'm Beau Ruston."

Her hand was engulfed in the warmth and strength of his. For a split second she saw something in his Hershey-brown eyes and tension-filled square jaw that found a corresponding response right in her core.

Desire. Hot. Urgent. Primal.

And wholly unexpected.

Oh, she was used to being admired. Even wanted. But that flash of sexual heat went beyond the surface physical reaction of a man and a woman meeting for the first time. And the fact that it mirrored her own response was as close to frightening as facing down the wrong end of her own favorite Ruger P95 semiautomatic.

He blinked, and just like that, the brief blaze of desire was banked. She didn't doubt it had been there, any more than she could deny the involuntary tightening of her inner thigh muscles or the way her nipples were still peaked behind her designer-suit jacket.

Grateful for the thickness and opacity of the fabric, she pulled her hand from his. "It's a pleasure to meet you, Dr. Ruston."

"Beau, please." The subtle twang in his voice reminded her of his origins.

His file said he'd gone to USC on a football scholarship and made his home here afterward, rather than return to his native Texas. Right then, she felt an absurd gratitude that he had done so.

She dipped her head in acknowledgment of his request. "Elle."

"Good. We don't stand on ceremony much around here."

Standing this close, it was easy to believe that this man had once played college football and that he'd had a reputation for breaking hearts ... until he'd gotten engaged. His file said he'd been faithful to his fiancée right up until the woman dumped him his senior year.

She'd gone on to marry one of his teammates who had gone into the NFL. A favorite for the draft himself, Beau had opted to continue his education and had gotten a doctorate in quantum physics. He'd chosen brain over brawn, and although he might be highly compensated as a lead scientist at ETRD, it was nothing compared to what he could have made catching footballs in the NFL.

His choices fascinated Elle. She'd spent a good portion of her week off going over his file. The information on his life before and outside his job was not nearly as sketchy as that on his hours spent at ETRD.

Elle had to tilt her head back to meet his eyes. "That's good to know."

He'd moved closer and she hadn't even noticed. This was so not good. A giant like him shouldn't be able to move an inch without her taking note, much less right into her personal space.

She'd known he was tall. The file said six feet six inches, but standing so close made him seem even taller. Bigger. Okay, so maybe that was due to the numerous well-developed muscles filling out his tight blue T-shirt and snug-fitting jeans. Not that six and a half feet was average height by any stretch, but her brothers were all within one to three inches of it. She was only two inches shy of six feet herself.

She'd never felt so flippin' small next to a man. She didn't like it. He was messing with her equilibrium in ways no one else ever did and they hadn't even said more than twenty words to each other.

She distinctly remembered The Old Man telling her that this assignment was going to be a cakewalk. And she'd agreed. *After* seeing Beau Ruston's file. More the fool, her.

She took a hasty step back.

A single dark brow rose in question, but Beau didn't comment. "Come with me and I'll introduce you to the boss."

Did his drawl have to be so damn low and sexy? Wasn't it enough that in person he was unstable C-4 where her feminine desires were concerned? Did his voice have to be more effective than a state-of-the-art weaponry display at gaining her attention? And holding it. Sheesh.

Cakewalk.

Right.

So not.

The Old Man was going to owe her big-time for this assignment.

# Chapter 2

Sporting an annoying but impossible-to-deflate semierection, Beau led Elle down the corridor on the way to Frank's office. She'd been untalkative since entering the building, speaking only when asked a direct question. Not that her all-business attitude managed to deflate this annoying attraction he felt. The fact was, he found her cool facade damn sexy.

Knowing it covered a highly trained federal agent was a turn-on he would never have expected.

She'd shown her ID to the security guard in the lobby and taken her visitor's pass with a minimum of fuss. Yet Beau got the distinct impression that she was surveying their current security setup with each step she took. The stunning security-consultant–slash–federal agent was hyperaware of her surroundings. Beau recognized the quiet intensity she exuded, like she was operating on more levels than the average person.

He was used to that. The scientists he worked with did the same thing, but for different reasons. Himself included.

However, as a rule, he wasn't dangerous. *Elle was.* Very dangerous. And instead of repelling him, that piece of information excited him as much as her physical attributes. Unfortunately.

The knowledge that she was there under false pretenses should turn him off fast and fully. It didn't.

That seriously sucked. The unfamiliar desire pulsing through him was a complication he neither wanted nor needed. He hadn't gone in for major emotional entanglements since his last disaster in that department. Two-for-two failure in the relationship stakes was enough to teach a man a hell of a lot dumber than Beau that he wasn't meant to play that game. However, casual coupling or not, he didn't make it a habit to have sex with women he knew up front he could not trust.

That was just stupid. And it put Elle Gray 100 percent in the off-limits category. Now, if only his body would catch up with his brain.

He was so caught up in the argument between his brain and body that he'd gone several steps before he realized Elle had stopped in the corridor, her blank look focused on the empty hallway behind her.

"Is something the matter?" he asked.

She shook her head, but her rigid stance belied the denial.

"Are you sure?"

"No, it's fine," she replied.

He got the impression she had to force herself to look away from the vacant hallway behind her. What—or who— had she seen? He made a mental note to try to ascertain who might have been in the corridor when they were. "Okay, then. Shall we continue?" he prompted.

"Certainly."

"Frank is looking forward to meeting you."

"That's good to hear."

"As you are aware, we've had a recent problem with security."

"So Mr. Ingram said when he engaged my services."

"You'll have to excuse my ignorance, but I don't see how you or anyone else can protect the company from an employee motivated by greed."

"I suppose I'll just have to show you then, won't I?"

Frank's secretary waved them toward his office without breaking conversation with whomever she was talking to on the phone. She whispered, "He's expecting you," as Beau and Elle walked past her desk.

Beau nodded and gave the woman a smile of thanks.

She blushed and he wondered what the person on the other end of the phone had said to make her react like that. He'd mentioned the woman's tendency to pink cheeks and girlish giggles to Frank one time, but his mentor had simply laughed and said she wasn't always like that.

She certainly was every time Beau saw her.

Frank was reading through some reports when Beau and Elle came into his office. He stood and extended his hand. "Ms. Gray, I presume."

Elle shook the older man's hand, her lips quirking in a barely there smile. "Nice to meet you, Mr. Ingram. Thank you for calling me in on this consultation. I'm looking forward to improving security and the safety of your employees."

"Frank, please," he said, indicating the chairs facing his desk with his hand in a clear invitation to sit. "I'm sure Beau told you we don't stand on ceremony around here."

Elle gracefully lowered herself into one of the chairs. "He did."

Beau followed suit, laying both his backpack and bike leathers beside him.

"Well, then . . ." Frank began.

"Frank, it is," Elle said.

"I'm very happy to have you here, especially after the unexpected disappearance of one of our top scientists," Frank said.

Elle frowned and sat up straighter. "You've had a disappearance? Of one of your employees?"

So, her agency didn't know of Bigsley's disappearance. Beau didn't know if that made him feel better or worse.

"Yes," Frank replied.

"Did you file a missing persons report?"

"Yes, but according to local law enforcement the man is an adult, and without evidence of foul play, they won't pursue it. Apparently, people walk away from their jobs and fully furnished apartments all the time," Frank replied.

"Bull," Elle said.

"Yes, well, our belief that a single missing suitcase and a few sets of clothes does not preclude foul play isn't shared by our local authorities," Frank said.

Elle's eyes went that flat gray that had fascinated Beau in her pictures. "Why wasn't I told about this?"

"I just told you, Ms. Gray."

Her frown did not diminish. "Who was it?"

"Dr. Gil Bigsley," Frank said.

"He was in charge of one of our material reclamation teams," Beau added.

Frank nodded. "Luckily we've just hired someone who was able to step into his position with little upheaval."

"Was he on the list of employees you provided?" Elle asked Frank.

"I'm not sure. It's Dr. Matej Chernichenko. I don't remember if he accepted the position before or after that list was compiled."

Elle's mouth opened on a slight gasp. She snapped it shut, still silent, her expression curiously open. Total shock masked her features for a full second before she schooled her look to one of blankness.

"Is that a problem, Elle?" Frank asked.

"No."

"Are you sure?" Beau pushed, more than a little curious about her reaction. Was Mat the person she'd seen in the hall who had caused her to stop in her tracks? If so, was that something they had to worry about? Or was he simply someone from her past who might be able to blow her cover?

Elle turned those fascinating eyes on Beau. "It's not a problem. Just a . . ." She paused, took a quick breath and let it out as if she wouldn't give herself the luxury of a complete sigh. "It's a surprise, that's all."

"Surprise?" Frank asked delicately.

"I should have gone home between jobs." She looked at Frank and then Beau, her expression giving nothing away "I considered it, you know.

It was Beau's turn to open his mouth and discover he had nothing to say.

"Are you saying you need a break before you can begin the security consult for Environmental Technology Research and Design?" Frank asked.

"No, nothing so dire. I'm just lamenting my own lack of foresight, that's all."

Frank and Beau shared a look of confusion and then turned that same look on Elle.

She smiled, looking somewhat self-deprecating. "It's nothing that need worry you." This time, the sigh was full and drawn out. "You see, Matej Chernichenko is my brother. My *big* brother."

That could definitely explain her reaction to seeing him this morning. Talk about a complication the TGP agent had not expected.

"You didn't know he had taken a job with ETRD?" Beau asked.

"No. The last I heard, he was working for a think tank in the Midwest. I guess he decided it was time to return to his roots."

Elle Gray's family was from Southern California? Beau wasn't sure why that fact interested him, but it did. And her brother was their newest scientist? That was not only interesting but an almost unbelievable coincidence, though stranger things had happened. Still, could he trust Elle's evident surprise?

Beau made a quick mental click through the other scientist's personnel file. The man had sent his résumé for consideration months before the information leak on the antigravity experiment. He'd been hired when the budget had allowed for taking on another scientist.

His credentials were impeccable and he'd spent years working with the same think tank. Despite the suspicious coincidence of his being hired and Elle coming in as a spy for the government, it was unlikely Mat was one as well.

That didn't mean the man wouldn't bear watching. Mr. Smith might be sanguine about Elle's reasons for being at ETRD, but Beau wasn't. And if he found out her brother was feeding her information beyond what was necessary for the scope of her security consultation, Beau would see the man sent back to that think tank in the Midwest faster than he could write $E = mc^2$.

Matej pounded the top of his worktable and swore, "*Sukin sin.*"

"What is that? Like 'damn it all to hell' in Russian, or something?" asked one of his new coworkers.

His subordinate, really, but who was keeping track?

"Ukrainian. It means 'son of a bitch.' "

"Oh. Something got your panties in a wad?"

Matej frowned at the tech who worked on several of the projects Matej was now responsible for overseeing in his new role as project manager of material recovery. "I do not wear panties."

The other man laughed.

Matej had not been making a joke and he didn't share the other man's misconceived amusement. Idiot. "Did you have a question for me?"

The tech shrugged. "Just wondered why you came in here pounding on the lab table and swearing in Russian, that's all."

"U-krai-ni-an," he said again, pronouncing each syllable with slow precision. If this was the kind of density Bigsley had faced on a regular basis, the man had probably dumped his job and run just to get away from it.

"Oh, sorry . . ." The technician winked. "*Ukrainian* swear-words."

"It is nothing to concern you." Matej stifled a sound of annoyance that would no doubt have caused only more questions from the curious staffer. It bothered him how his speech pattern slipped into that of his parents, who spoke English with a decidedly Eastern European accent, when he was angry or upset.

Right now, he was both.

It had been a hell of a couple of weeks and seeing his baby sister walking beside the second in command at Matej's new company had only added to his stress level. He'd been hired to work on material reclamation with a brilliant scientist he'd eagerly looked forward to working with.

Only Bigsley had disappeared before Matej had finished relocating to California, leaving Matej in the position of having to take over as project leader without so much as a handshake and good luck from his predecessor. Matej had led projects before, but he wasn't fond of being responsible for personnel and their morale. Hand-holding was not in his genetic makeup, and cheerleading others on his team was anathema to him.

From the way the team acted, Gil Bigsley had been good at

both and apparently the team members expected the same from him. It was enough to cause Mat a few sleepless nights.

Not that he'd been sleeping all that great regardless. Not when he'd been working in the same building as Chantal Renaud. Their shared past was one of the few things he regretted in his life. What were the chances he'd run into her here—at his new job? Okay, considering how small the field they worked in was, maybe the chances were better than slim.

And it wasn't as if he didn't have plans to find her.

But now his baby sister had shown up at ETRD?

Matej couldn't help feeling that someone upstairs had it in for him.

"Hey, I guess I'll just make myself scarce then," the technician said after several seconds of silence on Matej's part.

"I'm sure you have work to do that is of more interest as well as greater importance than my personal frustrations."

"Sure. I mean, they're personal, huh? Don't let it impact the job—that's what Dr. Bigsley always said."

"Right." As if *he* needed a reminder to do his job with his utmost. He had never done less.

The other man walked away.

"*Sraka,*" Matej muttered, barely restraining the impulse to inform the other man that the word meant "ass" in Ukrainian.

Elle would know. And she probably would have laughed to hear him use it.

What was she doing here? When he'd heard the news that a security consultant was being brought in because of a breach on another project, it had never occurred to him that the consultant would be Elle. He knew damn well that her job as a security consultant was deep cover for her real job as a federal agent.

He didn't know what department she worked for, and

their brother Mykola, an INS agent, hadn't been able to find out either. But Mykola *had* confirmed that in addition to the wages she received as a security consultant, Elle deposited a check once a month that could be traced—after concentrated effort—to the federal government.

She had all the marks of a government agent, no matter what she told their parents she did for a living.

He and his other brothers had not enlightened the older generation of Chernichenkos. Nor had they told their other baby sister, who was in her last year of college, that Elle was a black ops agent. Damn it, why had she never confided in one of them? As the oldest, Matej felt it was his right to be her confidant, but he realized the role fell more naturally to Mykola. However, the brother only a year older than Elle's twenty-eight years had been given no more truth on the matter than any of the others.

If Elle was here in Southern California, that meant the government was interested in ETRD. The question was, why?

Matej had every intention of finding out. Right after he called their mother to inform her of Elle's presence less than an hour from their family home.

His sister deserved a little shake-up after the one she'd given him.

Paybacks were hell. Hadn't he always told her so?

She should have listened to her big brother.

Elle's cell rang with the distinctive tone assigned to family. She flicked a brief glance at the phone while listening to the current head of security drone on about their state-of-the-art protection system.

It wasn't bad, but she'd identified more than a dozen weaknesses already. Some minor . . . one or two potentially major.

She had a text message. From her mother. Mom never used text. Elle clicked to the message. It read 911 and that was all.

Tension ratcheting through her body, Elle said, "Excuse me, but I've got to check on this."

The head of security stopped midword, looking like he'd lost his place in a book and wasn't sure where to start again.

Beau, who had insisted on accompanying her on the tour, said, "No problem."

She turned from them and dialed her mom's cell phone.

"Elle, is that you?" her mother said, by way of an answer. Clearly not trusting caller ID. Nothing new in that.

"Yes, Mama. What's wrong?"

"Wrong? You ask me what is wrong?"

"Yes, Mama. That is exactly what I'm asking."

"Do not take that tone with me, young lady."

"Mother, I am at work."

"Yes, this I know. And when were you going to tell me you were in California? You leave it for me to find out from someone else that my only grown daughter is near enough to visit but has not done so."

Matej! She was going to kill him. Slowly. Right after she finished paying penance with her mother.

"I don't think Danusia considers herself not a grown woman. She is twenty-two, Mama." It wasn't a bad diversionary tactic, but she didn't expect it to work.

And it didn't. "We are not discussing your sister. *She* called me only this morning. She did not fly three thousand miles and neglect to mention the travel to me."

Elle knew better than to mention the fact that she rarely told her family what she was up to. She went for diversion again. "I didn't fly. I drove."

"In that crazy insect car? Three thousand miles? It is so tiny, you cannot be safe on the freeways."

"A Lamborghini Spider is not an insect."

"What is a spider if it is not this?"

"Mama, this is crazy. We don't need to talk about my car right now."

"No. Only that you spent days driving it closer to home and did not bother to pick your phone up and call to tell us of your imminent arrival."

"Mama, you would not want me to talk and drive. You hate that."

Silence. Then, her mother said, "Your grandmother is heartbroken."

"Don't bring Baba into this." Please.

"Why should I not? Has she not as much a desire to see you as I? Who knows if she will live to the next visit, heh?"

Oh, great. The Queen of Guilt Trips was waving her wand and darned if Elle wasn't going under. Death would be too good for Matej. She was going to tell Baba he broke her favorite pie plate when he was sixteen using it as a Frisbee.

"Mama, I was going to call."

Silence met her assurance.

Crud.

"Really, Mama."

"This is about your name, isn't it? I wanted to name you after my dear friend, but the name made you feel less a member of our family. I will always regret this."

"It's not about my name. I love my name."

"As do I, but still . . . it was a disservice to you. My mother always said so. She said, 'Give the girl a good Ukrainian name, just like all the boys,' but I did not listen to her any better than my daughters listen to me."

Now it was "daughters," in the plural. "What has Danusia done to upset you, Mama?"

"This is not something to talk about on one of these contraptions. You come to the house."

"I will, Mama."

"Tomorrow."

"I can't, Mama. I have to work."

"Very well. I will tell your *baba* you cannot come. She has already started on the cooking, but I'm sure she will understand."

How could an undercover agent who routinely faced down perps that were not only armed but dangerous be steamrolled by a woman who was barely five feet two with the face of a middle-aged angel? Once Elle had an answer to that question, she might just be able to stop it from happening.

Maybe.

"I'll be there tomorrow. For dinner."

"Early dinner. Your sister will come from the university."

"I'll be there by six."

"You cannot come earlier?"

"No, Mama, I can't."

Her mother grunted. It was a sound only mothers could make. It meant, "Well, if that's the best you can do, I'll have to accept it, but you're going to hear about this later."

"I love you, Mama." The words, even more than this discussion, probably destroyed a good 90 percent of her tough-image credibility, but she wasn't so stupid she would forgo saying them. At least she'd remembered to speak in Ukrainian.

Though, somehow, she just knew Beau Ruston had guessed exactly what she had just said to her mother. His smug grin implied as much.

"I love you too, baby. You be careful driving that tiny car. Maybe if you got a more steady job you could afford something bigger."

Before her mother could get her teeth into her second-favorite rant regarding her oldest daughter (the first being how it was time for Elle to settle down and start popping out babies), Elle told her again she loved her and cut the connection.

"Your mother?" Beau asked, not in the least embarrassed to be poking his nose in her so obviously personal business.

"What gave it away?"

"Well, you did call her Mama, but there was also the tone of voice."

"Oh?"

"Yeah. You know the one. The 'crap-I'm-in-trouble-how-do-I-get-out-of-this-one' tone."

Elle found herself smiling, even chuckling a little. "Oh, that one."

"So, you're in big trouble?"

"Definitely."

"You think your brother ratted you out? It was him you saw this morning, wasn't it?"

"Not only are you beautiful, but you're smart too, doctor. Yes on both counts. I thought I was seeing things and then found out I wasn't."

He bowed, a teasing glint in his brown eyes. "Why, thank you."

Oh, man . . . this guy was dangerous. And where had she heard that before? Inside her own head, right? It was probably time that she listened.

So, why did she hear her own voice saying, "You ever have a traditional Ukrainian meal?"

"No, I can't say that I have."

"Would you like to change that tomorrow night?"

"Are you inviting me to join you for dinner with your family?" Beau asked, sounding genuinely shocked.

"I am."

His eyes narrowed in apparent revelation. "I get it. You want a witness, so they can't hide the body."

"Something like that. The drama will be contained in the presence of a stranger and you get a fabulous meal. Everybody wins."

Beau threw his head back and laughed.

"Does that mean you'll come?"

His grin sent a burst of warmth through her. "You bet. I'm always up for a new experience."

"Funny, I never knew scientists were such risk takers."

"If I wasn't, I'd be working at the think tank we stole your brother away from. Total job security."

"Security is often an illusion."

"I have a feeling you're going to teach me some more about that concept."

"Considering that's my specialty, I'd say that's a given."

"I can't wait."

Dangerous? Try lethal. This man was one she was going to have to watch out for. Big-time.

# Chapter 3

Elle made it a point to arrive early at ETRD the next morning. She wanted a chance to walk through the facility before most of the scientists and their staff arrived. She scanned her badge into the secured entry, waited for the green light and then headed for her brother's office.

She'd spent the previous evening studying the building schematics and memorizing the employee workstation assignments. It would have helped if she'd had access to the information before her arrival in town, but ETRD security had said they preferred to turn that sort of thing over in person.

She didn't blame them for their caution. In fact, she lauded it even if it had been inconvenient for her.

She did a quick scan of her brother's office, pleased to note that he had not left anything out for her to find on his current projects. There were pictures of the family on one of his bookshelves, the rest stuffed to overflowing with books on his field of applied physics and environmental science. His desk was spotlessly clean. Not only were there no stray pieces of paper, but there was no dust or personal paraphernalia either.

Other than the pictures on the bookcase, the office was almost disturbingly sterile.

Elle grabbed a piece of paper from the memo cube arranged with perfect parallel precision on the desk. She wrote a couple of lines, signed it and left it in the middle of the desk, a defiant and crooked mark on the pristine décor.

She turned to go and ran headlong into a warm wall of muscles. A wall that did not budge. Not even a little, despite her momentum. She wasn't so lucky. She bounced back but didn't have a chance to fall. Not only was she not that clumsy, but the wall was attached to two large hands that grasped her waist with a perfect hold. Not too tight, but not so loose she'd be at risk of falling. Or getting away.

No wonder this man had been counseled to go pro with his football career. If he caught footballs with even a tenth of this finesse, he would be a darn fine player.

He made a pretty fine wall too. A wall that smelled temptingly yummy. She was leaning forward and inhaling before she realized what she was doing.

Delicious.

She loved men's cologne, and on this man? It smelled way better than the trial cards in her favorite department stores. It was the underlying natural male scent that had her olfactory senses so blissed out, though. It not only mixed perfectly with the cologne but was amazingly appealing all on its own. Before she could even think of stopping herself, she inhaled a second time and might have even made an embarrassing noise of appreciation.

"You like CK Man?" Beau's dark, sexy drawl rumbled above her.

"Yes." She took another deep breath, making no effort to hide her enjoyment. "But I think it might be the scientist under the scent that smells even better."

"Do you flirt this hard with everyone?" His laughter went straight to the place that had started pulsing between her thighs when she made her initial accidental body contact with him.

She looked up at him through her lashes—that was such a high, to be around a guy who was tall enough to make that move actually possible. "Maybe."

His brow rose in question. She was quickly learning that this man did not waste words, using only a gesture to communicate when possible. Talk about typical alpha behavior. He expected those around him to be paying close enough attention not to miss his nonverbal clues.

Of course, this close, that would be pretty hard.

She shrugged, deciding to push a little. "Then again, maybe not. You're pretty hot, doctor."

He chuckled, the sound going through her like a warm caress. "I bet you say that to all the scientists."

"I can guarantee you she does not. Elle's got an issue with brainiacs. Just ask her."

Embarrassed to be caught flirting by her big brother, no matter how old she was, Elle started to push away from Beau at the sound of Mat's voice. But the muscle-bound scientist showed how good his hands were at holding on to something he wasn't ready to let go of. She found herself not budging so much as an inch.

"What about it? You got a problem with me?" Beau asked.

"I've been known to get more than a little irritated by men with more book smarts than common sense," she admitted.

Kyle hadn't been like that. He'd been one of the few brilliant men she'd known who hadn't used all his smarts up in academia, but had left a few over for human interaction as well. It was one of the reasons she'd fallen so hard and so fast for him.

But he was gone and she wasn't about to fall for another brainiac. Her brother had that right at least.

Beau's brown gaze bore into hers. "I didn't ask what you

thought of other scientists. I asked if you had a problem with *me*."

"Uh . . . no problem." Well, not one she wanted to admit to in front of Mat. She was pretty sure he didn't want to hear about her inexplicable lust for the other scientist.

"Well, I have a problem with the two of you taking up space in my office when I need to work. Get a room, or something, why don't you?" Mat said.

Elle gasped. Now *that* she hadn't expected from her overprotective oldest brother. With unmasked surprise on her face, she looked at him over Beau's shoulder.

Mat rolled his eyes. "What? You think I haven't realized you're a grown woman. *Hello?* You were married, Elle."

"You couldn't tell that by Papa," she muttered, still shocked.

"Hell, he probably thinks you're still a virgin. Kyle was much too happy with you for that to have been the case."

Had she really spent so little time with the family in the past four years that she didn't know what to expect from her brother? "I can't believe you just said that."

"Maybe if you had seen me more than a handful of times in four years, you would not be so shocked," Mat said, echoing her thoughts. "And as much pleasure as I find in this little reunion, I have work to do."

Elle felt the rejection like a slap.

But Beau laughed, and finally releasing her, he turned to face his newest scientist. "Hey, man. You in a hurry to get going this morning?"

"Aren't I always?" Mat asked, with a sigh.

Elle looked her brother over with concern. He looked tired and stressed. She wanted to ask if he was all right but didn't think he'd appreciate the sisterly concern in front of his boss. In light of his words, she wasn't sure he'd appreciate it at all.

When she'd lost Kyle, she'd pulled away from everyone she loved and only now realized the damage she might have done to those relationships. She'd spent the last four years living her job. New assignment notwithstanding, it felt like the rest of her life was catching up with her all of a sudden.

And she wasn't sure she was ready for it.

"You've done an incredible job coming up to speed so quickly in a position you didn't hire on for," Beau said to Mat.

Mat shrugged away the praise. "Thanks."

"I mean it. We're damn lucky we hired you."

"Did you hear that?" Elle asked in a forced, teasing tone. "They're glad they hired you away from the think tank. You'd better not mess up, big brother."

"I'm fully aware," Mat said, eyes the same gray as hers full of serious lights.

She was still his sister and she loved him, no matter if he was justifiably angry with her, or not. It was time to remind him of that. She moved forward and gave him a tight one-armed hug. "Don't worry. There's not another brainiac on the planet who can outdo you."

He surprised her by turning and returning the embrace full on, his eyes telling her that he loved her too and maybe even understood the last four years. Then he stepped back and focused on Beau again. "I just wish I'd had a chance to work with Dr. Bigsley before taking over his job."

The admission came as close to acknowledging weakness as she'd ever heard him make. This job really was getting to him.

"Gil was a brilliant scientist, but I agree with your sister. He had nothing on you, Mat."

"Was?" Elle asked, her professional instincts taking over. "Frank said he disappeared. You're talking like he's dead."

Beau looked unhappy. "You want the truth?"

"I prefer it," she said.

"Do you?" he asked, an expression on his overtly masculine features that lent a cynical tone to the question that had not come through in his voice.

"Yes, of course."

Beau stared at her in silence for several long seconds. What was going on? Why the look? And why was Matej looking between the two of them with an indecipherable expression as well? What was going on?

"Gil Bigsley loved his job. He believed in what we're doing here. I have a hard time accepting he just blew it all off to run away to South America, or something," Beau explained.

"So, you think something bad happened to him?" Elle asked.

Beau shrugged, but his words hadn't left a lot of room for interpretation. That was exactly what he thought.

"I agree." Mat interjected. "I hadn't met him in person, but I admired him. A lot. For him to abandon the goals he wrote so passionately about, he had to have had a pretty compelling reason."

"What do you mean, he wrote about his goals?" Elle asked.

"He published several articles on environmental theory," Beau said.

"I see."

"He also kept a blog, which he hasn't posted to since three days before he disappeared," her brother added.

"He kept a blog?" Beau asked with the same disbelief Elle felt.

She hadn't come across any such thing.

"He used a pseudonym, but he told me his real name when we started e-mailing privately after I said he sounded like one of my favorite authors," Mat said.

"You met him on his blog?" Elle asked, for clarification.

"Yes. It was one of the few I visited frequently. His posts were always relevant to today's environmental issues. He talked about some of his projects here in vague terms, but I knew he was as committed to finding solutions as I am."

"No wonder he was so adamant about hiring you sight

unseen. Gil was the reason we didn't go through the usual in-
terview process before we offered you a position," Beau said.

"He was the reason I took the job without meeting you all
as well. He'd told me a lot about the company once we got to
know each other. Nothing that would compromise security,
but enough that I knew I'd be happy working here."

"Is that why you sent your résumé in?" Beau asked.

"Yes."

Elle had been planning to include news of the scientist's
disappearance in her weekly report. However, in light of this
morning's revelations, she changed her plans to call her boss
about it as soon as possible.

"What was the name of his blog?" Beau asked.

"The Emerald Hope."

Beau made a strange sound. "I used to visit that blog too.
I never realized Gil was the author. I feel like an idiot."

"Don't. He was careful to protect his identity. Probably so
nothing he said could be connected to ETRD."

"Probably," Beau said.

"And you say he hasn't posted there since before he disappeared?" Elle asked.

"Right. Not only that, but my last e-mail from him said he
was looking forward to working with me."

"And the local authorities still refused to investigate his
disappearance?" Elle asked, shaking her head.

"Yes."

"Do you have the name of the officer who made that determination?" she asked Beau.

"Frank does."

Elle nodded, making a mental note to get it. She wasn't
supposed to be working on a live case, but things changed.
She could feel Beau watching her while she considered the
ramifications of the scientist's disappearance. He didn't

sound like the type of man who would have been involved in the security breach Alan Hyatt had discovered on his last case as an active operative.

Which meant either something else was going on, or that case wasn't as neatly closed as they'd all thought.

"I hate to bring this up and feed the rumors of my brusque manner and borderline lousy interpersonal-relationship skills, but . . ." Mat paused meeting first Elle's eyes and then Beau's. "Out."

Elle smiled. First because this was so like the brother she'd always known. Mat was done discussing his cyber-friend's disappearance. That didn't mean that he wasn't interested or concerned, but that he'd said all he thought was important on the subject.

She was also smiling because if Mat really were worried about his job he wouldn't be so rude to his boss.

"I believe that's our cue to vacate the premises," Beau said.

"I believe you're right, but maybe I should be the one to go. After all, you clearly came here to talk to Mat."

"Actually, I came here looking for you."

"You did?" How had he even known she was in the building?

He had to have checked the security log for her arrival, but why would he have done so? She supposed it wasn't too odd that he wanted to know when the new security consultant was in the building. However, if this kind of micromanagement continued, it was going to make it difficult for her to fulfill her other assignment of finding out what projects the company was working on. Not impossible, but slightly more challenging.

Her dual assignments of snooping and ensuring ETRD's security were of equal importance to TGP, but now she had the possibility of yet another objective: finding a missing scientist.

She definitely needed to talk to The Old Man.

"See you later, Mat," Beau said as he took her arm and steered her out the door.

"You said you came looking for me. Why?" she asked.

"What were you doing in your brother's office?" Beau gave her another one of those enigmatic looks tinged with cynicism. "You obviously weren't waiting for him."

"You assume that because . . ."

"You're here with me, not back there with him."

"Maybe I didn't want to make a big deal out of talking to him."

"Nope. If you wanted to talk to him, you would have said so.

"You've known me less than twenty-four hours and you think you can make that kind of call?"

"Yes." No explanations, just a simple agreement.

"Arrogant much?"

"Call it what you want, but my brain isn't only good for figuring out quantum physics."

"You trying to say that you're not just a brainiac with a pretty face, but that you actually pay attention to the other human beings that inhabit your space too?"

"Why were you in Mat's office?"

"You know, you've got a bad habit of answering a question with another question."

"I've got to have one or two bad habits or I'd intimidate people with my perfection."

"Oh, you are more than a little arrogant. I bet you've got more than a couple of bad habits."

"You'll have to let me know if you discover them."

"I've already discovered three. You're arrogant, you jump to conclusions and instead of answering questions, you ask your own."

"Technically, the third falls under arrogance. Wouldn't

you agree? So, really that's only two. And one is a character trait, not a habit. Which leaves you at one."

"Not. You may be right that arrogance is a character trait, but that doesn't mean you get to dismiss the bad habits that are a result of it."

"So, two."

"Right. And I'm sure there are more."

"I'm sure you've got lots of experience ferreting out information that interests you."

"What do you mean?"

"Being a top-notch security consultant and all."

There seemed to be another message in his words, but despite her yes, extensive experience "ferreting out information," she couldn't figure out what it was.

They walked in silence, Elle not sure where Beau was taking her. Certainly not toward his office. That was the other direction at their last turn.

"Well?" Beau asked.

"Well, what?"

"Don't play dumb; it doesn't suit you."

"You think I'm smart?"

"I know it. In fact, I'd guess you could give your brother a run for his money in the brains department."

"There you go jumping to conclusions again."

"You going to deny it?"

"Nope. Maybe you should tell Mat too."

"He already knows."

"Unfortunately, you're right."

"Unfortunately?"

"He and the rest of my family are disappointed that I chose to use my intelligence in the field of security rather than plugging myself into a think tank or academia. You know, making the world a better place."

"They don't think you do that with your job?"

"Do you?"

Beau was silent so long, Elle was sure he was going to give her a negative.

"Look, don't worry about it. I do what I do because it's what I love. No one else has to understand. Or approve."

"But it hurts that they don't."

"Maybe." She sighed at her own honesty. What was the matter with her around this man? She kept finding herself saying stuff she hadn't meant to. "Sometimes."

"But you don't let that stop you from doing what you know is right for you."

"No."

"I respect that."

"Thanks."

"And for the record, I do think you are making the world a better place, just in a different way than your brother is."

"Thanks."

"I understand, you know."

"Yeah?"

"Yes. The only people who understood and supported my decision not to go professional with football are Frank Ingram and my little sister. Well, my granny did too, but she's gone."

"The rest of your family didn't approve?"

"I haven't been invited home for Christmas dinner in this century."

Okay, so the century was pretty new, but that still meant his family had been practicing active rejection of his choices for close to a decade—maybe more.

"That sucks."

"I agree."

"They're that angry that you chose to pursue your academic career rather than one in sports?"

"Furious."

"You're serious?" she asked, though she could tell he was.

"They figured I could do the physics thing *after* I made a few million playing pro ball."

"That's supposing you weren't injured in a way that made that difficult or impossible."

"Now see, that's how I looked at it."

"But they didn't?"

"My little sister did. Well, not at first, but she got it eventually."

"Good."

"You'd think so, but it was her acceptance that triggered my parents' final rejection."

"You're not serious?"

"I am." Beau tugged Elle into a cavernous laboratory. "A couple of years after she made vocal support of my decision, she joined the Peace Corps."

"And your parents blamed you for that decision?" Elle guessed.

"You got it. In their minds if I wasn't such a 'raving environmentalist,' she wouldn't have gotten the idea that she should 'waste' her education helping others."

"They call you a raving environmentalist because of your job?"

"They called me that while I was still in college, because I made once-a-week trips to the recycling plant to drop off recyclable materials, rather than leave them for the garbageman to pick up."

Elle chuckled. "I guess they'd call me one too."

"Maybe." Beau stopped at a long lab table and powered on a laptop sitting beside experimental apparatus.

Elle mentally catalogued the apparatus and what it would be used for. "But I have to tell you, Beau, my family would approve one hundred percent of both you and your sister's choices."

"You think?"

"I know."

"Potential multimillion-dollar paychecks sway a lot of people's thinking."

"My mother calls my Lamborghini an insect car."

"So she doesn't know any better."

"Oh, she knows, but it's her way of letting me know that that kind of stuff doesn't matter. That it doesn't impress her."

"Does that bother you?"

Elle grinned. "Nope. I bought the car for me, not to impress other people." And maybe because owning one had been a dream she'd shared with Kyle, but that wasn't something she had to dwell on or admit.

"You like your designer labels, but you don't care what other people think of them?"

"You got it in one."

"See, my jumping to conclusions isn't always a bad thing."

"When you're right, I guess."

"Are you saying I was wrong earlier—that you were in Mat's office to see him?"

She glared. "You know always being right can be pretty irritating."

"So my team tells me."

"Oh, man, you really are arrogant."

"Is truth arrogance?"

"If you're so darn smart, you tell me what I was doing in Mat's office."

"Leaving him a note."

She stared at him, momentarily nonplussed.

Beau laughed and shook his head. "You don't have to be a super security consultant to know how to pay attention to detail. I saw the paper in the middle of your brother's otherwise immaculate desk."

"You so sure it was from me?"

"Yep. Anyone else would have left it in his in-box."

"Unless they wanted him to bitch about leaving a mess on his desk?" she guessed. She did know her brother.

"Exactly."

"Whereas I get a typical sisterly kick out of annoying him."

"Are you saying my sister waxes eloquent about some new man every time she calls just to annoy me?" He did a good job of feigning surprise.

But Elle wasn't buying it. "Pfft. As if you didn't know that."

"I think my sister would like you."

"Maybe I should meet her. My little sister thinks I'm a sell-out, just like the rest of the family."

"At least they're still inviting you to family dinners."

Not that she'd taken them up on many invitations in recent years. "Oh, they love me for sure, even if they don't exactly approve of me. My mom even said once that she just wants me to be happy. Of course she followed that with a treatise on what she thinks would make me that way."

"Let me guess—it starts with getting rid of your insect car."

"Not quite. She thinks my widowed, therefore single, status is far more a travesty than the car I drive."

"You're a widow? That Kyle guy your brother mentioned?"

Elle bit her lip. Why had she offered that bit of information? "Yes."

"How long?"

"Four years."

"And you don't date?"

"I date." Well, you could sort of call it that.

"Just not men your mother approves of."

"Right." Though some of the men she had gone out with for her job in the past four years would have thrilled her mother, her father and her *baba*. What they disapproved of was that she wouldn't bring any man home to meet them, thus proving she was not seriously pursuing a relationship.

They were oh so correct in that. Elle'd had had her heart shattered once. She'd managed to glue it back together enough to function, but that had left the organ brittle. No way was she putting it at risk again. She was perfectly happy committed in a long-term relationship with her job.

"So, if you knew why I was in my brother's office, why did you keep asking me about it?"

Again that odd look. "I wanted to know if you'd tell me the truth."

"What? Why?"

"You are redesigning the security for my company. I don't just work here, I believe in what we're doing . . . in the vision of ETRD. Most of our projects are highly classified and some could be misused in the wrong hands. Is it so strange that I want to make sure you are trustworthy?"

"I would think you would trust Frank and your mysterious benefactor, Mr. Smith. After all, they chose me for the job."

"Frank hired the security guard who turned out to be dirty, as well. Frank's as fallible as the next man."

"And Mr. Smith?"

Beau shrugged. "Let's just say that I'm more comfortable testing and calling my own plays than someone else's."

"I thought it was the quarterback who called the plays."

"I started out as a quarterback. I took our high school team to state three years in a row. It wasn't until I got to college that the coaches decided I was even better at catching and making touchdowns than I was at throwing."

Well, he'd certainly caught and held her that morning. She had a feeling if he ever touched her with intent, he'd score just as easily as he had on the field.

And that scared the bejeebies out of her.

Sex had not gone beyond physical release for her in four years. It was fun, but not necessary. She could always walk away. However, if Beau bent his considerable brainpower—and yes, charm, darn it—toward seduction, Elle wasn't sure she'd be able to do that.

# Chapter 4

Another foreign curse came from the new project manager's end of the lab.

Chantal bit her lip and looked over her shoulder to find Mat scowling at one of the technicians. Again. The poor tech looked ready to cry.

Who could blame the tech? Mat was well over six feet tall with the solid muscles found in many Ukrainian men. The only colors she'd ever seen him wear were black and shades of gray. Even his lab coat was a special-order slate gray. When she'd told him the monochromatic dressing made him look like a hit man for the Russian mob, Mat had admitted he was partially color-blind—after giving her a lecture on the difference between the two nationalities. He'd told her that dressing like this was his way of preventing himself from leaving the house looking like a circus clown. But added to that, his black-as-coal hair, trim mustache and close-cropped beard gave him a decidedly intimidating look.

Especially when he was angry. Like now.

Mat never had been the warm-and-fuzzy type. Calling him a people person was a stretch even she hadn't been able to make when she was head over heels for the man. He wasn't the worst manager in the world. In fact, he was actually pretty decent at it and even better when his scientists and technicians were efficient. Only he had an abrasive way of dealing with them if they weren't.

Abrasive as in almost scary until you got to know him better.

Deciding their department really couldn't afford to lose another team member after their former PM's disappearance, Chantal got up from her lab stool and headed toward the minicontretemps.

"Wake up on the wrong side of the bed this morning?" she asked Mat, with a smile and a nod for the technician.

Mat turned his scowl on her while the tech he'd been upbraiding stared at her as if she'd just stepped in an electromagnetic field and then tried to use her electron scan microscope.

She turned up the wattage on her smile and made sure it included both men. "Is there a problem here, gentlemen?"

"I . . . uh . . ." The technician swallowed twice and gave Mat a sidelong glance before continuing. "I was trying to explain to Dr. Chernichenko that we'd already done the tests on mercury reclamation from fluorescent bulbs and that the ROI was too low to make it a viable project."

Chantal remembered the tests. "Unless a different reclamation process can be developed, I agree." She looked up at Mat, trying to ignore how being this close to him made her body go haywire. "Were you thinking of trying a different process?"

"I want more information on the one already tried," he said, with a stubborn tilt to his chin.

"No problem," she said.

It was the technician's turn to glare at her.

"I can get that for you and fill you in on the preliminary trials if you like," she added.

The sense of relief from the tech was palpable as he realized she wasn't setting him up for more of the same with his new PM.

Mat frowned, however. "I don't want to take you away from something important."

"Bringing the project manager for Material Reclamation up to speed on all our current and recent projects *is* important."

Mat sighed and rubbed his eyes, a gesture she remembered from their college days that meant he was more stressed than tired. The man was almost inhuman when it came to getting tired—he could go for hours. In more arenas than academia. The thought brought the heat of a blush to her cheeks while her thighs clenched together involuntarily. Thank goodness for lab coats that hid embarrassing reactions.

"Thank you. I would appreciate that," Mat said.

The look of shock the technician gave Mat's polite response was comical, but Chantal didn't crack a smile. Mat might think she was laughing at him, and even she wasn't going to beard this bear in that way.

To stop herself from reaching out and touching that particularly tempting bear, she crossed her arms under her chest. "It's past lunchtime and I don't know about you, but I could use something to eat."

Mat nodded, his gray gaze skimming her body like a barely there caress. "We could meet in the cafeteria . . . or we could go off-site."

"The cafeteria would probably be better." Less chance she would make a fool of herself. "We can talk freely without worrying about being overheard."

Mat's scowl was back. "I suppose."

"Would you rather eat off-site?" *And if so, why didn't you just say so?*

He shut his eyes and tensed his jaw like he was trying to bite back words.

"We could eat in your office," she suggested, wanting to take that look of strain off his features. "We'd have privacy without the distractions."

Which wasn't going to do a thing for her own strain, but she had to deal with her attraction to him or quit her job. And she had no desire to leave Environmental Technology Research and Design.

"You'd think so, wouldn't you?" He opened his eyes, the irises storm-cloud gray now.

She remembered that shade, but not from frustration at work. Stifling a groan, she gave herself a strong mental shake. Her attempts to deal with her reaction to him were not going to succeed if she couldn't stop memories of the past from intruding on the present.

The reminder should have been enough to bolster her flagging self-control. It wasn't. The problem being that she'd been using the same self-lecture for two weeks and it wasn't getting any more powerful with repetition.

"What do you mean?" she asked.

"Nothing you need to worry about."

"Okay then. We'll meet in your office."

"Yes." The clipped single-word response wasn't all that he was thinking, but typical for the stoic scientist, he wasn't sharing whatever else was on his mind.

Chantal had enough of her own worries; she should not be concerned with his. Only it never worked that way. By nature, she was too empathetic to others, and it was even worse when it came to this man. She had to watch it to stop his moods from dictating her own, even when they hadn't said a single word to each other.

The last two weeks had proven one truth beyond the shadow of a doubt: she was not and probably never would be completely over Matej Chernichenko.

Not that she was going to do anything about that fact, but

facing the truth was the first step in dealing with it. Isn't that what someone had told her after her parents' deaths? She'd hidden in her room, wanting to pretend that they were still alive, that the world was not what it was.

She hadn't been allowed that luxury. She'd known the people around her, the ones forcing her to face reality, were only trying to help. She just hadn't understood why truth had to hurt so much.

She forced a smile. "Good. I'll pick up lunch at the deli and bring it to your office."

"Good, that will give me a chance to finish up here."

The technician who had looked so relieved got a worried expression on his face again and turned to hurry off without another word.

Mat ignored his defection. "You remember what I like?" he asked her.

"Yes." She remembered far too much.

Her suggestion they meet in his office was probably the height of idiocy. Off-site would have been better, even if they had spent the hour whispering over a table in some dark corner of a crowded restaurant. But making bad choices when it came to men was a failing of hers, she thought cynically.

Matej Chernichenko had been her first object lesson in how poor her judgment regarding men was, but he hadn't been the last one.

She was absolutely not going to let him be a repeat, though, lunch date in his office notwithstanding. She might be unforgivably gullible where men were concerned, but even she was savvy enough to know that the same man was bound to hurt her the same way if she gave him the chance.

She wasn't about to do so, no matter how foolish some of her choices in the past might have been.

"I'll see you in about thirty minutes then." She turned to walk away.

"It wasn't waking on the wrong side of the bed that made me cranky this morning, little one."

The endearment she had not heard in ten years stopped her more forcefully than if he'd grabbed her physically. She looked back over her shoulder at him. "It wasn't?"

"No."

"Are you going to tell me what was?" she asked fatalistically.

"Waking up alone."

Mat almost felt guilty about the way he terrorized the scientists and technicians under him. But was it really that hard to answer a few simple questions? Chantal was ready to do it. And she was willing to tease him to boot. She wasn't afraid of him and that pleased him.

She might be shy, but Chantal Renaud was no wilting flower.

The petite blonde had grown more beautiful with maturity. Once kept in a haphazard ponytail, her golden hair now framed her delicate features in a straight silk curtain. She dressed with more style as well and had replaced her thick and geeky-looking glasses with frameless lenses that did nothing to detract from her hazel eyes. Those eyes still changed color with her emotions, and she still blushed like a virgin for no apparent reason whatsoever. It was cute. Sweet. Arousing.

Too much so. He didn't relish spending his working days with the boner from Hades. And no hope of alleviating it.

Which was why he'd made that comment to her about sleeping alone. It was the truth. Probably a truth that should have remained unsaid, however, if the speed of her exit was anything to go by.

He muttered a curse.

"Still using the swearwords your dad taught you?" The sexy, soft voice with a very slight French accent he had never been able to forget came from his doorway.

Mat couldn't count the number of times in the last ten years he had woken with a hard-on and the memory of dirty words being uttered in that exact tenor. Words he was sure that sweet-as-candy mouth would never utter in a million years.

He looked up to find Chantal standing just inside the door of his office, her laptop in one hand and a bag from a local deli in the other.

"Thanks for picking up lunch. As for the swearwords, they protected me from censure from my teachers for a good many years."

Chantal set the laptop on the two-person conference table he kept in the corner of his office. "I bet they got you in trouble with your mother, though."

"And my *baba*." He took the bag with their lunch and apportioned the food. "Would you like a soda or water with your lunch?"

"Water please." Chantal sat in the chair facing her computer. "I remember the stories you told about your grandmother. Is she still living?"

Mat grabbed two bottles of water from the minifridge behind his desk before detouring to shut his office door. "Yes. She's ninety, but she'll live to see her centenary and then some."

"I bet she's a crackerjack."

He opened Chantal's water and handed it to her. "More like the bouncing ball you play jacks with. She's never still."

"She sounds wonderful," Chantal said wistfully.

He remembered that her parents had died when she was a teenager. She'd come from France to the United States to live with family she barely knew.

"Do you still see your aunt and uncle?" he asked, twisting the cap off his own water before taking a sip.

"They're my second cousins."

"That's right." He felt an unfamiliar sense of embarrassment wash over him for forgetting. "Do you see them?"

"Every few years we manage something."

"Why so long between visits?" he asked, not caring if it was nosy and none of his business. He wanted to know.

"They retired the year after I finished university, sold their place and bought a motor home the size of a small house. They've been on the road ever since. We see each other when they make it back to this part of the continent."

He sat down and their knees brushed. She visibly jumped and he found himself smiling. "You could fly out to see them wherever they are."

He couldn't imagine a family so disconnected. His drove him nuts, but he loved them and would never go even a whole year without seeing them. Which was why Elle's infrequent visits hurt so much.

He tried to understand, but he missed her—they all did.

"They've never invited me and I don't make an issue of it. They chose not to have children for a reason. It was more than decent of them to take me in; it was amazingly unselfish. But I'm a grown woman now and there's no reason their retirement should shape up differently than they'd always planned."

"I'm sure they miss you, even if they don't say so."

Chantal's lips quirked in a small smile. "Whatever you say."

"You're a sweetheart, Chantal. Of course they miss you."

"A sweetheart?" she asked, her voice tinged with humor.

"Yep. A total sweetheart."

That blush he found so distracting tinged her face a soft pink and her lips opened and closed with nothing coming out.

He grinned. "You must be. Only a woman as sweet as honey would have saved that hapless tech from the big, mean PM. Not to mention manage to undermine my fully justified snit."

"You admit to having snits?" she asked, her face now a fire-engine red.

He grimaced. "Baba says I have them, and no one messes with that woman."

"So you take her word in all things?"

"Pretty close to it." Everything but that one demand he always pretended not to hear—the one about him getting married already.

He was beginning to suspect the reason he had not found the right woman was that he had left her behind ten years ago. And he didn't mean the faithless witch he had almost asked to marry him either.

"I'll have to remember that the next time you start terrorizing the staff."

"And how will that help you?"

"I know how to look up a phone number online. How many Chernichenkos do you suppose there are in Southern California?"

"Two, and one of them is unlisted."

"I'm guessing that's yours."

"Yes."

"So, Grandma should be easy to track down through your dad, yes?"

He tapped her pert nose with his forefinger. "You are one sneaky scientist."

Chantal blanched, flinching back, her teeth clamping on her bottom lip with what looked like painful intensity.

He reached out and brushed under the abused lip with his thumb. "Hey, you okay?"

She nodded, but then tears filled her eyes. Jumping up, she grabbed her laptop. "Uh, I need to go. We'll have this meeting later, okay?"

Then she was gone, the sound of him calling her name echoing in the empty office.

What the hell had just happened?

* * *

"That is one sweet ride," Beau said as he got out of the passenger side of Elle's Spider.

"I like it."

"It's easy to see why."

They'd pulled up in front of a sprawling mission-style home an hour east of L.A. in the desert. The neighboring houses were far enough away to ensure real privacy. Used to the cramped and crowded conditions of Los Angeles, even in their smaller community to the south of the city proper, Beau took a deep breath, enjoying the sense of space. "Nice."

"It was a good place to grow up."

"It reminds me of home."

"Where is that?"

"East Texas."

"So, that's where that sexy drawl comes from."

"You think my drawl is sexy?" he asked, purposefully stretching his syllables with Texan twang.

Elle grinned. "It's sexier when you aren't doing a Keith Urban impersonation."

"Bite your tongue. That good ole boy is from Down Under. Not the sacred state of Texas. His drawl ain't anything like mine."

"I didn't know there was such a thing as a sacred state." She rolled her eyes for emphasis.

Beau leaned forward until he was whispering right next to her ear. "That's because you weren't raised in Texas."

"Oh," she whispered back. "So, it's some kind of secret, huh?"

He moved even closer until he was as close to her super-model body as he could get without actually touching. Then he leaned in so his lips actually did touch the shell of her ear. "I'll share my secrets with you if you share yours with me."

Her whole body shuddered and if that didn't send him

zero to sixty from one breath to the next. His cock ached and pressed insistently against the fly of his good jeans.

He flicked his tongue out and tasted the sensitive skin just under her earlobe. "What do you say? You ready to share your secrets with me?"

Damn if she didn't turn just so and lean her forehead against his shoulder. She didn't say anything, but he could feel tension emanating from her.

He nuzzled into her neck, still whispering. "You got a lot of secrets, princess?"

"Who doesn't?" Her voice was quiet and muffled against his body.

Beau didn't know why he did it, but he rubbed her back in comfort. At the moment, the beautiful government agent who was lying to him and pretending to be nothing more than a security consultant seemed vulnerable. And he realized he wanted to protect her. Take all her cares away.

What a sap.

Vulnerable. Right.

It was probably part of her act. Her cover. Only he felt there was something growing between them. Something real and inescapable.

Dumb.

She was just doing her job and pretending to be something she wasn't to get information her agency wanted about his company.

He *had* to remember that.

If only he could convince his body to listen. Never mind the heart he was smart enough not to risk for a woman who was living a lie.

Elle couldn't believe she was leaning against Beau as if he were her boyfriend instead of a man she'd met only the day before. A man who was part of her current assignment. Nothing more.

He pushed her away and stepped back, his actions gentle but firm.

And darn if she didn't feel chilled even though the desert heat had not dropped for nightfall yet.

The door swept open behind Beau and Elle's mother stood framed in the door, just beaming. "So you have finally brought us a man to meet?"

Elle squeaked. And how embarrassing was that? Only her family could elicit such a response from her. "He's my current client, Mama, not a boyfriend."

How could she not have thought ahead to this reaction? She should have called and told the family she was bringing a client to dinner, but she'd wanted the element of surprise. She'd hoped it would further forestall the usual family drama and lectures on her single status and her working on what was in their opinion the wrong side of the country, followed by the common refrain that she didn't visit often enough.

That she rarely visited was true and maybe something she was going to fix, but the rest of it wasn't going to change.

Beau turned and faced her mother, reaching his hand out. "Dr. Beau Ruston, ma'am. It's a pleasure to meet you."

"*Dr.* Ruston?" her mother asked, with an unmistakable glimmer of pleasure in her eyes.

"Just call me Beau, ma'am."

"And you may call me Mama."

"Mama!" Elle practically screeched.

"What?" her mom asked, all innocence. "I'm only being friendly."

"Her name is Lidia," Elle told Beau, trying hard not to grit her teeth.

Beau winked at Mama. "It's a lovely name, though I don't mind calling you Mama if you prefer."

"You see? He has manners, this one."

"Who has manners?" came the voice of Elle's *baba* from inside the house.

"Come inside." Mama grabbed Beau's arm and dragged him into the interior. "You must meet the rest of the family. Valeri, my husband, he is still at work, but he will be here in time for dinner. Roman, he is like our Elle and works too far away to make it home often."

"He's in the military, for goodness' sake," Elle slotted in.

Her mother shrugged. "Mykola is off catching the bad guys, but our dear Matej and Danusia are here for dinner. They will be happy to meet you, I'm sure."

"I work with Matej, ma'am."

"He's my boss."

Mama turned to face Matej, who had come from the living room to the entryway. "This one is your boss?"

"Yes."

"Ah, a successful man, then," Baba said as she gave Elle a significant look that even a blind Russian could interpret.

Ignoring the heavy hinting, Elle moved forward to hug her tiny grandmother. "Baba, it's good to see you."

The old woman hugged her back with strong arms. "I wouldn't mind seeing you more often, that is the truth."

"I'll be in California for a few weeks, maybe even a couple of months. I'll make sure to visit often."

"That is right, you are in California. Working."

Elle rolled her eyes and turned to hug her mother before she could start that tirade all over again. "I love you, Mama."

"I love you too, my dear daughter."

Elle glared at Matej over her mother's head.

He just scowled back.

Hmm. Not in a good mood, then. Or still angry with her. She gave him a questioning look, but he ignored it and turned away.

She still had to greet her little sister and then her father arrived and proceeded to grill Beau just as if he really was Elle's boyfriend. He took it good-naturedly but managed to ask a question about Elle or her family for every one that he answered.

If she didn't know better, she'd think he had experience in covert ops. The man was entirely too good at getting other people to talk. Everyone but her brother Matej.

He spent dinner in a dark funk that not even Baba could penetrate.

# Chapter 5

After they'd eaten and Papa had taken Beau on a tour of his outdoor workshop, Elle cornered Matej in the courtyard while Danusia helped Mama clean the kitchen and Baba took a rest in the living room.

"What's the matter, Mat?"

He didn't answer, just stared into the fountain in the center of the flagstone.

She laid her hand on his shoulder. "Come on, you can tell me."

"Like you told me you are a federal agent?" he asked in a voice that sliced through her.

"What? What are you talking about?"

"Please, Elle. Do you really think we're so dumb we don't know the truth?"

"We who? Who have you told you suspect such a thing?"

He spun to face her, his expression stony. "Don't worry, we haven't told Papa, Mama or Baba."

"We who?"

"Who do you think? Roman, Mykola and I figured it out years ago."

"Danusia?"

"Of course not."

"Why? Do you think she is too weak to know because she is a girl?"

"Did you think we were too untrustworthy to know because we are men?"

"Don't be ridiculous. I'm not like that."

"So, why did you not tell us?"

"Maybe there was nothing to tell."

"Don't lie to me, Elle. Mykola doesn't lie to us. You shouldn't hide your life from your family. That's not right."

Pain lanced through her. "Mykola works for the INS. He has the luxury of admitting that to the people he trusts."

"And what, you don't have that luxury?"

She didn't say anything. She didn't want to lie, but she couldn't tell him the truth either.

"We know you work for the federal government, Elle. Mykola traced the money."

She probably should have been angry at her brother for invading her privacy like that, but she wasn't. Because she knew in a similar situation, she might have done the same.

"He must be good. The connection to the federal government paying me is supposed to be impossible to trace."

"He's a Chernichenko."

Elle nodded. "I'm good at my job too."

"And what is that?"

"I can't tell you."

"Can't or won't?"

"The Old Man . . . my boss . . . he's worked for the agency for decades and his wife still doesn't know what part of the State Department he's employed by."

"So, your agency is under the State Department?"

"Honestly? I don't know. I only know that's his cover. Probably. The truth is easier to hide behind than a lie."

"Like your cover as a security consultant."

"Yes."

"What are you doing at my company, Elle?"

"Nothing you need to worry about. Really. I'm not on an investigation so much as a fact-finding mission." Well, after that morning, she wasn't sure that was true any longer, but the status had not officially been changed.

"You realize I have to tell Beau."

Elle stared, totally shocked. "No. You can't blow my cover, Mat."

"I have a responsibility to my employer."

"What about your obligation to your sister?"

"The sister who has all but forgotten she had a family for the last four years?"

"It hurt. Coming home. Seeing people I loved. I couldn't handle it after Kyle died."

"It's been four years."

"I realize that. I let it go on too long. It became a habit to keep to myself; I'm not planning to keep doing it."

"That will please Mama."

"And the rest of you too, I hope."

"You don't need to worry. We've missed you, little sister." He pulled her into a hug. And while she sensed he was still upset about something, she could tell he had forgiven her.

Just like that. She didn't deserve it, but that was one of the blessings of family love.

He let her go to scowl at her again, but this time it didn't make her heart hurt. "We're a privately held company, Elle. The government has no right to our research."

"I'm not trying to get your research. I'm not. It's just my job to keep tabs on *what* the projects are. That's all."

"So you can use what you decide is worth having?"

"No, that's not how it works. My agency has supported many important technological advances. We do a good thing, Mat."

"You're saying your agency never steps in and claims technology for the government."

"It's more complicated than that. We're not the FBI or the INS or even the CIA. Trust me."

"You've been lying to the family for four years. Why should I trust you?"

She almost laughed because she knew he didn't mean it. He was trying to push her buttons, just like he had when they were younger. She wasn't so easy to get to anymore. "Because I'm your sister and I've never done anything to prove I'm unworthy of your trust."

"Except lie to us."

"Lying by omission only."

"Still lying."

"Everyone has secrets," she said, remembering her conversation with Beau before coming into the house.

Mat sighed and nodded. "Promise me you aren't after our technology."

"I promise."

"This is a bad position to be in, Elle. I don't like it."

"I'm sorry. Is it why you've been in such a bad mood all night?"

"Maybe I've been worried about what you plan to do to pay me back for telling Mama you're in California before you had a chance to do it."

"I don't think so."

"Your note was pretty threatening."

"Right. Like you've ever felt threatened by me."

"The last couple of weeks have been hard," he admitted in a voice laced with mental fatigue.

"You weren't expecting to be a project manager."

"No."

"Bigsley's disappearance really messed you up, huh?"

Mat shrugged. "I don't hate the job, but I'm worried about him. Are you going to investigate his disappearance?"

"It's not technically part of my assignment, but I told my boss about it. He's deciding whether to give the disappearance over to the FBI, or pursue it as part of a reopened case for us. Unless he's convinced Dr. Bigsley's disappearance puts important technology at risk, he'll probably turn it over to the FBI."

"Bigsley's a brilliant scientist and a good man, Elle. I want him found."

"And you expect me to find him?"

"I expect you to make sure his disappearance isn't ignored, like it has been.

"Why didn't you call Mykola about it? He probably has connections with people who could have looked into it sooner."

"He's on a case and can't be reached. Don't tell Mama. She thinks he's e-mailing her once a week."

"But you're doing it from his address?" She wasn't surprised to hear one brother was covering for the other.

And it made her feel warm inside to realize they had all covered for her in regard to keeping her job a secret. She had pretty great brothers.

"Yes."

"More secrets."

"Yes."

"I'll make sure Gil Bigsley's disappearance doesn't get dismissed any longer."

"Thank you."

"No problem. Don't push yourself too hard for this new job, please, Mat." She would never have guessed her oldest brother would end up in a position of managing other people.

He didn't like a lot of them.

He shrugged again. "We all do what we have to."

"That darn Chernichenko overachieving gene at work."

"Better that than an underachiever."

"You think that's what I am?"

"What the hell are you talking about?" He looked and sounded genuinely shocked.

"I know the family thinks I'm wasting my intellect in my job."

"Are you happy with your job, Elle?"

"Yes." It was all she had and all she wanted after she'd lost Kyle.

"Then, it's not a waste. We can't all live in an ivory tower looking for ways to save the environment. Some of us have to save the world in a more dangerous way. I won't pretend I don't wish the danger wasn't there for my baby sister, but it is what it is."

"Thank you. That means a lot to me."

"Don't start blubbering."

"Won't happen."

"Good."

"Why hasn't Mykola ever told me he knows I'm an agent?"

"He's probably like me. He's been waiting for you to trust him enough to tell him."

"I didn't mean to hurt you."

"I know."

"But I did anyway, huh?"

"We'll get over it. We're not little kids. Life's not perfect and we don't expect it to be."

"I can't tell Mama and Papa."

"That's probably for the best. They would only worry, and they do enough of that already."

"You saying you don't worry?"

"Of course I worry. You're my little sister, no matter how

good you are with a gun." He pulled her into a bear hug. "But I trust you not to take risks you don't have to."

She hugged him back. "Thanks."

"Did you make your sister cry again?" Papa asked, his voice censorious. "These two, you've got to watch them. They push each other so hard, you would think Elle was second oldest, not second youngest, yes?"

Elle pushed away from her brother and wiped her cheeks, only then realizing she *had* been crying.

"See? I told you that you made her cry. Did you bring up Kyle? You know Baba told you not to talk about him to her. What's done is done."

Elle choked on her laughter. Trust her father to stomp all over tender feelings while trying to protect them. Tactful was not a word in his personal dictionary.

Elle and Beau were on the way back to his place when he said, "Tell me about Kyle."

"He was my husband."

"I know that from this morning. He died."

"Yes."

"And your family isn't supposed to talk about him?"

"I guess so. I never knew Baba put the moratorium on it, but I'm grateful. For a long time after he died, I felt like I had too, and hearing his name hurt more than anything I'd ever known."

"And now?"

"It still hurts, but I can think about him with pleasure too."

"Remembering the good times?"

"Something like that."

"What happened?"

Memories that at one time had been sharp and suffocating now played through her mind like an old movie reel. "He was a witness in a bank robbery gone bad. They took him as a hostage and then killed him."

"Shit."

"Yeah."

"Were you on the recovery team?"

"I'm not a police officer. I'm a private consultant and I was consulting." She hadn't even been in town when it had happened. Losing her husband had nearly destroyed her. Knowing that if she had been in town maybe she could have saved him added salt to a wound that would never completely heal.

"I'm a damn good security consultant, but I never taught him self-defense. How stupid was that?" Oh, man, she'd never admitted that particular guilt out loud. "He didn't even have a pocketknife for use as a weapon. I could have taught him how to use one to effect, but I thought he was safe. He was a professor, you know? What was going to happen to him? A poisoned apple from a disgruntled student? We used to joke about it. Doesn't feel so funny now."

What was the matter with her? Did she have diarrhea of the mouth?

"Elle, sugar, I think you should pull over."

"What?" She swiped at her cheeks. "Why?"

"You're crying."

"No, I'm not. Crying is for the weak, and I'm strong."

"Princess, stop the car. Now."

Elle found herself obeying, pulling into a lay-by and turning off the sports car's purring engine.

Beau unbuckled both their seat belts and then pulled her against his chest, and damned if she didn't let loose a sob.

"Why didn't I teach him, Beau? Why was I so stupid?"

"Did he want to learn?"

"No. Kyle was a pacifist. He hated weapons and fighting." But he'd loved her. He'd never once asked Elle to change careers. He'd always supported her. "I failed him."

"It doesn't sound like that to me. He wouldn't have let you teach him if you'd offered."

"I did offer." And Beau was right. Kyle had turned her down. "I should have made him."

"When you love someone, you respect his or her choices. You can't force yours on that person." He said it with such certainty, she could tell he knew exactly what he was talking about.

"But he would be alive right now."

"No. You can't change the past no matter how much you want to, not even in your own mind. If Kyle was a pacifist, he wouldn't have fought the kidnappers regardless."

"To save his own life . . ."

You can't change who he was and you wouldn't want to, would you?"

"No." She had loved Kyle so much. "He was an amazing man."

"It's not your fault he's gone."

"It feels like it. I should have been there to save him."

"Maybe then you would be dead now, along with him."

"I'm good at what I do."

Beau chuckled. "All right, princess, no slurs on your deadliness, but all the what-ifs in the world aren't going to bring Kyle back. They just make you miserable and I'm sure that's not what he would have wanted."

"How do you know?"

"He loved you. When you love someone, you want that person to be happy."

Elle let the words sink in as she laid that particular ghost to rest. Kyle would not have wanted to learn self-defense and might very well have refused to use it if she had succeeded in bullying him into the lessons. She would never lose all the guilt she felt about being on assignment when her husband's life was taken, but like Beau said . . . the past couldn't be changed.

She realized she was snuggled in his muscular arms, having soaked his shirt with tears. Mortified at her weakness, she pushed away from him. "Maybe you should drive the rest of the way."

Her eyes were still blurry.

"No problem." The glee in Beau's voice brought a small smile to her lips.

He definitely liked the idea of driving her car.

Mat knocked loudly on Chantal's apartment door and then stepped back so she could see him through the peephole. He heard her on the other side of the door, but it didn't open.

"Let me in, little one. We need to talk." It was past time.

"It's not a good time," she said through the door.

He leaned against the wall facing the door. "I am not going anywhere."

After a few seconds, the door swung inward. Chantal frowned at him from the open doorway. "You are very stubborn."

He shrugged, pushing himself away from the wall and toward her.

Dressed in a fuzzy robe, bare feet peeking out from below the hem, Chantal retreated from his advance into her domain. He followed her, closing and locking the door behind him.

She stopped in the middle of the combination living-dining area. "What are you doing here? How did you find me?"

She sounded panicked. That was a little over the top for him showing up on her doorstep unannounced. He didn't have to be a superspy, like his younger brother and sister were, to recognize that something was going on.

"I'm here because we need to talk. As for how I found you, you aren't the only one who knows how to look an address up on the Internet." Which wasn't actually how he'd found her, but admitting he'd looked in her employee file might make him sound like a stalker, or like he was desperate, or something.

Her face lost all color, right down to her bow-shaped lips. "I thought I was unlisted."

"Okay, so I looked in your employee file. You going to tell Frank?"

"No, I . . . Uh, what do we have to talk about?"

"Why did you run out of my office this afternoon?" She hadn't just left his office; she'd left the building. He'd tried to call her, but gotten her voice mail. He hadn't left a message.

He would have been here right after he got off from work, but he had promised Mama he would be there for dinner with Elle at the family home. He'd wanted to talk to his sister about Gil Bigsley anyway, but now he was starting to wonder if he should have gone with his first instinct and come directly to Chantal's.

"I had things to do."

"They weren't work related. You left ETRD entirely."

Her gaze was filled with worry; she bit her lip in a gesture that was growing familiar as well as more and more arousing.

Just like earlier in his office, he couldn't stop himself from reaching out to save that sweet little bit of flesh. He gently pressed against it with his thumb. "Stop that."

She released her lip with a small gasp, her hazel eyes dilating.

"You were starting to cry. In my office," he reminded her, in case she'd forgotten.

She looked on the verge of tears now. "I . . . I had something in my eye."

"You are a lousy liar."

"Maybe because I'm so rotten at telling when someone is lying to me," she said sadly, her small shoulders drooping.

"Who has been lying to you, little one?"

"I . . . it's not important."

"It is to me."

"Why?"

"We're friends."

"Are we?" She spun on her heel and walked quickly toward the kitchen area.

He followed her but stopped short when he saw the packed suitcase beside the two-person bistro-style table that comprised her dining room.

"What's going on? You have a trip planned?"

She ignored him and walked into the kitchenette. It was separated from the rest of the living area by only a set of waist-high cabinets. "Would you like something to drink?"

"No, I want to know what this is for." He tapped the suitcase with his foot.

She tried for a casual shrug, but it came off jerky and more than a little false. "I decided to take your advice and go visit my cousins."

"When did you make this decision?"

"Tonight." She turned and grabbed a glass from one of the upper cabinets on the far wall above the sink.

"They must not be too far away."

"Actually, they're out of the country," she said, then snapped her mouth shut as if she regretted saying that.

"So, what? You're going to spend tomorrow flying, spend a few hours with them and fly back Sunday? Sounds to me like you should plan this trip a little better."

"I'm not coming back on Sunday."

"You haven't cleared a vacation with ETRD." He would know; technically, she was his subordinate.

"You can tell Frank I'll be gone."

"How long?" His frustration grew with her vague answers, each of which only increased his growing certainty that she was in some kind of trouble.

"I don't know."

"What the hell is going on?" The words exploded out of him. Okay, so patience wasn't his strong suit.

She jumped and dropped the glass she'd taken out of the cabinet. It landed in the sink, shattering. She stared down at the broken glass as if it held answers to the secrets of the universe.

Enough was enough. Something was frightening his little one and he damn well was going to find out what.

He was in the kitchen in a heartbeat, pulling her into his arms. "Tell me what's wrong, Chantal."

"I can't."

"You can." He cupped the nape under her silky blond mane. "You will."

She shook her head.

"Yes. Little one, I can help you. You need to trust me."

"Like I did ten years ago?"

# Chapter 6

Mat had known the travesty of what had happened ten years ago would come up. How could it not? He had made a huge mistake and was only now realizing the cost it had on his own life.

He'd seen the cost to Chantal in her beautiful, vulnerable gaze ten years ago.

"That was a different time. I was younger. An idiot." The words were a lot easier to say than Mat would have thought. Perhaps because he now knew how true they were.

"No, I was the stupid one. I thought a superhunk like you could really be interested in a geek like me."

"I *was* interested."

"In adding my virginity as a notch on your bedpost maybe."

"It wasn't like that."

"Yes, it was."

"My girlfriend had just dumped me. We were talking marriage and then suddenly she wanted out. She wanted to date other guys; she said I bored her. I was proving something to myself."

"That you could seduce a geeky virgin? Doesn't seem like you proved all that much."

"You were shy, not a geek. But your shyness wasn't the

problem; my feelings were. I still loved my girlfriend, or thought I did. I realized the next morning I'd been totally unfair to you."

"So, you dumped me and walked away."

"I thought it was the right thing to do." He wasn't going to make the same mistake again, though. He would not be walking away. He would prove he was trustworthy too, no matter what the past held.

"You might as well walk away right now too." She sounded resigned, but unhappy at the prospect. "Trust me, it's for the best."

It was her evident unhappiness that gave him hope. "That's not happening."

"It has to. Please, Mat. You've got to leave."

"I'm not going anywhere." He rubbed her back through the fuzzy bathrobe. "Now, tell me what's going on."

"I'm scared, Matej."

He loved the way she said his full name with that slight French accent. It made him hard, but it touched his heart too.

He tipped her head back with his hold at her nape. Their eyes met and he wouldn't let her look away. "What's scaring you?"

She just shook her head.

"Tell me, little one."

"You need to go."

The hell with that. He wasn't leaving her like this, scared and all teary-eyed. She needed him.

He picked her up and held her cradled against his chest.

"Yipes!" She really said *yipes*.

Adorable.

"What are you doing?" she demanded.

"You broke a glass . . . you have bare feet."

"It broke in the sink!"

"A piece could have landed on the floor. We can't risk you cutting yourself."

"*Sacre bleu!* You are being ridiculous."

"You think?"

"*Oui.* Yes."

"Did you know you slip into French when you are agitated? I noticed it when we made love ten years ago. You are still doing it."

"That wasn't making love; that was sex," his little kitten spat. "There were no feelings attached to it."

"You were in love with me. That is a feeling."

"You . . . you . . . I . . ." she sputtered.

"Yes, you and I. And it was good. Very good. I was a fool to walk away from what we shared, but I will not be that misguided again."

"We shared nothing."

"Oh, but we did. We shared our bodies. We shared our hearts."

"Your heart wasn't involved."

"I did not realize it, but it was. I now know that I left a big chunk of it behind with you. I want a full heart again."

"You don't mean that," she said on a gasp.

"Have I ever lied to you, even when it would have been easier on both of us?"

Chantal stared at Mat, for once her fear fading in the face of a stronger emotion. He could only hope it was what he hoped—that she still had feelings for him. He would fan the flame until it consumed them both. He was done being alone and so was she, even if she didn't know it yet.

Finally, she spoke. "No." She cleared her throat, her eyes glistening with suspicious moisture. "No. You have never lied to me."

"And I never will."

She nodded, swallowing.

He smiled at her and then walked around the counter into the other part of the room.

"You're acting like a real Neanderthal," she said in a conversational tone.

"Is that a good or bad thing?"

She laughed, shaking her head.

He smiled. Laughing was good.

He sat down on the sofa, placing her in his lap in the process. "Now, talk."

"We can't sit like this."

"Why not? I like it." He liked it a lot. In fact, he was pretty sure if she moved half an inch to her left, she'd feel just how much he liked it.

Chantal wasn't sure how to answer. She had been on the verge of losing it when Mat arrived, and now she was dealing with a whole other set of emotions on top of the fear and desperation.

Licking her lips, she said, "You are my boss, not my boyfriend."

"What if I want to be both?"

He couldn't mean it. "No."

"Why not?"

"You dumped me ten years ago." She needed to remember that, but he'd said he was sorry, tried to explain. Even claimed he regretted walking away from her. And he'd never lied to her. Not once. Even when she wished he had. Nevertheless, she said, "I won't let you hurt me like that again."

"I won't let me hurt you like that either. I'm playing for keeps here, little one." His gray gaze was clear, hiding nothing. Or so she hoped.

"How can you say that? We barely know each other. What we had ten years ago is not now."

"Neither of us has changed that much."

"And that is exactly why we can't date." Only her arguments sounded hollow even to her own ears.

Chantal had never forgotten Mat and she never would. She'd compared every man she'd dated since to him. She'd daydreamed about him finding her again and telling her he was wrong to let her go. And here it was happening.

How could she trust him, though? Especially now.

"I wanted you then, but I was too stupid to realize it. I've gotten smarter in the ways that count." He grinned down at her. "Mama and Baba are going to be thrilled. But it will not simply be relief that I am finally settling down. They are both going to love you. Papa too."

Settling down? As in marriage? He couldn't be talking about something that big. Only, knowing him, she figured he could be. Matej Chernichenko did not live life by anyone else's rules. He hardly ever smiled at anyone else either. Only her. Why did she have to think of that *now*? "This is impossible. Stop it. *We can't*."

"Not impossible. Easy actually. It is right."

She so wanted to believe him, but she shook her head.

"Tell me what's got you so scared," he prodded.

Could she? Could she *not*? "I don't know where to start."

"My father always told me the beginning is a good place to start with explanations."

"Your father is a smart man."

"He is."

"I was dating Eddie."

"Who?"

"Eddie Danza. The security guard who got let go for leaking company secrets."

Mat's usual frown was back. "The one who disappeared afterward? The security guard disappeared, too."

"Yes." Mat must have heard the rumors on the company grapevine. That's how she found out Eddie had disappeared.

"How long were you dating?"

"A few months."

"Were you sleeping with him?"

Chantal bristled. "What business is that of yours?"

"Probably no business of mine at all, but you'll answer the question anyway."

"I will?"

"Yes."

"Why?" She might, if he didn't say something dumb like because he'd told her to.

"You brought up dating him as part of something that's scaring you enough to send you running to family who don't want you around."

"You told me they miss me."

"And I'm sure they do, but *you* don't believe it, and yet, you're going to see them. I want to know why."

"What has that got to do with me sleeping with Eddie?"

"I don't know, but he's part of this thing that has you wanting to run away. Everything should be out in the open."

"Yes, all right?" She glared at Mat. "I was as stupid with him as I was with you. I haven't managed to learn anything about telling the good guys from the creeps in ten years."

Mat jerked back as if Chantal had slapped him. "I am not a creep."

"You used me. He used me."

"I did use you and I regret that more than anything else in my life. I will never use you again."

"I want to believe you," she admitted.

"I will help you."

"I'm sure you will."

"How did Danza use you?"

She turned her face away, not wanting to see Mat's expression when she admitted to her naiveté. "I thought that he wanted me . . . that maybe he even loved me, but he just wanted an in with one of the scientists. I was the one dumb enough to fall for it."

"Has he been threatening you?"

"No, he disappeared—I told you."

"But you're frightened of something."

"The people he was working with still want the plans he got for them."

"What plans?"

Chantal forced herself to meet Mat's eyes, but she saw no disgust there. Just concern. "You heard that security was breached on the antigrav project?"

"Beau's project? Yes, I heard that. That's why they hired my sister to beef up security."

Shock coursed through her. "Ms. Gray is your sister?"

"It's Elle, and yes. She can be a pain in the butt, but she's going to adore you too."

Ignoring the last comment, Chantal said, "I guess I can kind of see the family resemblance. You two have the same eyes. She's tall too. Like you."

"You're getting sidetracked, sweetheart."

"Sorry. It's just I don't want to think about it."

"About what? You still haven't told me exactly what's scaring you."

"They called me."

"The people Eddie was working with?"

"I think so. They want the antigrav plans and they want me to get the schematics for them."

Mat looked confused. "But you aren't on the project."

"They don't care. They said that they could make trouble for me. That if I told anyone about them contacting me they would make it look like I was dirty even if I'm not, and they said . . ."

"They said?"

"That I could disappear just like Gil Bigsley if I didn't cooperate."

"They took Gil?"

"I don't know. I think so. That's what they implied, but maybe he just ran away, like I've been thinking about. I'm so scared, Mat. I don't know what to do." She grabbed his shirt and tried to shake him.

Of course, he was as solid as a rock and didn't move a centimeter. "You are not running away."

He stood up and made sure she was steady on her own feet before he let her go. "Is everything you need in that suitcase?"

"Everything but my laptop. And Gervaise."

"Gervaise?"

"My pet betta fish. I named him after my father." Her eyes got all watery again and she had to blink the moisture away. "I didn't want to leave him, but you can't take a fish on the run with you. I was going to call you, ask you to feed him and talk to him. He likes that."

"You talk to your pet fish?"

"If I didn't, he would be lonely. He can't have little Betta friends because they would eat each other."

"Okay. Get it."

"Gervaise?" Was Matej going to take care of her pet for her? "You're going to take me to the airport?" That didn't make any sense. He'd told her that she wasn't going to run away, which really was her decision, but still, he'd said it.

"I'm taking you to my place."

"You can't." No, no, no. *He really couldn't.* "What if they're watching? What if they go after you next?"

"Bring it on." He smiled, and this one made her shiver, glad she wasn't the one that scary expression in his eyes was for. "Besides, tomorrow morning, I'm taking you to an expert."

"Expert?"

"My sister."

"Your sister?"

"She'll figure this mess out. It's her job."

"As a security consultant?"

"Listen, Elle is better with weapons than a marine with a hard-on for his rifle, and she can kill with her bare hands. With both of us watching out for you, you aren't going to disappear."

"She can kill with her bare hands? That sounds scary. She looks so chic, like a supermodel who knows how to dress like one *all* the time."

"Yeah, well, appearances can be deceiving."

"I suppose." But still . . . that gorgeous security consultant was deadly? Wow. Matej's offer sounded so good, but she didn't want to bring danger to him and his family. "I don't know. Maybe I should go with my plan of just disappearing. I feel like I'm putting more and more people at risk. I don't like it."

"We can't stop the people threatening you if all you do is run away."

He was right, and if they were responsible for Gil's disappearance, they needed to be stopped. "I'm still not sure *this* is the right route to take. Maybe I should risk them trying to make me look like a thief and go to the authorities. I don't like putting you or your sister at risk."

"It is my choice and Elle's job is already high risk. She's used to it."

"I didn't realize security consultants had dangerous jobs."

"If only you knew."

"I—"

Mat put his finger against Chantal's lips to stop her words. "It is no use arguing. We won't rule out talking to the authorities, but first we will get Elle's opinion on what is happening. I will not allow you to be hurt. In any way."

Chantal knew that last promise regarded her emotions and she wanted to believe him. So much. But could she trust her own judgment where Mat was concerned? She didn't know.

She did trust him to protect her person and that meant talking to his sister and getting this mess straightened out. For right now, that was what she was going to focus on.

"What happens tonight?" He'd said he wanted to take her to Elle tomorrow morning.

"You come home with me."

"It would probably be better if I stayed here." Less risk to him. She could stay with Gervaise.

"That's not happening. Now, you can get your pet fish and your laptop and walk out to the car, or I can carry you. Your choice."

"You *have* changed in the last decade," Chantal grumbled even as she headed to her bedroom to change out of her pajamas.

"How?"

"You've gotten bossier."

Elle watched lights flash by in the dark. Beau wasn't going so fast that he had her adrenaline pumping, but he sure wasn't sticking to the speed limit either.

"So, what do you drive?" she asked.

"A Suzuki Hayabusa."

"That's a sports cycle."

"I shouldn't be surprised you know your motorcycles."

"My mother would kill me if I bought one, but they fascinate me."

"D.C. isn't exactly practical weatherwise for a rider either."

"You've got that right."

"On the other hand, Southern California practically begs for that type of transportation."

"Do you race?"

"Officially?"

"At all."

"Sometimes. I'm in a cycle club. We do road trips into the desert, and sometimes that leads to a race or two."

"I bet your bike kicks ass."

Beau laughed, the sound rich and warm, filling the small interior of the car. "That it does."

"You can take the cowboy out of Texas, but you can't take the need to ride out of the cowboy. Is that the way of it?"

"I don't know. My dad was a banker, not a rancher. I never did ride a horse, but I sure do love my cycle. This little baby isn't bad either." He patted the dash of her Lamborghini.

"I think you owe me a ride on the Hayabusa since I let you drive."

"Sure, princess. Anytime."

"What is it with the 'princess' thing? I'm hardly a girly-girl."

"You are so kidding, right?"

Was *he* joking? "No."

"Elle, you dress in designer labels, keep your nails manicured and your hair sleek and gorgeous, and wear your makeup just right. You are not exactly butch."

"Hey, I can kill a man with my bare hands."

"And while that's a serious turn-on, it doesn't make you any less of a princess."

"You don't mean that."

"Hey, not all princesses are whimpering damsels in distress. Haven't you ever watched *Xena*?"

Elle laughed, "Xena's got a serious wardrobe problem."

"She doesn't have your style, but she knows how to fight."

"And that excites you? Really?" She had a hard time believing he found her training a turn-on.

"In you? Oh, yeah." He flicked her a sensual grin. "But then pretty much everything about you turns me on."

"I don't know if this is a good idea."

"What?"

"This whole being attracted to each other and working together thing."

"So, you admit the attraction is mutual."

"I haven't made a secret of how sexy I find you."

"You could have just been flirting."

"I was, but I meant it too."

"So, what's the problem? We don't actually work together."

"I'm working for your company."

"You're consulting for Mr. Smith. That hardly places us in a position of needing to keep our libidos under control."

"You're very blunt, you know that?"

"Would you prefer I wasted time dancing around this thing between us?"

"This 'thing'?"

"I want you, Elle and I know you want me too. We can pretend it's not there, but it is. Some kind of connection that neither of us was expecting."

"Of all people, you know I'm not completely over what happened with my husband."

"You probably never will be."

"And that doesn't bother you?"

"I want sex with you, Elle, not happily ever after. Hell, you'll only be in California for a couple of months. On the outside. So, I don't see what point there would be in getting serious."

He was right. She wasn't going to be here forever and trying to start anything lasting with their divergent careers and home-base locations would be useless. It could never work.

When she was younger, that knowledge would have prevented her from pursuing the mutual attraction. Before loving and losing Kyle.

But tonight? She wanted, maybe even needed, the physical connection sans emotional entanglements. Her desire for Beau was intense and uncomplicated. She wasn't contemplating intimacy with him for the job. She wasn't looking to create a long-term bond. She was seeking catharsis for pain and loss she was maybe finally coming to terms with.

"You just want sex?"

"Exceptionally good sex. Probably even great sex. Maybe even mind-blowing sex. Yes."

"Mind-blowing? Your arrogance is showing again," she said, with a laugh.

"We get within a foot of each other and sparks shoot between us. I get hard as a rock and if you aren't getting wet enough to drown my dick, I'll give up the pink slip on my cycle."

"You've got a dirty mouth for a PhD."

"You like it?"

"I . . ." For the first time in her memory, she was speechless. But then honesty won over confusion. "You know? I think I do."

He laughed and the car accelerated. "Yeah, I thought so. You're perfect for me, Elle."

"For your bed, you mean."

"My bed, my body . . . it all works."

"I guess it does." He wasn't asking her for anything she couldn't give and he was offering her pleasure that sounded darn enticing. "My place or yours?"

"Yours. Frank's been known to show up unexpectedly at mine on the weekends."

"And you don't want him to catch me naked in your bed?" she teased.

"It wouldn't bother me, but I was thinking to protect your sensibilities."

"Thanks." And she meant it. She wasn't used to anyone looking out for her. She was the trained professional, after all.

It was more than a little pleasant having Beau thinking about how to protect her feelings. Most people in her life these days assumed she didn't have any. And while she might have worked to cultivate that belief, it still felt nice to have someone not buy into the total tough-girl image.

She really didn't care if that made any sense, or not.

Beau drove straight to Elle's, enjoying the way her car handled in town as much as he had driving it on the freeway. He couldn't wait to take her for a ride on his bike. He knew she wanted to drive it too.

He'd have to borrow another cycle from someone in the club so they could go on a nice, long, *fast* ride together. As opposed to the long, slow, pounding ride he planned for her tonight.

After pulling the powerful sports car into a spot outside the temporary corporate housing apartments ETRD had put Elle up in for the duration of her stay, he cut the engine. "Sweet ride, princess."

"Thanks. It was worth taking a week to drive out here so I'd have it with me."

"I buy that."

Neither of them said another word until they were inside Elle's furnished apartment. It looked like an upscale hotel suite, but Beau wasn't here to study the décor. His attention was firmly fixed elsewhere, like on her derriere, where her slacks clung tightly.

"Nice," he said, letting his appreciation color his voice in vibrant hues.

She shrugged out of her short jacket and dropped it along with her purse on the white leather sofa, leaving her in a clingy tank top and the sinfully formfitting pants. "It is a nice place."

"I wasn't talking about the apartment, sugar."

She went still and then turned slowly to face him. The look she gave him was pure enticement, her eyes glittering silver. "Is that right?"

# Chapter 7

"Oh, yeah." Beau leaned back against the door, crossing his arms over his chest. No doubt, he looked a hell of a lot more relaxed than he felt. But it was that, or charge across the room and take Elle down in a tackle worthy of a defensive lineman. "Do you know how good your pert little ass looks in those slacks?"

She made a show of trying to look at her own backside. "You think my bottom is pert?"

"I do. Of course, I could give a more educated opinion if I saw it without covering."

She tapped her chin, like she was thinking. "Uncovered?" She turned around. "You mean like this?"

Then she shimmied out of her slacks, letting them fall to the floor and stepping out of them.

"She-yit," he whispered.

She had struck a classic pose, her elbows up, fingertips touching at her nape under her silky black hair. The pose brought the hem of her top just above the small of her back, leaving the succulent globes of her ass framed by the thin straps of a blood-red thong. The shadowed apex of her thighs teased him, drawing his gaze downward along legs that would make a showgirl proud. She was still wearing her shiny ankle boots with four-inch spiked heels.

He groaned. "Sugar, you are a wet dream come to life."

She looked back over her shoulder and gave him a sexy wink. "I'm glad you think so." The husky tone of her voice told him she was as turned on by showing off for him as he was by the sight.

Elle spread her legs just a little and bent from the waist until her hands clasped her ankles and her hair brushed the carpet. The tiny triangle of blood-red silk barely covered her labia. Damp, it clung to the swollen folds, revealing their lush shape to his heated gaze.

Beau's knees tried to buckle and he figured he'd have fallen on his ass if he hadn't been leaning on the door. "Gah . . ." was all that came out of his mouth.

Throaty laughter trickled from her. "You like?"

"I want."

Her thighs visibly tightened at his guttural tone. "Yes?"

"*Yes*." He wasn't sure how he got there, but the next thing he knew, his hands were holding her hips in an unbreakable grip and he was thrusting his denim-covered erection against her backside, rubbing right up against that damp triangle of silk. He'd never been with a woman as tall as Elle, and in her heels, he barely had to bend his knees for perfect alignment.

Maintaining that amazing pose, she pressed back against him. "You sure you want?"

"You know it." He was surprised his mouth could form words. He was heading toward that place where single syllables and grunts had to do for his attempt at communication.

"Have."

The single-word invitation sent pre-come spurting out of his rock-hard cock. He thrust against her, grateful he still had jeans on. If he didn't, he wasn't totally sure he wouldn't already be buried inside her, and he didn't even know if she had condoms.

"Gloves?" he asked in a graveled voice.

"Bed . . ." She moaned and shimmied against him. "Room."

Beau tucked his arm into the crease of her body, pressing it against her pelvis and lifting. She was surprisingly light and easy to carry. As he headed toward the door he hoped led to the bedroom, she straightened with the strength of a gymnast and looped her arms around his neck.

The temptation to touch her now accessible breasts too much for him, he stopped. Keeping her body slightly off the floor and flush against his, he used his free hand to slide under her top. The skin of her stomach was silky smooth and hot. He got sidetracked exploring it, tracing the indent of her belly button and measuring his big hand against the flat expanse of skin.

Elle turned her head and kissed the side of his neck and his jaw, nipping him gently between each tender caress of her lips. Her hair caressed his skin with each movement of her head, adding extra sensual stimulation to their embrace.

Damn . . . everything about this woman was designed to make his libido explode. He'd never been so turned on. Never wanted so many different things at the same time. To strip her naked. To touch every inch of her skin. To be inside her. To leave love bites and mark her as his, for now at least. To taste—both her skin and her feminine nectar. And, man . . . he wanted *her* to taste *him*. He wanted her hands on him. He wanted her legs wrapped around his waist, her body under his or on top of his, riding him and bringing them both pleasure.

It was going to take every night of the weeks she would be in Southern California to do everything he wanted.

But right now, he was going to get his first feel of her breast.

Beau slid his hand higher until he felt the bottom of her unfettered mound. "No bra, princess?"

"Don't . . . like . . . them," Elle said between nibbles along his jaw.

Her tongue flicked out to taste him, rasping along his five o'clock shadow. She didn't seem to mind and that heightened his arousal. He'd never been with a woman so earthy and in touch with her own sexuality, so accepting of every aspect of his maleness. She didn't play coy, but met him desire for desire.

" 'M glad," he said as his fingertips skimmed the curve of her breast. She wasn't huge, but he wasn't disappointed. Not a bit. He gently squeezed the resilient flesh. She was maybe a B cup and deliciously firm with nipples just the right size for her understated curves. "You don't need one."

"Nnn . . . OOOH . . ." Her voice went up an octave as he rolled her turgid peak between his fingertips. Goose bumps rose around the hard bud.

"Damn, woman, you are molten." Go him, talking in whole sentences.

"You . . ." She bit his chin—this time just enough to sting.

A raw sound came from deep inside him as he jerked his head around so their lips could mesh.

"Too . . ." she whispered against his mouth just before their lips converged.

The kiss was amazing. No shrinking violet, Elle met his tongue thrust for thrust and changed the angle only slightly when their teeth clashed. No complaints about it being too rough. She wanted it as much as he did. She was squirming against him, her fingers digging into his nape and, man, didn't that feel fine.

Beau didn't know how long they stood there necking right outside her bedroom door, but his arousal grew so intense, he was on the verge of coming in his jeans. He could deal with that—he knew he was good for more than one go-round tonight—but hell if he was going alone. Changing the angle of his hold on her, he tunneled his long fingers into the honeyed depths at her core.

Her body went rigid and she keened against his lips.

He dipped into her wet center, spreading her natural lubricant upward so his fingers slid over her clitoris as easy as pie. Oh, shit—she was perfect there too. A hard little nub that pulsed with her desire. He was careful not to press too hard, but rubbed with a gentle rhythm as his own balls drew up in preparation for shooting.

He felt the point of no return coalesce in the base of his dick and he pinched her clit, once . . . twice . . . three times. She ripped her mouth from his, a harsh cry sounding as her body convulsed and he let his own pleasure explode out of him.

He milked her pleasure with his fingers until she gave another set of miniconvulsions, and then whimpering, she sort of just went limp against him. He carefully adjusted his hold on her so that he wasn't pressing directly against her overstimulated clitoris.

Letting her head rest back against his shoulder, she gave a very satiated sigh. "Mmm. Nice appetizer."

His laughter rang around them as he finished carrying her into the bedroom. She was perfect for him.

Elle decided that there was something incredibly decadent about being carried the way Beau was holding her. He still had one hand cupping the apex of her thighs, the tip of his middle finger sliding just into the opening of her vagina. His other arm was crossed over her chest, his hand pressed protectively over her breast—or was that possessively? Either way, it felt good. Right. For now, anyway.

When they reached the bed, he stopped and let her down

so she was standing, his hand sliding up and brushing her pleasure spot and making her body jolt. He didn't let her move away, though, but kept her close with a hand on her hip. "Stay there."

"Okay."

"I like it when you're all agreeable."

"Don't get used to it."

"Oh, I won't." His voice was laced with laughter, though, and she got the impression that that humor was directed at her.

"You're only in charge if I let you be," she warned him.

"You think I'm not aware? We Texans aren't that stupid, princess."

"All right, then."

He laughed softly. "Don't you worry, sugar. I know you're a warrior under all that fierce feminine desire."

"And you're still a brainiac under all that alpha attitude."

"We make a good pair, then, don't we?"

"Why? Because we're more than what you see on the surface?"

"I like your surface and what's underneath."

Elle believed him. Beau wasn't intimidated by her dangerous side or her uninhibited desires. A lot of men weren't comfortable with a woman who gave as good as she got. She liked the fact that Beau wasn't one of them. Maybe even adored it.

"Ditto." It wasn't hearts and flowers, but it was truth and a rare one.

He kissed her temple in acknowledgment of that unspoken reality. "Thank you."

Without another word, he pulled her tank top off over her head. Then he skimmed his hands down her sides until both thumbs hooked in the elastic of her thong. "Let's get this off."

"Yes."

He pulled the thong down and she stepped out of it. She could hear him inhaling behind her and she turned to see.

He was sniffing her wet panties with a feral expression that sent more pleasure pulsing between her legs. His eyes narrowed, the brown irises glittering with primal hunger. "I want to taste this."

She fell back on the bed, spreading her legs, and waved her hand airily, belying the gush of pleasure his words had caused. "Be my guest."

"Oh, I plan to." He dropped to his knees and leaned forward to plant a single kiss to her moist curls before lifting his head. "These boots are going to have to go too, princess. Sexy as they are, I'm not risking my John Thomas to those stiletto heels."

"John Thomas?"

"You bet. J.T., he's my best friend, don't you know?"

She laughed, delighted by his silliness. "You think my feet are going to get close to your groin in the next round?"

He winked. "You never know, what with wild sex and all, anything could happen and those stiletto heels are dangerous."

"You think sex with me is wild?"

"I'm from Texas, sugar, and you're a warrior princess, for sure. Tame ain't gonna cut it."

Elle found herself grinning in a way she hadn't during sex since Kyle. In fact, she wasn't sure she'd ever been this amused and hot at the same time even then. She schooled her features into a facade of seriousness. "Then the boots definitely have to go. We can't put J.T. at risk."

"Exactly." Beau removed first one and then the other, along with the footy socks she wore under them, leaving her finally completely naked.

Her legs dangled off the bed, her body open to him, but she wasn't even remotely embarrassed. Again that odd sense of rightness had settled over her. Being naked with him felt good. And yes, right.

"What about you?" she asked in a voice that came out more breathy than she'd intended.

His expression the epitome of innocence, he looked at her. "What about me?"

"You're still dressed."

"You want to see this magnificent body, you've got to earn it."

No way would she admit it to him, but his arrogance was starting to charm her more than a little. "How am I supposed to do that?"

"It's real simple, sugar. You just lie there all nice and quiet like."

Beau's drawl was thickening, his words elongating until even single-syllable words had more than one beat. Elle took that as evidence of his arousal and felt proud about bringing the primitive man out from the highly educated scientist's shell.

"I'm just supposed to lie here?"

"That's right." Then he tipped his head to the side as if considering. "Well, maybe we could alter things just a hair."

"How?"

"Let's put your feet up here." As he spoke, he lifted her feet so they were situated flat on the bed, her legs spread wide.

His dark chocolate gaze sizzled with heat as he looked at his handiwork. "Yeah, I think that'll work."

"Good," she croaked out, her throat gone dry.

He grinned. "You like being all open to me, don't you?"

"Yes." He'd tapped into her deepest fantasies, arranging her as a sexual display about to be devoured.

"Fine. Now, remember . . . you just lie there. Got it?"

She nodded, then swallowed before speaking. "What will you be doing?"

"This." And then his mouth was on her.

The sight of his dark head between her thighs and the feel of his mouth pleasuring her sent rational thought flying out into the ether.

He knew not to go directly for her clitoris after she'd already climaxed so hard, so he began with his tongue on her labia and the opening to the heart of her. He knew exactly what to do with his lips, teeth and tongue. He knew when to use his fingers and where in order to intensify her pleasure. By the time he moved his attention to her clitoris, she was moaning and thrusting her pelvis toward his mouth.

He brought her to the brink of climax not once, but three times.

She was swearing, demanding and finally begging when he took her over. Her scream was almost as long as the climax, which wrung her out until she couldn't get enough breath to make more sound.

He kissed all over her inner thighs and soothed her with gentle caresses before lowering her legs so they once again dangled over the side of the bed.

At some point, he disappeared from between her legs, but she couldn't make her head move so she could see where he'd gone. She could just about manage to lie there and wallow in a sense of repletion unlike anything she'd ever known.

She didn't know how long he was gone, but she felt his presence when he got back. Felt his eyes on her even though he said nothing.

Cracking her eyes, she looked up at him. He was naked. Finally.

She licked her lips and then smiled. "I earned naked Texan, huh?"

"You did, princess. You came so good."

She laughed, shaking her head. "I think you're the one who earned a reward."

"I plan to have one too. Bath?"

Oh, that sounded good. "Carry me there?" She didn't even feel bad about asking. It was his fault her legs were now limp noodles.

"My pleasure."

Elle hummed with pleasure as Beau lowered her into the water. He'd guessed she liked her bathwater good and hot. The blissful expression on her face told him he was right. He'd found some of that stuff that makes water all soft and slippery against your skin and added it. He now took advantage of the slickness to begin a full-body massage.

Her eyes fluttered, exposing their clear gray depths. "I thought you were going to take a bath with me."

"Naw. This little tub's too small for both of us."

"But—"

"I want to rub nekkid bodies together."

"Yes."

He smiled at her emphatic agreement despite the way her body lolled in the water, obviously exhausted.

"First we gotta get you a little revived."

"Giving me a bath is going to do that?"

"It'll get you ready for what I've got in mind." The nice, long, slow ride he'd promised himself earlier.

She met his gaze, hers as serious as a heartbeat. "You're an exceptionally generous lover."

"That presupposes that I don't get as much out of giving you pleasure as you do." Didn't she know how unbelievable her own level of response was. He was already addicted to the sounds she made in passion. "The way you react to my touch gives me a high better then aged Kentucky whiskey."

Elle shook her head. "You're a very special man, Dr. Beau Ruston."

"You go right on thinking that, princess, but I don't know a man who wouldn't gladly drown himself in your desire."

"No one ever has before. Not even . . ." Her voice trailed off, as she closed her eyes, as if she couldn't deal with giving voice to what she was thinking.

But he could guess. Kyle. "A man learns a thing or two about appreciating the good things in life by the time he's thirty-two, sugar."

"Thank you."

He wasn't sure if she was thanking him for the surfeit of physical pleasure or making excuses for the man she had given her heart to, but it didn't matter. "Welcome."

He continued the body massage, pressing into muscles that had been rigid during her orgasms. Her limbs were toned and a pleasure to touch. But then he enjoyed touching all of her. He spent several minutes using a deep, Swedish-style massage, bringing her down completely from her earlier arousal. When her breath was even and her muscles were relaxed, he changed to subtly enticing touches.

He watched in fascination as her body went from total lethargy to renewed need.

She undulated sensually in the water. "You're exciting me again."

"That's the plan."

"It's different this time."

"Yep."

"Intense, but not so edgy."

"Getting you ready for a slow ride that just might last 'til dawn."

Her eyes flew wide open. "You're serious."

"As a heart attack, sugar."

"You can't possibly have enough energy."

"You ever heard what a football player goes through during preseason training?"

"Um . . . no."

"Riding your pretty little body isn't going to be a patch on that physical challenge and it's going to feel a million times better."

"You're a competitive bastard, aren't you?"

"You think?"

"I should have known. Nobody puts himself through college on a football scholarship and then goes on to be one of the youngest PhDs in the country without having a competitive streak about a mile wide."

Beau just shrugged. He wasn't about to deny it. That would require a lie, and unlike Elle, dishonesty wasn't built into his job description.

Her eyes narrowed. "It's been a while since football training, though, jock-boy. You sure you're still up to challenging physical feats?"

Oooh . . . he might be competitive, but she was a professional when it came to throwing down the gauntlet.

"I think I'm up to it, but you'll just have to let me know what you think tomorrow morning." He still ran five miles a day and did weight training six days a week. The exercise kept his body in shape and the blood flowing to his brain.

Beau popped the plug on the tub and then lifted Elle from the water. Before he had a chance to dry her off, she pressed herself to him from lips to toes and gave him a kiss that engaged his whole being. She was certainly doing her part to make sure he could meet her challenge.

He liked a woman who played fair.

Her hands were everywhere, rubbing, smoothing, scratching lightly with her nails, and he realized that rather than helping meet the challenge, she was upping the ante, driving his arousal up notch by notch.

He liked a woman even more when she pushed his limits.

They dried each other off, since she'd gotten him wet, and then kissed on their way to the bed. By the time he got the condom on and went to slide inside her, she was soaking and his cock was so hard it hurt. But he wasn't going to come right away. No, sir. They were taking that long, slow ride.

He stopped once he was fully seated in her slick, tight channel and looked down into her eyes. Their gazes locked for several seconds before he started to move. This wasn't lovemaking in the strictest sense because they weren't in love, but it was as close to it as it got.

And damned if it wasn't going to end up the real McCoy unless he watched himself.

Falling in love wasn't on his imminent to-do list, but falling at any level for a woman who was lying to him about who she was? That would never be on his list of things to accomplish before he died.

That didn't mean he couldn't enjoy the physical intimacy. Damn right he could. And would.

And did.

It wasn't quite dawn when they finally culminated their intercourse with another simultaneous orgasm, but it was enough past midnight to be respectable.

Elle skipped her morning workout and opted for a long, hot shower instead. She was sore in places she'd forgotten she could even feel. The steamy water helped, but oh, she was going to be feeling it today. Which probably made her perverse, because she liked it. Aching muscles and borderline tender flesh were witness to how different the night before had been from anything she had allowed herself to experience in the last few years.

She felt like she'd taken a necessary step forward. She had no desire to know the emotional vulnerability she had experienced with Kyle, but having amazing sex was something else. She might not have been prepared for it, but she realized now that she didn't mind knowing that aspect to her sensuality wasn't dead. She was surprised not to feel any guilt, but maybe four years of penance—of sex as nothing more than a tool and/or a physical release of tension—was enough.

Even for her.

Then again, while every unfamiliar twinge she felt reminded her of the incredible pleasure she'd experienced the night before, there was also a subtle tension clenching her insides. So, maybe not completely guilt-free after all.

Still, she refused to regret what had indeed been mind-blowing sex.

She was drinking her second cup of coffee and making breakfast when Beau came out of the bathroom after his own shower.

Biting back a moan at how yummy he looked in nothing but his jeans from the night before, she gave him a leisurely once-over and smiled. "Good morning."

Still wet, his dark hair looked as black as hers and his brown eyes glinted with sensual lights that said he was remembering last night's ecstasy as well. The dark whorls of hair on his well-defined chest led down in a sexy-as-sin treasure trail that ended enticingly at the waistband of his low-slung jeans. She knew exactly what the snug denim covered and her womb clenched in anticipation of experiencing it again.

# Chapter 8

"You like what you see?" Beau's morning voice was a sexy rumble.

"You know I do."

He gave Elle a smile laced with smug male confidence.

She shook her head. "That arrogance again."

"I thought we agreed it wasn't arrogance if it was based on the truth." He poured himself some coffee.

She turned the bacon. "I remember you argued that point, yes."

"Let me help." He took up the spatula for the pancakes and flipped them. "You don't think I've got anything to feel smug about?"

She gave him a sidelong glance. "Oh, no, you are so not going to trick me into challenging you again." She poured egg substitute into another pan for scrambling. "I'm only walking this morning because my muscles are accustomed to hard use."

He leaned over and kissed her on the cheek and then reached around so he could get her lips. "You taste good."

"It's the bacon. I was taste testing."

He gently tugged her chin around so his lips could claim hers again, this time with more intent. This kiss lasted several seconds and involved tongue. When he pulled back, she was dazed and he was shaking his head. "Nope, not the bacon. It's definitely you."

She laughed and smacked his bare chest. "You are a goof."

With his own hand he covered where she'd hit him and staggered backward. "You wound me."

"Not only are you a goof, you're a ham too."

He bumped her hip with his own as he flipped the finished pancakes into the ceramic dish she'd been using. "Nah, I'm one hundred percent Grade A prime Texas beef."

"You are that, stud." She pursed her lips as if in thought. "It's pretty surprising considering what a brainiac you are."

He poured the remaining pancake batter into three circles in the pan. "You know what they say. What you see ain't what you get."

"I think you've got that backward. It's what you see *is* what you get."

"You sure about that?"

A loud knock on the door saved her from making another foolish challenge that might leave her downright sore, because she'd have to meet it herself, now wouldn't she?

She moved to the fridge so she could pull the package of bacon back out and laid it on the counter before going to answer the door. "Would you mind getting some more of that cooking, hon?"

He gave her a questioning look but said, "No problem."

Only three people in town knew where her temporary apartment was located. One of them was already with her. She doubted sincerely that Frank Ingram would show up at her door on a Saturday morning. That left Matej. And that meant she'd better make more bacon if she wanted any.

Sure enough, her oldest brother, dressed in his signature monochromatic black, was standing on the other side when she swung the door wide. His hair was still wet from the shower and his beard was neat, no stray hairs where they shouldn't be on his face, but he looked tired. Like he'd gotten very little sleep the night before. He also had that tic in his jaw that meant he was stressed about something, or angry.

Elle was guessing stressed and she figured the reason for his lack of sleep was standing right beside him. What was Chantal Renaud, a team scientist for ETRD, doing with Elle's brother on a Saturday morning? They must be dating, but Mat hadn't even hinted at having a girlfriend. Baba would say it was about time, though.

And personally? Elle would agree with her. Matej needed a softening influence in his life. He was far too hard edged for a research scientist.

Elle gave them both a blinding smile. "Come on in. Have you two had breakfast?"

"Yes," Mat said as he pulled Chantal inside, his arm around her waist. "But if that's bacon I smell, you might as well fry me up a piece or four."

"I'm already on it. How about you, Ms. Renaud? Would you like anything?"

"No, thank you."

"You sure, sweetheart? You barely ate anything at breakfast," Mat said, giving the small blonde a frown tinged with concern.

Chantal moved her shoulders in a half shrug. "I'm not hungry."

"You sure about that, Chantal? I make a mean pancake," Beau said, from where he stood lounging in entrance to the kitchen.

Half naked and clearly unworried by that fact.

Mat's head snapped up from his focus on Chantal and his gaze narrowed with an expression she knew well as it fell on Beau. "What the—"

"Okay, then," Elle interrupted with the speed of light.

"Breakfast. Right. Mat, you want to put plates and cutlery out? Chantal, have a seat. If you didn't eat much before, you should consider something now. It's the most important meal of the day. Beau, can you finish the bacon while I get juice and coffee for anyone who wants it? Mat, once you've set the table, you can carry the other food in. Eggs and pancakes are done."

Elle had grown up with three older brothers, yes, but under the tutelage of both her mother and grandmother. Those two worthy women knew how to keep men busy when the situation demanded it. Elle figured her oldest brother walking in on what was obviously the "morning after" between her and Beau would be labeled a demanding situation by anyone with half a brain.

She had a fully functioning one with a high IQ to boot.

She ran further interference asking everyone's drink preferences and managed to get Mat seated at the table with Chantal while she and Beau finished up in the kitchen.

Once he'd put the bacon on the table, he made a quick trip to the bedroom. He came out wearing his T-shirt.

Elle just managed to stifle a sigh of relief. She didn't need the distraction of his half-naked body when dealing with her brother. And she didn't think Mat needed the continued reminder that Beau had been lounging around her apartment barely dressed when Mat had arrived.

Elle might be independent, but again, she wasn't stupid.

Mat surprised her once they were at the table, though. Instead of glaring Beau into the carpet, he seemed preoccupied. He munched on his bacon and a single pancake with less than his usual enthusiasm. His gaze kept sliding to Chantal, and he encouraged her to eat more than once while giving her these intense looks of reassurance.

Was the female scientist that worried about meeting a member of her boyfriend's family? Elle couldn't think of another reason for her brother's behavior, but the vibe didn't feel right.

So, she ate her own breakfast and waited for Mat to tell her what was up.

They were all done eating and sipping on their coffee when he reached out and took Chantal's hand. "It's going to be all right, little one."

"What's going on?" Beau asked, the subtle authority in his voice not lost on Elle.

And darn if she didn't like it.

Chantal bit her lip, looked up at Mat, and then at Elle. Finally, she met Beau's gaze with what looked like resignation "I am in trouble."

"None of it is her fault," Mat pronounced.

Chantal turned her pale gaze on him. "How can you say that? I'm the idiot who got involved with that creep."

"He deceived you. This is not your fault." Mat looked as fierce as Elle had ever seen him.

"Are you saying you were mixed up in Eddie Danza's scheme to sell corporate secrets?" Beau asked in a flat tone.

Mat said a word in Ukrainian that Mama would wash his mouth out for, and then he surged to his feet and leaned over Beau. "She is not saying any such thing. Did you hear her say this? I didn't. Are you looking for scapegoats for your own lack of foresight in security?"

Oh, man, Mat had it bad.

Beau didn't so much as flinch. He shrugged, like Mat's words were so much buzzing, and then fixed Chantal with an unreadable gaze. That was so not going to work for the oldest Chernichenko brother in his current mood.

Elle jumped up and laid her hand on her brother's arm. "Calm down, hon." She led him back to his chair, knowing that to simply suggest he sit down would not be enough. She also knew he wouldn't fight her. That would go against the way he'd been raised. "Beau was just asking a question, not making an accusation," she soothed further.

"I don't need a scapegoat," Beau said in the same flat tone he'd used before. "I do need an answer."

Elle shot a look of reproach at him. Heaven save her from having two alpha men together in the same room.

Mat popped right back up out of his chair. "Like hell."

Elle was ready to clock both of them.

However, humor was leaking through the worry in Chantal's eyes, and she turned to face Mat with a small smile. "I don't think this will work if you leap to defend me like a mad grizzly every time a question is asked."

He frowned at her, though his expression was not nearly as fierce as it had been when he'd been looking at Beau. "I will not have you feeling like a criminal."

"I don't. I may feel like *un imbécile*, but I know I've done nothing unethical. If Beau believes I have, then I know you will help me convince him otherwise. Though, please remember, he has not said so. Now, sit down, *s'il vous plaît*."

Elle watched in shock as her brother did exactly as the petite woman had requested. "Wow. You don't mind Mama that well. You didn't even give a token grumble. Mama will be jealous, but I think Baba is going to dance with joy."

Elle almost felt guilty for teasing him when the big, tough, highly educated, thirty-four-year-old eremitic scientist blushed, his expression more than a little pained. Chantal looked pleased, however, so maybe it had been worth it.

"So, tell us what you mean by being in trouble," Elle invited before either of the men could start pounding their chests again.

"I broke up with Eddie when I found out what he'd done. I didn't know anything about it beforehand. I want you to know that." She was talking to Elle, but the words were obviously meant for Beau.

He nodded.

"Is that why you're feeling dumb?" Elle asked. "Because he was an unethical creep and you didn't know it?"

"Yes. He was just using me." Chantal bit her lip, her hands twisting in her lap. "I thought he wanted *me*, but all he wanted was information."

Mat scooted his seat around so he was beside Chantal and then put his big arm over the back of her chair. Elle had to bite back a smile. Oh, yeah . . . big brother had a terminal case all right. She didn't try to hide the smile, though, when Chantal relaxed into him.

"Did you give it to him?" Beau asked and then raised his hand toward Mat as if anticipating an argument. "Not on purpose, but did you share information that he could sell?"

"No. I only ever talked about work in general terms with him. As for the antigravity project, I'm not even on the official team. There wasn't much I could have told him if I had wanted to."

"Our resources get stretched thin. Team members move around. You did some work for me early on," Beau said.

"Yes, and I think Eddie knew that. He probably assumed I played a bigger role than I did, but it didn't matter. I knew how big that project was, how important it was not to let word leak out about your findings. I didn't talk about it at all except when he brought up how exciting the potential was and I agreed."

"You didn't think it was odd that a security guard knew what one of our top-level projects was?" Beau asked.

"No. Everyone who works at ETRD pretty much knows what's going on in the labs."

Elle nodded. It was one of the aspects of security she meant to discuss with Frank and Beau.

Beau didn't look happy, but he matched Elle's nod. "That being the case, while you may have made a bad choice in whom you chose to date, you certainly weren't and are not an imbecile. We don't hire mental deficients to work on our projects at ETRD."

"And trust me, Chantal," Elle said, grateful for Beau's attitude, "anyone can get taken in by someone who pretends to be something he or she is not." She'd seen it too many times to count.

Beau gave Elle an unreadable look, then focused his gaze on Chantal and said, "Absolutely."

"But the problem didn't end with you and Eddie breaking up, right?" Elle asked.

Chantal shook her head. "I've been getting phone calls since Gil Bigsley's disappearance."

"What kind of phone calls?" Beau asked, an edge to his voice.

"From whom?" Elle asked at the same time and then clamped her mouth shut. Bad interrogation technique with a friendly witness, having two people asking questions at once. And technically, though her brother and Chantal had come to her, Beau was their boss and this was his gig.

"Frickin' scary phone calls," Mat growled.

Chantal's hand shook a little as she poured herself more coffee from the carafe, but she managed not to spill. "They want me to get the plans for the antigravity project."

"Who does?" Beau asked.

"I don't know. Maybe the people Eddie was working with?"

Elle shook her head decisively. "Unlikely."

"Oh, really? And what exactly do you know about it, Ms. Gray?" Beau asked.

"Frank said that the problem had been taken care of."

"We can't assume anything," Beau said.

"We can assume it's not them," she said with certainty.

Even before Beau turned a skeptical expression laced with curiosity on her, Elle wanted to kick herself. Talk about making a rookie mistake. Okay, it wasn't out of bounds that she knew the basics of the breach of security on the antigravity project. After all, that was why she'd been hired, but to be so sure about Eddie's cohorts when even Frank had only been told the threat had been neutralized was over the top.

Now both Matej and Beau were giving her looks intended to make her squirm. She knew what her brother wanted—for her to tell his boss the truth so he didn't have to feel guilty about keeping a secret. She wasn't sure what the source of Beau's expression was, but it was making the base of her spine itch.

"How do you know that the people Eddie was working with are no longer interested in the antigravity project?" The tone of Beau's voice was borderline taunting, and Elle wasn't sure why.

"I assume if the case were still open, then a government agency would have an active investigation going," Elle replied.

"How do you know there isn't?" Beau asked.

"Frank didn't say there was one."

"He didn't say there wasn't one either. The fact of the matter is that we don't know if there is, or not. Since Mr. Smith chose not to press charges against Danza, the FBI agent who apprised us of the security breach opted not to share any further information. He said it wasn't necessary."

"I have contacts. When Frank Ingram approached my security company, I made it a point to find out everything I could. The men involved in the sale of the plans are not in a position to continue pursuing them," Elle countered.

"You sure about that?" Beau asked in his slow drawl.

She shrugged. "Pretty much. But maybe I'm wrong and it *is* the people he was working with. Let's leave that for now so Chantal can finish her story."

"Agreed," Beau said.

"Whoever the f . . ." Mat gave a sidelong glance to Chantal and then Elle and then cleared his throat. "Uh . . . who-ever called, *threatened* her."

Chantal nodded, doing a pretty good job of holding it to-gether. "They said if I told anyone, they'd make it look like I was in league with Eddie. That I was actually the one behind it all and Eddie had just been my pawn."

Beau made a noncommittal noise and Mat glared at him.

Elle sighed. "Could we lower the testosterone level in here just a tad? Mat, stop reading accusation into every word or expression Beau gives. Or maybe the two of you would like to take a walk while Chantal tells me the details."

"No way!" her brother growled.

Beau sat back in his chair and crossed his arms over that magnificent chest, let his legs stretch out in front of him. "Not gonna happen, princess."

Mat's eyes narrowed at the endearment and Elle remem-bered why she'd gone to university on the East Coast. Three older brothers could be stifling. She gave him her own frown to remind him that she was a big girl and could more than take care of herself.

He ignored her, but Chantal smiled. As if she found the sibling dynamics amusing.

Elle returned her smile with a wry one of her own and shrugged. "Is that all they said, the only threat they made?"

"No. They told me that if I didn't get the plans I could dis-appear just as easily as Gil had done." That seemed to really shake the blonde.

And why wouldn't it? No one wanted to be hunted.

"Whoever these people are, they have Gil." Beau was clearly well and truly pissed at the prospect too.

Elle shook her head. "Not necessarily. If they threatened him like they did Chantal, he might have run rather than come forward and ask for help."

"I was going to run," Chantal admitted, sounding ashamed. "But Mat talked me into coming to you."

"Why is that, by the way?" Beau asked. "I'd think you two would have brought the problem to Frank or me. After all, Elle is just a hired security consultant."

"Mat said she'd help him make sure I didn't disappear."

Warmth at her brother's obvious belief in her spread through Elle and inexplicable moisture filmed her eyes. She blinked it away, of course. She wasn't that much of a girly-girl, no matter what Beau said.

"I will," she promised, though she wasn't sure it was a job she could do all on her own. Not and work on her primary objectives as well as this new element being added to her current assignment: an active rather than a passive threat to key technology.

Beau made another one of those noncommittal sounds, and this time Elle frowned at him. What was his problem?

"Do you doubt my ability?" she asked him.

"No, sugar, I surely don't."

That was okay, then. She nodded. "Chantal can move in here with me, for now."

"She's staying with me." Mat said it like there was no choice in the matter, and Elle was sure that in his mind, there wasn't.

"Is that okay with you, Chantal?" Elle asked her.

Let her brother glower like the grumpy grizzly Chantal had compared him to. The other woman needed to feel like there were some things still under her control.

Chantal bit her lip and then looked up at Mat. Something passed between the two of them and Chantal nodded. "If he doesn't mind, it's where I want to be."

"Okay, then I'll be moving in with both of you."

"*What?*" Mat demanded.

Again, Beau was there putting his oar into the water. "Why?"

"I'm a professional in the area of security. As strong and big as my brother might be, he's a scientist, not a bodyguard. Frankly, I'd feel better knowing both of them were under my protection."

Mat opened his mouth, no doubt to argue, but Elle shook her head.

"It's my job, Mat. I know what I'm doing."

Beau said, "I think we need to bring Frank and Mr. Smith in on this."

"What if the people who want the plans make good on their threats?" Chantal asked.

"We won't let them take you," Elle assured her.

"No, I mean what if they have something that will make it look like I was in on Eddie's deal? What if Frank believes them? Or Mr. Smith does?"

"If you're innocent, Chantal, you have nothing to worry about," Beau said.

"Are you implying you doubt her innocence?" Mat demanded in a dangerous voice.

Elle recognized that tone and she didn't want to have to deal with the aftermath if this situation continued. Her instincts were telling her that Chantal was on the up-and-up. Besides, Mat cared about Elle, and her brother might be borderline antisocial, but he *was* a good judge of character.

Elle jumped up and indicated her bedroom with a jerk of her head. "Can I have a word with you, Beau?"

# Chapter 9

Beau got up without a word and went straight to the bedroom. Elle closed the door behind them and turned to join him by the window on the far side of the room.

She whispered angrily, "Your confrontational attitude is not helping anything here, Beau."

"Listen, I want to believe Chantal is as innocent as she appears, but it's my job to protect the company. Both Frank and Mr. Smith are smart enough to figure out if she's telling the truth."

"You told me that Frank was fallible. After all, he hired Eddie, right?"

Beau just shrugged.

"Darn it. What is your problem with trusting someone? You didn't trust me when we first met, and now you're showing a ton of unjustifiable skepticism where Chantal is concerned. This is ridiculous. Do you really think she would have come forward about the threats if she had been in league with Eddie?"

"I've got my reasons for thinking the things I do. Like you said to Chantal, lots of people are good at pretending to be something they aren't. Like innocent."

"Oh, for goodness' sake. I wasn't talking about Chantal. Has *she* done something to indicate she might be untrustworthy?"

"She was going out with Eddie Danza."

"You told her that didn't mean anything."

"I don't think it does." Beau rubbed his eyes, like he was tired, but he didn't look tired, just frustrated. "I have to be sure. It's too easy to be deceived."

"Listen, Beau. She came to me for help. She told us what was going on. She could have run."

"I know." Beau swiped his hand down his face. "I know. My gut says trust her, but then it tells me to trust you too."

"You can, Beau."

His jaw hardened and he looked over her shoulder, rather than at her. "You're damn good at sounding sincere. So is Chantal."

"Then believe us."

"I'll be more careful of what I say, but I'm still watching her."

Elle couldn't say she didn't understand his cynicism. He'd already been betrayed by at least one employee. The jury was still out on Bigsley. But somehow Beau's distrust of Chantal felt personal, like it reflected a lack of belief in Elle's integrity. And that hurt in a way she had no desire to examine.

"Just remember, she's on the edge of losing it, Mr. Paranoid. Don't push her over, or she might do something that could put herself at further risk. Like run. Not to mention, if you want her cooperation investigating this issue, you don't want to antagonize her past the point where she'll give it." He was already almost there with Matej. Thank goodness Chantal seemed to be more even tempered than the man so interested in her.

Beau frowned. "Understood."

Elle shook her head, feeling like there was more to be said but not knowing what it was. "Fine."

"Fine," he repeated with a boatload more belligerence. Then he grabbed her shoulders and pulled her into a kiss.

A very steamy, no-holds-barred, passion-drugging kiss. She was swaying on her feet when he was done.

"That feels real at least," he said.

She blinked. "It is."

There was an angry tinge to the desire darkening his eyes that she didn't understand. But rather than say anything that might explain it, he shook his head and stepped back. "Let's go find out what else Chantal has to tell us."

She nodded.

They returned to the living area to find Chantal and Mat sitting side by side on the love seat. They were talking in hushed tones that ended when they saw Beau and Elle.

Beau sat on one end of the couch. "I'm sorry if I made it sound like I think you're a suspect, Chantal. I don't, but I have to be cautious for the sake of the company. You've got nothing to worry about with Frank and Mr. Smith, though."

Elle took the other end in silence.

"That's easy for you to say," Chantal replied with a definite spark. "Frank treats you like the son he never had, but I'm just another underscientist. I don't want to lose my job or my reputation."

Mat rubbed her back. "It won't happen."

Chantal straightened her shoulders and squeezed Mat's forearm. "I hope not, but regardless, Mr. Smith and Frank deserve to know that someone is trying to steal ETRD's technology."

"Someone is always trying to steal new technology," Elle said, with a sigh. "But, you're right. They need to know about what is happening right now."

"Then we're all in agreement?" Beau asked.

Elle nodded. "You call Frank and set up a meeting. I'll go

home with Matej and Chantal and secure the premises. Do you have my cell phone number?"

Beau shook his head.

"Where is your phone?" she asked Beau.

"On the small table beside your bed. I left it there last night."

Predictably, Mat was back to scowling.

Elle ignored them both and hopped up to go get the phone so she could program her number into it. She handed the phone to Beau as she came back into the room. "It's in there under Elle."

"What quick-dial number?"

"I don't know, whatever the next one available was." She never used quick dial.

Beau flipped the phone open, and being the curious cat that she was (it came with the territory of her job), Elle watched him alter her place on the numerical list to number two, right under Frank and before everyone else. Okay, so it shouldn't matter, but she liked it.

Was she turning into some kind of sap?

Mat fixed Beau with a look that Elle knew all too well. Kyle'd had to withstand the same one from all three of her brothers and her father. "So, you want to tell me what you're doing at my baby sister's apartment on a Saturday morning wearing nothing but the jeans you wore to my parents' house last night for dinner?"

It was a testament to how worried he was about Chantal and how much he cared for the petite blonde that Mat had waited to pull the big-brother protector card until now.

"That would be none of your business," Elle said before Beau could answer.

Mat ignored her, his gaze fixed firmly on his boss.

Beau looked supremely unworried. "I'd think the answer was self-evident."

She was going to kill him. Later. After she'd had a few more nights like the one they'd just spent. He didn't need to be so blatant.

Mat puffed up with anger.

Elle groaned. "Here we go again."

Chantal giggled. "Soon they will be beating their chests, no?"

It was so like what Elle had thought earlier that despite the annoyance she was feeling, she laughed as well. "I think maybe."

Her brother made a noise that sounded suspiciously like a snarl.

Elle had to bite back her own sound of irritation. She didn't think her private life was her family's business, nor did she rub it in their faces. Especially not when it came to her brothers. Of course, if her mother knew about last night, that grand dame would have her and Beau as good as married and headed off to the Poconos for a honeymoon.

Beau gave her another one of those looks that made her spine itch, then said, "I'm not into lying, Elle."

"Keeping your mouth shut isn't exactly miring yourself in dishonesty," she said with exasperation.

"Sometimes it is, princess. Sometimes, that's exactly what it is."

And Mat, darn him, was nodding his agreement, giving Elle another one of those looks that said he wanted the truth on the table. All of it.

"I'm not denying what happened last night, but I don't think it's any of my brother's concern either."

"I don't agree," Mat said. Of course.

"*Mat*," Chantal said with open censure.

"It doesn't matter if you agree, or not." Elle kept her voice even but firm. "My private life is my own business. I won't hide things from you, but I won't dissect it for you either. We are here to discuss Chantal's problems and deal with them. Full stop. Period."

Beau had the effrontery to laugh while Mat was back to glowering. This time at Elle.

"She really doesn't get it, does she?" Beau asked Mat.

Her brother shook his head. "She does not understand what it is to be an older brother."

"Gee, you think?" she asked with sarcasm.

"I know," Mat replied, all serious.

"I know that I give you the respect of privacy." In the spirit of full truth she added, "Mostly."

"I respect your privacy," Mat said.

Chantal made a noise of disbelief that echoed Elle's feelings.

"But he has a natural desire to know what I was doing here this morning, sugar. He now knows. Case closed," Beau said.

"Really?" She didn't think so. Either she was going to hear more about it, or Beau was. She gave her brother her best die-later-in-pain-if-you-ignore-me glare. "If you rat me out to Mama again, I'll get you good with Baba. You get me?"

Mat actually grinned. "Don't worry, I'm not going to say anything. For now."

"Forever."

"You know you can trust me with your secrets, Elle."

Chantal looked pleased with that statement.

Elle nodded, feeling better. He and her other brothers had kept the truth of her job from their parents for several years now. He wasn't going to go blurting out stuff to Mama that would end up hurting her in the long run.

Okay, time to get back to the matter at hand.

"I need to make a phone call." She pointed to Chantal and then Mat. "You two stay here." Then she looked at Beau. "I'll see you at the meeting with Frank."

"What, you're kicking me out?"

"I'm not kicking you out. I just assumed you'd want to go home, get some clean clothes and call Frank."

"I could call Frank from here, but some clean clothes wouldn't hurt."

"Right. So, see you later."

He shook his head, smiled, and stood up. Then he bent down, getting right into her personal space until her head was leaning back on the sofa. "You will definitely be seeing me later."

He planted a kiss smack on her lips. And it wasn't a friendly little peck either. If her brother had had any doubts about what they had been doing last night, he didn't now. Elle was panting when the kiss ended, and Beau looked altogether too pleased with himself.

It was pure claim-staking behavior, but he had no claim on her to stake. What in the world was going on?

She didn't have any better of an answer a couple of minutes later when Beau came out of the bedroom wearing his shoes and tucking his wallet into his back pocket.

He put his hand out. "I'll need the keys to the Spider. You picked me up last night, remember?"

Elle grabbed the keys from her purse and handed them over. "Bring it to the meeting. We'll work out your transport home from there."

"Will do."

Then he was gone and Mat was giving her a look of utter disbelief. Chantal's sweet face wore an expression of introspection.

"What?" Elle asked her brother, when he kept giving her that look.

"You're letting him drive your car?"

"He drove it last night. He knows how to handle the powerful engine."

"You're letting him drive it . . . *a second time?*" Mat whistled. "It must be love."

"Not. Listen, brother mine, Beau and I enjoy each other. I'm sorry if that offends you, but it's the way it is. Since he's the first man I've wanted to be with in the last four years without an ulterior motive, I'm not about to dismiss this thing between us. But trust me, it's *not* love."

"Whatever you say, *princess.*"

"Matej, my dear brother, did you know that I have the skills to maim a man twice my weight more easily than fixing a run in my panty hose?"

"Elle, my darling *little* sister, did you know that though you might do it for a living, you can't lie to family for shit?"

"I am not lying. Beau and I are not in love!"

"Fine." That word was getting a lot of use this morning. And she didn't think it had been said once with real sincerity. She turned to go.

"Just don't forget to invite me to the wedding."

She pivoted on one heel, and faster than he could blink, she flipped him right onto the carpet. She was careful not to actually hurt him, which might be why instead of being properly impressed, he was laughing his grumpy grizzly ass off.

Yelling out instructions over her shoulder for them not to leave or open the door to anyone, Elle slammed into the bedroom to make her call.

The Old Man wasn't happy to hear the threat to the antigravity project still existed, but he didn't sound surprised either.

"You're sure that Ms. Renaud is trustworthy?" he asked Elle. "That she's telling you everything she knows?"

"That's what my instincts are telling me, sir."

"You've got damn fine instincts."

"Thank you. I'd like to ask her some questions about her former boyfriend and his associates, though."

"Good idea. Clearly we need to deal with this threat."

"I'd like to find Gil Bigsley, sir."

"He might have information for us."

"Yes, and he's definitely in danger if they don't already have him."

"Agreed. So, is Ms. Renaud."

"I'll be watching over her and my brother."

"You're going to need help."

"I've considered that, sir. I would like to bring in outside resources."

"You want to pay for bodyguards for them?"

"Yes, sir." She wasn't going to let her brother or the woman he was clearly smitten with lose their lives, like Kyle had.

And Elle knew her limitations. She couldn't be with them twenty-four-seven, not without removing herself from her current assignment. She could do more to assure their long-term safety staying on it.

"We could bring in another agency, but that's not our way," The Old Man said.

No, it wasn't. "For good reason, sir."

He made a sound of agreement. "I concur that Ms. Renaud and her lover need full-time supervision at present. TGP will see to it."

"If you don't mind, sir, I would prefer to choose the out-side resources."

"Whom do you have in mind?"

"Do you remember that friend of Alan's? He and his associates were mercenaries and now they run a security consultation firm almost as good as mine. It's called Elite Security Force."

"I'll make the call."

"If you are sure. I'm fully prepared to fund this endeavor."

"That won't be necessary, but I'll make it clear to them that you are the agent in charge on this case."

"Good. Will you be calling Alan in?"

"I think you can get what you need from him in a phone consult. His investigation didn't extend to anything thorough in California. Which is why your assignment was created."

"Okay." The call-waiting click sounded on her phone. "I've got another call, sir." She looked at the display. "It's Beau. He's probably calling with details on the meeting with Frank Ingram."

"Take it. I'll call you when I have information on Elite Security Force."

"Got it." Elle beeped through to the other call. "Beau?"

"Yeah, it's me, sugar. Frank wants to meet in his office at ETRD as soon as we can all get there."

"I'll get Chantal and Matej on the move."

"See you there soon," he said, then hung up.

Both Beau and Frank were waiting in the controller's office when Elle walked in with her brother and Chantal.

"Mr. Smith is joining us on speakerphone," Frank said as they all took chairs around the six-person dark-wood conference table that dominated one side of the room. "The other three have arrived, sir."

"Hello, Ms. Gray, Dr. Chernichenko, Ms. Renaud," came the cultured male accent from the high-end speakerphone on the table near where Frank was sitting.

The phone's quality was so good it sounded like the other man was in the room with them. None of the tinny acoustics so many speakerphones were plagued with.

Elle said, "Mr. Smith, it's good to talk to you again."

"Hello, Mr. Smith," Chantal said, hiding her nervousness admirably.

Elle's brother was back to his normal unsmiling self, but he managed to grunt a greeting to the founder of ETRD. She loved her brother, but she bet the employees on his team would be really happy to see Gil Bigsley back. If the man could be found.

"Ms. Renaud, I must apologize for the stress you have been put through as an employee of Environmental Technology Research and Design."

"Uh . . . thank you, Mr. Smith."

"For my personal edification, would you mind going over what exactly transpired between you and Mr. Danza in regard to the security breach that occurred before as well as the recent phone calls you've received?"

"Can we hold off for a moment on that?" Elle asked.

Without waiting for an answer, she pulled the minilaptop she carried with her at all times out of her Coach bag, bought specifically because it was both stylish and the perfect size to carry the small computer. It also held a few other necessary things she was sure other women didn't carry in their purses. She retrieved one of those items now and plugged it into the USB drive on the computer.

It looked like a transmitter for a wireless mouse. It wasn't. It doubled as a scanner for electronic listening devices as well as a subsonic scrambler for long-distance spyware. The scan took less than a minute, announcing the results on her system. There was in fact a device in the room, but she was guessing Frank didn't know about it.

She got up and crossed to the bookcase behind his desk and started a search with her fingertips on the underside of the top shelf. She found what she was looking for on the third shelf down. She pried the small bug away and brought it to the table. Everyone else was staring at her in silence.

She removed the tiny battery from the bug. "We're clear."

"Good work, Ms. Gray," Mr. Smith said.

"Is that a bug?" Chantal asked, looking a little green around the gills.

Elle nodded shortly. She didn't mention the fact that it ran on a long-life battery, but one that would be dead if it hadn't been replaced since Eddie Danza had left the company. That was something she would discuss with Frank and Mr. Smith at a future time.

"Now that Ms. Gray has assured our privacy, Ms. Renaud?" Mr. Smith prompted.

Chantal repeated what she'd said at Elle's apartment, giving more specifics about the times Eddie Danza had asked her questions about her work. Mr. Smith coaxed her into repeating word for word the three phone calls she had received. He also elicited the information that the most recent one had happened the day before yesterday and that the threats had escalated.

"I told them I couldn't get the information even if I wanted to—since I wasn't on the project. They didn't believe me. They're convinced I'm on the team and told me that if I didn't get them a copy of the plans and filmed test flight by next week, they would . . ." She stopped and swallowed, turning moisture-sheened eyes to Mat, who looked back with such steady support and tenderness, Elle felt a lump of emotion form in her own throat.

Which she immediately swallowed. This was a job. Principles involved, family or not. There was no room for emotion, maudlin or otherwise. Still, they were a sweet couple.

"They said they would take me out of the equation." Chantal's voice trembled as she spoke, but she did her best to maintain a calm demeanor.

For the second time that day, Mat moved his chair close to the small scientist's so he could lend her his physical support. Chantal gave him a grateful look and he rubbed her back, whispered something in her ear that made her lips tilt in an almost smile. His expression clearly pleased, he rested his arm over her shoulders and leaned negligently back in his chair.

Frank's eyes widened in clear surprise while Beau grinned evilly. Elle had a feeling she wasn't the only one who would be teasing her brother about his relationship and new tender side. Though honestly, it wasn't new, so much as it had always been reserved for close family.

"Frank has mentioned that Ms. Gray has offered her services for your protection as well as that of her brother," Mr. Smith said. "Though I'm still a bit unclear as to why the latter is necessary. Have you been approached by these unsavory characters as well, Dr. Chernichenko?"

"Matej has taken a personal interest in Chantal's safety and welfare, going so far as to insist she stay in his home. Therefore putting himself in the line of fire, as it were," Frank said before anyone else could speak.

Elle was watching the phone in a natural if useless reaction when talking to someone via speaker, so she saw the small eye on the unit move. Mr. Smith had video. Which wasn't a problem except Frank hadn't informed the others present that that was the case. And she wouldn't have noticed the miniature lens if it hadn't moved. Not good. Although it was tiny, as many minicams were nowadays, other than being the same color as the speaker unit, it wasn't camouflaged.

The fact that she hadn't noticed it earlier said she was more off her game today than she'd realized. There was no place for an off day in an investigation.

The fact that Frank hadn't mentioned the video feed made Elle wonder what else he wasn't mentioning.

"Ah, I see," Mr. Smith said.

"Damn right." Mat's fiercely protective nature for those he loved was spilling over into his tone. "Nothing is going to happen to Chantal on my watch."

"Those are laudable sentiments, to be sure," Mr. Smith said.

"I agree," Elle said. "However, while my brother may be a strong and intelligent man, he is not trained in the field." He might scare his technicians out of their wits with his surly nature, but his patented scowl wasn't going to stop a bullet, or a professional intent on kidnapping Chantal. "They both need someone accustomed to protective services watching over them."

"This is in no way a criticism of your abilities, Ms. Gray. Your qualifications for such an endeavor are undeniable. However, I believe that might spread your resources somewhat too thin."

"I agree. I plan to bring another security team in to handle the bodyguard detail. They're unknowns, so they should be able to maintain a lower profile than I could."

"Excellent," Mr. Smith said.

"There is no reason to let the would-be technology pirates know that Chantal has told you and Frank about the threat, or that she is being looked after professionally," Elle said. Chances were, the best way to flush out those responsible for the threats was to use Chantal as bait.

That couldn't happen if they believed she was working with a professional.

"I agree," Mr. Smith said.

"I don't," Mat said, with a frown. "If she tells them she's exposed them, they'll leave her alone."

Elle shook her head. "We can't be sure of that. The only way to guarantee Chantal's safety is to find out who is threatening her and to report them to the proper authorities. We have a better chance of doing that if they don't realize their plans to obtain stolen technology have been exposed. We have a better chance of doing that if your bodyguards go unnoticed."

Mat didn't look happy, but he didn't argue. Her brother was big on justice, and bringing the bad guys in would motivate him only second to Chantal's safety.

Beau, however, was giving Elle a look of censure. "Don't you think bringing in an outside security detail is overstepping your authority here, princess?"

She let the endearment slide. "No. This is my brother and his girlfriend's safety we're talking about. I'm not asking ETRD to pay for it, if that's what's worrying you."

"We will happily do so, however, Ms. Gray," Mr. Smith said. "We take the safety of our employees very seriously at ETRD."

"If that's true, Mr. Smith, why weren't more concrete actions taken when Gil Bigsley disappeared?" Elle asked. That was something that had been bugging her since Frank told her about it. "Did you assume he was in league with Eddie Danza?"

If so, it would have been in keeping with their initial response to learning of their security guard's duplicity for them to write off the disappearance of the project manager as good riddance to bad rubbish. Aside from Mat, only Frank talked like he hoped the scientist would return.

"Dr. Bigsley was not in league with our former security guard," Mr. Smith replied.

"You sound awfully certain," Elle said.

"I am."

"Why?"

"Gil Bigsley received threats much like Ms. Renaud did. Unfortunately, because he is close to his elderly parents, they were also threatened. He brought his concerns to me."

"How did he do that?"

"Employees of a certain level at ETRD have access to a phone number they can use to contact me. It is very rarely used, but it is nevertheless available."

"And Gil Bigsley used it."

"Yes."

From the expression of shocked consternation on Frank's face, this was news to him. "You know where Bigsley is?" he asked in a tense voice.

"I know many things," Mr. Smith said.

Elle had to hide her smile at the rare frown Frank gave the phone.

"Perhaps the rest of us would benefit from that knowledge, were you to share it more generously," Frank said. "Though I now understand why you resisted hiring a new scientist and put Matej in as acting project manager."

Elle could guess too. Although he was fully qualified for the position, no one could have any doubts that her brother would gladly give the job back over to Gil Bigsley when he returned.

"I'd like to talk to Bigsley," she said.

"I would too," Mat said, sounding more than a little pissed.

Mr. Smith wasn't making points with his newest hire, that was for sure.

"Phone calls can be arranged. However, I feel it would be better for him to stay where he is, along with his parents, until this matter has been dealt with."

Elle agreed. Protecting Mat and Chantal would be enough surveillance work for a small detail. But something was bugging her. "I don't understand how you expected the matter to be 'dealt with' since you haven't brought any authorities in to investigate what has been going on."

"But I did, Ms. Gray. In fact, I brought in the best." Now Mr. Smith just sounded smug.

She stared at Frank. "You told me that no one was investigating Dr. Bigsley's disappearance."

"Officially," Mr. Smith said, "no one is."

"I don't understand."

"Perhaps it's time for full disclosure, Ms. Gray."

"I'm all for full disclosure, Mr. Smith."

Beau made a noise that sounded suspiciously like a snort, and Elle's gaze flew to him. What the heck had that been about?

"Good, good." No one said anything for several seconds. Then Mr. Smith said, "It might be best if Dr. Chernichenko and Ms. Renaud waited in another room for this part of the discussion."

Mat got his stubborn face on. "Absolutely not. If this concerns Chantal's safety, I'm not going anywhere."

"Unfortunately, that will not be possible. There are certain facts better kept between the other principals at the table at present."

"Like you kept the fact that Gil Bigsley was safe to yourself?" Mat could do sarcasm even better than Elle. "I don't think so."

"I'm very sorry, but in order to have full disclosure between myself and Ms. Gray, you and Ms. Renaud *cannot* be present."

Elle didn't know what Mr. Smith wanted to talk about, but she understood revelation of information on a need-to-know basis. He had decided her brother didn't need to know. Elle would judge that for herself, but for now, she would cooperate by helping to get her brother out of the room.

She turned to Chantal. "My brother is stubborn, and sometimes, that's a good thing. Sometimes, though, it can put his livelihood at stake."

Though she didn't think Mr. Smith would fire her brother for his insistence on staying, the possibility did exist.

Chantal, the intelligent woman who she was, got Elle's meaning immediately and nodded. She turned under Mat's arm until they faced each other. "Gil Bigsley's trust in Mr. Smith paid off; I think we can trust him too. I'm okay with leaving them to their discussion. More than, to be honest."

"But—"

"Please, Mat. No more stress right now. Okay?" Whether the vulnerable exhaustion lacing Chantal's voice was real or for Mat's benefit, it worked.

His appearance went from pissed off to concerned in a single eye-blink. "You could use a break."

"*Oui.*"

Mat stood and looked at Elle. "You don't let them talk you into doing anything you aren't comfortable with, you hear me?"

Oh, her big brother really wasn't in a space where he trusted the mysterious benefactor for his new company.

"You've got it. I'll come to your office when we're done here. Okay?"

"Okay." Throwing a glare at the speakerphone, he left the room, taking Chantal with him.

Elle shook her head, impressed all over again by the sway the diminutive blonde had over her bear of a brother.

"He really cares about her," Mr. Smith said, echoing Elle's thoughts. His voice was filled with satisfaction too. "They make a lovely couple."

Stifling a snort of laughter at the thought of her brother as a lovely anything, Elle asked, "So, what is it you wanted to discuss that you didn't want my brother or Chantal present for?"

"In actual fact, I asked them to leave for your benefit, Ms. Gray."

"Why is that?"

"You wanted to know the nature of the unofficial investigation into Dr. Bigsley's disappearance. Revealing that would no doubt make certain facts available to your brother and his girlfriend that they are not currently in possession of."

"What facts might those be?"

"That although you are arguably *legitimately* one of the best security consultants in the world, you are also a top agent for The Goddard Project."

Elle couldn't prevent the single gasp that escaped at those words.

Mr. Smith went on as if he had not noticed. Perhaps he hadn't. "That unless the decision is made to bring in a second agent, which is not the way TGP usually operates, *you* will be investigating this new attempt to procure the antigravity plans and thus the threats to both Dr. Bigsley and Ms. Renaud. And that it will be your responsibility to see that the culprits are apprehended and brought to justice."

He paused, but still working at hiding her complete shock, much less responding to it, Elle was silent.

"Correct me if I am wrong," Mr. Smith continued, "but TGP has always required its agents to conceal the true nature of their jobs, even from close family members. I assume your brother is unaware of the true nature of your primary job and has no more knowledge of the existence of The Goddard Project than the average citizen. Ms. Renaud is most certainly in the dark concerning such things."

# Chapter 10

Elle was stupefied.

No one had ever copped her cover. No one had ever even come close. To identify her as a federal agent, as her family had done, would be one thing, though implausible without inside information. But to know that she was an agent for TGP? She would have said that was not possible.

So few people were even aware of the existence of her agency that the risk of one of them ever running into her personally was almost nil. And even if someone did so? To know that she worked for said agency was beyond improbable. Without a leak in TGP, it should be *impossible*.

How, then, did Mr. Smith know about TGP, and further, how had he discovered she was an agent?

Was there a leak? Oh, man, she needed to talk to her boss.

While thoughts whirled in her head—speculation competing with prospective answers to Mr. Smith's words—she let her gaze fall first on Frank and then Beau. Neither showed the least surprise at Mr. Smith's words. They had known. *Beau* had known. This whole time.

"Before you attempt to deny your status as a TGP agent, or your assignment here to discover both what we are working on and the true status of the antigravity experiment, let me assure you, it would be useless. Not only do I know which agency you work for, but I know the name of your boss and, in fact, think it would be a good idea to bring him in on this meeting."

Elle crossed her arms and sat back in her chair. When in doubt, maintain silence. It was neither an admission nor a denial.

"Frank, will you please call the number I gave you earlier and request the man who answers to join our discussion?"

"Of course, sir."

Elle waited while the connection was made.

"Hello?" The Old Man's voice came over the speaker-phone, cautious but unmistakably his.

Adrenaline surged through Elle at this further evidence that Mr. Smith had way more information than he should have, but she maintained her calm facade while she waited to see what came next.

"Hello, Whit. We're having a meeting with your agent Elle Gray and thought you should be brought in on it," Mr. Smith said.

Several beats of silence and then, "I'm not sure what you are talking about. I don't have agents."

Mr. Smith laughed. "Ms. Gray is technically a Goddard Project agent and TGP is your baby, so that makes her *your* agent, wouldn't you say?"

"TGP?" The Old Man asked carefully.

"Please, let's dispense with the subterfuge," Mr. Smith said.

"Whom am I speaking with?"

"I'll answer that, since I seem to be the topic of this con-versation, as bizarre as it might be," Elle said.

When Mr. Smith had called Whit by his name, Elle was ut-terly convinced he did indeed know about TGP and her role as an agent. She didn't know *how* he knew and that was something they would have to investigate, but she didn't want The Old Man worried that she was at risk. So, she'd used her code word—bizarre—to let him know she was not in any known physical danger. It was not her code for all green, however.

This situation was too fantastic for her to be okay with it.

"You are speaking with Mr. Smith, benefactor and founder of Environmental Technology Research and Design. In the room with us is Frank Ingram, company controller. We're actually at the conference table in his office. The only other person in the room is Dr. Beau Ruston, second in command to Mr. Ingram. I am Elle Gray, a security consultant hired by the company. Although the room is clean since I disarmed the single listening device my equipment detected, I can't tell you whether or not our conversation is being recorded or listened to by anyone else via the one-way videoconference apparatus Mr. Smith is using."

There. She'd apprised her boss of the situation, let him know she hadn't admitted to anything and left any revelations made up to his discretion. If her fury at the situation leaked through her words, The Old Man would understand it. The idea that someone within The Goddard Project was feeding information to the outside was more than disconcerting; it was devastating.

The agents and support personnel for TGP were more than her coworkers; in a very real sense, they were a second family.

Beau was looking at her with that odd expression again. Only now, maybe she understood it. He'd met her knowing she was pretending to be something less than what she was. And because of that, he didn't trust her. A lot of things made more sense to her.

But one thing didn't. Why had he made love to her the

night before? It had been the first time she'd had sex in four years without some ulterior motive. The prospect that he'd had one left a hollow feeling in the pit of her stomach.

"I see," Whit said. "Mr. Smith, do you have a first name?"

"Of course."

"Do you mind sharing it?"

"I do."

"I see."

Silence again. "This situation certainly is bizarre," The Old Man said.

He might be giving Elle tacit approval for her handling of the circumstances and agreement that she did not appear to be in imminent physical danger, or simply stating the truth.

"I am sorry it seems that way to you," Mr. Smith said.

"Ahh . . ." The Old Man sounded like he was pleased about something. "I thought your voice sounded familiar, Mr. Smith."

"So, you recognize it?" the other man asked.

"Yes."

"If I assure you the conversation is neither being recorded nor listened to by anyone not already listed by Ms. Gray, will you believe me?"

Silence.

Elle waited. Everyone waited. Even Mr. Smith, who said nothing else.

Finally, "I will," came from The Old Man.

"Good. Can we dispense with the cloak-and-dagger regarding Ms. Gray's role here at ETRD?"

"It would be pointless to refuse. However, I expect you to tell me how you got into my computers and identified my agent."

"Will do. Later."

Mr. Smith and The Old Man knew each other? And trusted each other? This case was getting stranger by the minute. Elle didn't know there was *anyone* Andrew "Whit" Whitney trusted other than his precious TGP, but the way her boss talked made it sound like Mr. Smith himself was responsible for the leak in information. That he had somehow hacked into TGP's computers.

Which put him in league abilitywise with about three computer hackers in the world. Unless he had one of them working for him.

"I assume you are meeting about the threats made against Chantal Renaud," The Old Man said.

"That and the disappearance of Dr. Gil Bigsley. Apparently, Mr. Smith is responsible for Bigsley's disappearance," Elle said as she gave the camera eye a look of disgust. "He didn't see fit to share that bit of information with anyone else until now."

The Old Man snorted. "I'm not surprised."

Okay, she was now majorly curious as to who Mr. Smith was in her boss's world, but she knew better than to ask.

"Hmm . . . then you are light-years ahead of me. I don't understand why if Mr. Smith knew about our agency and my assignment, he didn't come clean from the beginning. If we had known about the threats against Dr. Bigsley, we might already have leads on those responsible."

"I fully intended to apprise you of the threats made toward Dr. Bigsley, but I wanted to see if you would discover the issue on your own," Mr. Smith replied.

The Old Man chuckled, but Elle wasn't amused. "You were testing me?"

"You may put it that way if you wish."

Oh, she was so going to find out who this guy really was. "I'm glad you seem to find your little games so appealing." She let the sarcasm drip from every word. "I don't think Chantal is enjoying the results of them nearly as much."

"I miscalculated both the impatience and tenacity of the

people who had threatened Dr. Bigsley. I did not anticipate them going after another of my scientists so quickly. They should have been wary of discovery since they knew that contrary to their claims to her, *they* were not responsible for his disappearance," Mr. Smith replied.

"You think? Maybe someone should have told them that. Oh, and maybe *you* should have been more concerned with the good of your company and the safety of its employees than with stratagems designed for your own personal entertainment," Elle retorted.

Her boss chuckled again and she had visions of spreading honey on his desk chair and dropping a hive of bees off in his office.

"That's telling him, princess." If Beau's voice hadn't been brimming with laughter, she would have been okay with it, but evidently he too thought this situation a lot funnier than it was.

She gave him a look meant to intimidate and then turned to his boss. "What do you think, Frank? Are you as amused as Beau and our bosses are by this situation?"

Below the perfectly styled salt-and-pepper hair, the older man's expression was resigned. "Perhaps I am more accustomed to Mr. Smith's peccadilloes. But amused? No, I am not. Had Chantal run or given in to the threats out of fear as a result of Mr. Smith keeping his secrets, that would have indeed been a tragedy."

At least one person had his brain in the right place. "I agree, but then I'm just the dupe in this little farce Mr. Smith has orchestrated."

Elle was more than good at her job; she was great. She hadn't been played like this ever. And she didn't like it.

At all.

Doing nothing to suppress the growl of irritation pushing to get out, she started typing. She was done playing the role of Bottom to Mr. Smith's Fairy King, though. If her boss wasn't worried about the breach of their agency's security, she wasn't going to make a big deal about it. Not that she didn't plan to bring it up in the next status meeting with the other agents. She so did. But for right now, she had a job to do.

No one spoke until she looked up from the notes she'd taken on leads she wanted to pursue and pieces of information she had already gathered from the meeting.

"Right. Okay, first things first. Dr. Ruston, *is* the antigravity project viable for commercial or government prototype?" she asked.

Beau gave her a look at the use of his title, but at least he wasn't trying to stifle laughter anymore. "Mr. Smith?"

"You may answer with full disclosure."

Beau's dark Hershey gaze shifted to Elle. "The short answer is no."

She did her best to ignore the effect those gorgeous eyes had on her. She'd made all the mistakes on this case she was going to. Wanting something with Beau beyond their working relationship had been one of them. "And the long answer?"

"Our antigravity theory is based on magnetohydrodynamics. We tested on a one-five-hundredths-scale model, but the electrostatic discharge was excessive. At this point, it would be fatal for crew or observers on a full-scale model. We're still working on the fix for that before we go back to testing on a modular level."

"But the ship looks full scale in the video of the test."

"The simple explanation for that is that your mind interpreted the other visuals in line with that supposition, as opposed to looking at it and realizing the camera was fairly close to the flying model." Beau shrugged. "It's a common technique used in special effects, but it wasn't intentional on our part. Of course, we didn't anticipate someone stealing the video footage and showing it to others without knowledge of the modular nature of our test."

Elle nodded, taking more notes as he spoke. "On another note entirely, do you have an electrolyte concentration analyzer in one of your labs here?"

"In fact, we do, but why do you ask?"

"I'd like to use it to see how long the battery on the listening device I found has been in place."

"Ah," said Mr. Smith.

"Unless it has a much longer life than I anticipate, it has been replaced since Eddie Danza's departure from the company," Elle said.

"That's not good news," Beau said.

"Unless you know something about it?" Elle asked, her question clearly directed at the speakerphone.

"I do not bug my employees' offices, Ms. Gray," said Mr. Smith.

"Really? Would you tell me if you did?"

"Elle—" her boss started to say.

"I don't want to waste time pursuing a useless lead because he's playing more of his games, sir."

"I assure you, the bug was not placed there by me or at my instigation," Mr. Smith said.

Elle wasn't sure she believed him, but she had no choice but to pursue the lead with his denial. He wasn't the first principal who hid things from her. Now that she knew he fell in that category, she would take a slightly different tack with her investigation. No matter how much The Old Man seemed to trust the mysterious Mr. Smith, she wasn't going to be caught blindfolded again.

"I'll need to speak to Dr. Bigsley as soon as possible. Please arrange it for sometime today," she said.

There were at least a couple of indrawn breaths at Elle's peremptory words toward Mr. Smith, but she ignored them.

He'd played her and she wasn't about to pretend she wasn't more than a little annoyed about it. She also was no longer technically merely his employee. His knowledge of her role as an agent played in her favor there.

She was indisputably the agent in charge on a federal investigation and they could all just deal with that fact.

"I'll see what I can do, Ms. Gray."

"Good. Have you been in contact with Elite Security Force yet, sir?"

"I have. Daniel Black Eagle and his wife, Josette, will be arriving this evening. They will be coming in on a private jet landing in a municipal airport south of your present location. A rented vehicle will be waiting for them. They should call your cell to confirm arrival, but their current plan is to meet you at Dr. Chernichenko's home."

Some of the tension Elle had been feeling drained out of her. "Perfect."

From everything she knew about him (and it was her job to know a lot about the others in the top of her cover field), Nitro and his wife would do a darn good job of watching over Elle's brother and Chantal. Nitro was a former Army Ranger, then mercenary turned security specialist. His wife was a former mercenary, trained from childhood by her father in the art of combat and warfare. Although she spent more time working on computers than in the field now, they were both the best of the best.

If Elle ever decided to leave TGP and move entirely into the private sector, she would be more than happy to join her resources with those of Elite Security Force.

"Is there anything else that could be pertinent to this situation that you have not shared, Mr. Smith?" she asked.

"No."

Elle waited, giving him a chance to change his answer and telling him silently that she took nothing he said at face value any longer. When the silence had stretched a full minute, she said, "Good. Frank?"

"There are a couple of personnel matters that may or may not play into this."

"Do you think so, Frank?" Mr. Smith asked.

"I think they're worth telling Elle about. She can decide if they are pertinent to her investigation or not."

Oho, so Frank wasn't above giving a subtle rebuke either. She nodded her approval to him.

"Just so," The Old Man said. "An agent never knows what bits of information will play a key role in an investigation like this. It's always better to err on the side of telling too much."

"Point taken," Mr. Smith said wryly. "From both of you."

Frank cleared his throat. "Lana Ericson, the PM for material transformation, has made it clear she is jealous and disapproving of the amount of resources dedicated thus far to the antigravity project."

"Material transformation?" Elle asked.

"Modern-day alchemy. Recycling resources or creating energy via conversion," Beau explained.

"And you think . . ."

"That if the people looking to buy the plans for the antigravity project had contacted her rather than Chantal, they might have encountered a lot more cooperation." Frank didn't sound particularly disturbed by that knowledge, simply more resigned.

Like he was about Mr. Smith's peccadilloes, as he'd called them.

Elle couldn't imagine being a company controller. And she'd always thought The Old Man had a tough job riding herd on TGP.

"Are the other PMs aware of the lack of success on the project's modular test run?" she asked.

"It flew; that was a success," Beau said, just a tad defensively. "But yes, she and the other project managers know that it is not yet viable for use as a prototype."

"So, she would what? Give the plans in hopes of undermining it both as a security risk and by exposing its lack of overall success to the public?" Elle asked Frank, making sure she wasn't off base on the motivations she was attributing to the other woman.

"Knowing her personality and the way her brain works? It's a possibility, yes."

"Why is someone you obviously consider a security risk in a lead position, or even working here at all?"

"Nobody is perfect, Elle. And brilliance almost always comes with a cost. For Lana, that cost is a borderline obsessive jealousy toward other scientists and projects not under her authority or part of her passion," Frank replied.

"But if a full-size prototype was built, as soon as it was powered up, people could, and probably would, die," Beau said, with a frown as fierce as anything her brother could come up with. "I can't believe Lana would risk that, no matter how jealous she is of my project."

"People don't always count the cost of their actions when an impulse grips them," Elle replied, giving the video cam a significant look. Then she looked at Frank. "You said a couple of personnel concerns."

He nodded. "The second one would be Archer Sandstone."

"He wanted my job." Beau looked pained.

"He's a PM, but he wanted both Beau's group and his role as my second in command."

"Any justification to his expectations?"

"No. Beau's worked here longer, and frankly, he's been my right hand since day one. His promotion to project manager only made that role more concrete. Archer's a fine scientist, but something of a prima donna."

"You think there's a chance he'd be interested in under-mining Beau and his project?"

"Unfortunately, yes."

"Sounds to me like it was lucky for ETRD that the perpetrators approached Chantal instead of someone else." Of course there was the bug to consider. Someone had planted that.

However, if it was someone with access to the plans, Chantal wouldn't have been threatened in an attempt to procure them, would she?

Frank shrugged. "Every company has its personality conflicts."

"I suppose." Elle finished typing in her notes on Frank's revelations, then faced Beau. "Anything you've been holding back?"

"Pertinent to the case? No."

"Pertinent to the case is the only thing that interests me." And she was going to remember that from now on.

"You think so?" he asked in that sexy Texas drawl.

She gave him a short nod and then turned to Frank. "I should have a preliminary report regarding proposed security changes for ETRD to you by the end of next week." Then she spoke toward the speakerphone. "I'll confer with our Vancouver operative this afternoon, sir. Maybe he's got some idea about who could be responsible for the threats to Dr. Bigsley and Chantal."

"Sounds good, Elle," The Old Man said.

She packed her laptop away and stood. "If that's all, gentlemen."

"She's no shrinking violet, is she, Whit?" Mr. Smith commented.

"Nope." The Old Man sounded like a proud parent.

Elle ignored both his and Mr. Smith's comments as she headed out of Frank's office.

Beau was with her when she reached the door. "Aren't you forgetting something, sugar?"

"Thank you for reminding me." Elle put her hand out for the keys to her Spider. It would have been a bummer to be stuck at Mat's place without transportation, especially once the Black Eagles arrived so she could return to her own temporary apartment.

He held the keys above her open palm. "I don't suppose you'd consider giving me a lift home." He paused, a grin flirting with his lips. "Or letting me drive this baby again?"

"I'm sure Frank can give you a ride. I need to stick by Chantal and Mat right now."

"What are the chances the bad guys realize she's with him?"

Elle shrugged. "Doesn't matter. *Any* chance is enough to maintain caution."

Even though federal stats indicated that a bank is robbed every hour in the United States, Elle had believed the chances of her husband being witness to a robbery, much less taken hostage, were pretty much nonexistent. She'd been wrong. She wasn't going to allow a false sense of security to diminish how carefully she watched out for her brother and his new girlfriend.

At least she assumed Chantal was a new love interest for her brother. Might be interesting to find out what had led to the other woman asking the irascible scientist for his help when she was threatened. If they'd been in a relationship for a while and he hadn't told Mama, he was *so* in trouble.

Hmm . . . something to bug him about once they got back to his place.

With a spring in her step, Elle headed for Mat's office to collect her charges.

Her sense of anticipation took a dive for the carpet when she realized Beau was still with her. "I'm sorry, but I really can't give you a ride, doc."

"I get that, but we need to talk."

"About the case?"

"No."

"Then we don't need to talk."

"What the hell do you mean?"

"It's simple. I need to focus on my assignment, not get sidetracked by a nice piece of ass. No matter how intelligent the brain attached to it."

Amazed laughter tumbled out of him. "Did you just call me a piece of ass? A *nice* piece of ass."

"Yes."

"I think I resent that."

"Why? It was just sex. You said so."

"So did you."

"Yes, and it's obvious we both meant it. Are we done talking now?"

"Has anyone ever told you that you could pass for a guy?"

"Seriously? No. But more than one person has mentioned that I don't look at life like a normal woman." Her beloved *baba* and mother included.

"She-yit. I didn't mean it that way. You might not fit feminine stereotypes, but, sugar, that sure doesn't make you Abby Normal."

Elle's lips tilted at the reference to *Young Frankenstein.* An absolute classic, in her opinion. "What did you mean when you said I could pass for a man, then? I'm pretty sure you weren't talking about my looks."

She'd never been accused of looking unfeminine, just acting it.

"You're as gun-shy as any guy I've ever known when it comes to talking about feelings."

She hadn't always been that way, or had she? Come to think of it, Kyle had accused her of something similar, though he'd never likened her to the male of the species while doing it.

"But you don't think that makes me abnormal?"

"Nope. My grandma used to say it takes all kinds to make the world go round."

"And that means what?"

"That the world would be worse off without the different kinds of people who live in it, not to mention damn boring."

"So, it doesn't bother you that I'm not a typical woman?"

"Is there such a thing? If there is and you aren't it, that doesn't bother me a bit. I already told you I find your dangerous side a hell of a turn-on."

He had, and she so didn't need to hear that again. So, why in the world was she pursuing this line of conversation? It was like her brain lost track of her mouth when she got within five feet of him.

"Are there some feelings you wanted to discuss?" she asked with as much enthusiasm as she would have shown for a conversation about the merits of one floor polisher over another. There was a reason cleaning services existed, after all.

Oh, man, she was getting sidetracked inside her own mind. That was a very bad sign.

"There are, but they'll keep." They'd stopped outside of Mat's office.

Something tightened in her chest. "You agreed it was just sex."

"I'm not talking about sex, but you're channeling a guy again—thinking everything revolves around that particular endeavor."

She rolled her eyes. "What are you talking about, then?"

"I'll tell you when we have more time and a bit more privacy."

The door to Mat's office opened and her brother stood there glaring at them both.

"You can relax, Matej. Your bosses knew all along that I'm an agent. It was apparently the elephant in the room no one wanted to mention while you were there." She turned and tilted her head so her and Beau's gazes met. "The name of my agency and the nature of its charter are on a strictly need-to-know basis and he doesn't need to know."

Mat's eyes had widened at her initial announcement, but now they narrowed and he looked at Beau. "So she says."

"Mat, do you really want to be responsible for me losing my job?" Elle asked.

"Of course not."

"Then drop it. You know more than you are supposed to and less than you want. Leave it at that."

# Chapter 11

Mat's home wasn't your typical bachelor pad. Instead of renting an apartment in one of the new buildings or buying an easy to monitor condo, her brother had bought a 150-year-old farmhouse with a wraparound porch on a large lot.

Obviously the original homestead, the two-story structure was surrounded by newer developments. There was a small stand of fruit trees, a gardener's shed and a detached garage, all of them around back. A majestic oak tree offered shade and an old-fashioned swing was in front of the house. Elle catalogued each item for its potential to compromise security.

Inside was a noticeable work in progress.

"I'm restoring it." Mat offered the explanation even though Elle hadn't asked for one.

"It's going to be beautiful when it's done." She could see where he'd already done some of the woodwork downstairs. "Man, I don't think I've ever seen a cleaner project area. Heck, Kyle and I used to make a bigger mess than this painting the bathroom."

"You know how I am."

"Yep, and I love you for it."

"So, it's okay to mention Kyle's name now?"

Elle stared at her brother for a few seconds in silence, then smiled. "Yeah, it is. I'm always going to miss him. I'll never stop regretting that I wasn't even in town when the robbery went down, but I'm done pretending like those years of my life didn't happen."

"That's good to know."

"Thanks. I think it is."

Chantal was looking at them in confusion.

Elle shrugged. "Mat can tell you all about my sordid past later, 'kay?"

"He doesn't have to tell me anything."

"I think he'll disagree, but I'll leave it up to him."

"Okay."

"So, what do you think of Mat's project here?"

"It's amazing." Chantal glowed with enthusiasm. "I couldn't believe it when Matej brought me here last night. I didn't expect this from him—a house that is so big and with such character. Such a fixer-upper, yes? But it has soul, you know? It would be a wonderful place to raise a family."

The blush that took over the small blonde's features as soon as the words escaped her mouth made Elle grin. "He pretends to be a total curmudgeon, but there's the heart of an artist beating in that grouchy bear's chest."

"*Oui.*" Chantal laughed softly and gave Mat a sideways glance. "He never had me fooled, though."

It wasn't just her brother that had it bad, and Elle couldn't have been happier. "Show me the kitchen?"

Mat and Chantal both turned and walked down a hallway that led to a kitchen that looked like it had been updated in the fifties, but not since then.

"Is it safe to bring tea water to boil on that thing?" Elle asked, teasing.

Her brother would have had the whole house checked for

safety issues before moving in. He would never have brought Chantal if the wiring, or anything else, was dangerously substandard.

"Of course. Is that your way of hinting you'd like some?" he asked.

"If you wouldn't mind. You both stay in here while I do a walk-through of the house, all right?"

Chantal's brow wrinkled as she was reminded of the reason for Elle having come to Mat's house initially.

Mat hugged her with one arm. "It will be fine, sweetheart. My baby sister knows what she's doing."

"I do. Don't worry. Either of you. Nitro and Josie will be here in a few hours too, and they are phenomenal at what they do."

"I just wish I knew who was threatening me. There is something so sinister about being frightened by a faceless adversary," Chantal said.

"They have faces all right, and we'll expose them," Elle reassured her.

"I told you, my sister knows what she's doing. You don't have to worry anymore, sweetheart."

"I just wish I'd never gotten involved with Eddie Danza."

"I think Eddie's wishing he'd never gotten involved with the people he did either," Elle said.

"Why do you say that?"

"Let's just say that there's a reason for the old adage 'Crime doesn't pay.' "

"Truly? Because I hate the idea that he profited from betraying his employer and me."

"He might have, at first, but trust me—Eddie Danza and the men who were involved with him in selling the plans for the antigravity project ended up regretting their choices," Elle replied.

"I'm glad."

"You've got the same desire to see justice done as my brother, don't you?" Elle asked.

Chantal shrugged. "I'm not all about tit for tat, but some things are just so wrong. If they had succeeded in selling those plans, innocent people would have died."

"What do you mean?"

"Hasn't Beau told you yet that the test flight of the scaled-down model was only a partial success?"

"He did. I wasn't aware you knew it."

Chantal shrugged again. "All the teams do."

"Did Eddie?"

"He wouldn't have been privy to the scientists' gossip. All he knew was that it had been a partial success."

"So he didn't know powering up a full-scale model could well have killed anyone within a certain radius?"

"What's wrong with it? An excess spillage of the electrical field?" Mat asked.

"That's what Beau said," Elle replied.

"I don't think Eddie knew how dangerous it was," Chantal said after a moment of thought. "I certainly didn't talk to him about it. You know, we were all pretty excited. Even with the drawbacks, it was further than anyone else has gotten with the concept of antigravity."

"So, it's safe to postulate that whoever he was trying to sell the plans to are just as ignorant of the danger," Elle said.

"Probably."

"This could get ugly if they get hold of the plans. It's a good thing that Eddie originally stole the wrong set of plans."

"He did what?" Chantal asked, with a laugh.

"He stole a set of plans that were for an unworkable model."

"You're kidding."

"Nope."

"Oh, that's bad."

"What an idiot," Mat said.

"I guess any non–technically savvy person could have made that mistake," Chantal said.

"Yes, but he didn't appreciate what he had in you either. The man is beyond ignorant; he's stupid," Mat said.

Chantal blushed again and Elle took that as a sign it was time to do her walk through.

The walk-through went quickly. Elle liked the layout of the house, though the attic was just a little too inviting to waiting predators. She would suggest Nitro and Josie use it for their command center. It would work as a good place to hide their presence as well.

There were four bedrooms, an updated full bathroom and a large linen closet on the second floor. Elle couldn't help noticing that apparently Chantal was using one of the extra bedrooms and not sharing the master with Mat. A small fishbowl with a gorgeous blue betta fish was on the small table beside the double-size bed.

One of the bedrooms was completely empty, and the other, the second largest, was patently Mat's office. The layout downstairs was just as simple. A living room, or what was probably considered the parlor when the house had originally been built. Then there was the formal dining room; a laundry room; another full bath, this one with a large clawfoot tub; and the oversize farm kitchen with enough space for a big table.

Right now, there was only a dinette set, which Mat had probably brought from his home in the Midwest. Surprisingly, he and Chantal were not in a clinch but were busy making the tea.

"What a picture of domestic harmony."

Chantal whipped around. "I'm not sure the ability to make tea together counts as a domestic accord."

"Trust me, being able to make *anything* with Mat and not have him growl at you definitely counts."

Right on cue, Mat grumbled something about annoying little sisters and both women laughed.

"If you are done being a pain in the backside," he said pointedly and then handed Elle a mug of steaming tea.

"Hey, you've had a pretty long break from my irritating little-sister shtick. I'm just making up for lost time."

Mat's eyes warmed. "It's good to have you around again."

She leaned over and gave him a kiss on the cheek. He laughed and grabbed her into a bear hug. Chantal, showing she really did fit in this little domestic scene, managed to save the tea while laughing with delight.


Mat rearranged the dishes in the kitchen cupboards for better efficiency of use and space. Organizing was just something he did. Couldn't stand a mess around him, but it helped him relax too—to put things in order. Chantal got that. At least she had ten years ago and she seemed pretty cool with his idiosyncrasies now.

She'd once told him that they were the cost of his brilliance.

Maybe she was right. All he knew was that he was the way he was and she didn't seem to mind.

The only other people on earth who got him like she did were his family. And even they teased him for his refusal to tolerate clutter.

Elle had made that joke earlier about how clean his house looked for a restoration project in progress. So, he put his tools and everything away when he was done with them. Nothing wrong with that. Little sisters could be a pain, but it was nice to have her back in California. Even if it was temporary. They'd all missed her since Kyle's death and she'd gone into a self-imposed isolation.

Baba told them all to be patient, that once her grief had muted, she would be back. Mama had argued that they could help Elle deal with her pain. But they hadn't been given the chance. Elle's job kept her on the go and she never seemed to have time to come home between assignments.

She was here now and Mat was really glad. He was even happier that she seemed okay with talking about Kyle. That meant she really was dealing with the past, not just burying it.

After their tea, she'd given him and Chantal a quick lecture on safety precautions, then retreated to the living room to make a phone call. She'd been there ever since, periodically talking on the phone and typing away on the mininotebook open on the coffee table in front of her.

Chantal had disappeared upstairs about the same time Elle had gone into the living room. Mat figured she was probably napping. He doubted she'd gotten much sleep last night. He only wished it had been for reasons other than worry. What he wouldn't give to keep that woman up making love to her delectable little body. Memories from ten years ago haunted him even worse now than they had been doing.

But he'd been a gentleman and put her in the one functioning guest room to sleep alone. She'd acted relieved when he'd taken her to it, so he knew he'd made the right decision. Even if it meant he spent a good part of the night fantasizing about the woman on the other side of the wall.

"You really think they'll find out who is trying to get their hands on the antigravity project plans?"

Mat closed the cupboard and turned to find Chantal standing only a couple of feet away. She was wearing a snug yellow T-shirt and a pair of purple sweats that hung loose on her trim hips.

His lips twitched. "Yes. Elle will find them."

"What's so funny?"

"You look like an Easter egg."

Chantal looked down at her clothes then up at him, putting her small fists on her hips. "I like bright colors. Do you have a problem with that?"

"Nope. Not a one."

"Good." She shrugged. "Bright colors make me feel better."

"I've been thinking of painting the house yellow with white trim, but maybe I should use a brighter color for the trim."

Chantal's eyes widened. "Uh . . ."

He crossed the short distance between them and looked down at her. She was so beautiful. "What's the matter, sweetheart?"

"I don't understand."

"What don't you understand?"

"Why are you helping me? I mean, now that the powers that be know about the threats, you don't have to put yourself out personally for my safety. I'm nothing to you, but you're talking about painting your house and everything."

"It needs an exterior face-lift too."

"That's not what I'm talking about. What difference does it make to you that I like bright colors? Why would you consider changing the color of your house's trim for me?"

"Because you aren't *nothing* to me. Haven't you figured that out yet? I staked a claim ten years ago and then I made the supreme mistake of walking away. I'm staking that claim again, but this time it's going to last a lifetime."

"What?" She jumped backward, her hip bumping into the counter. It didn't slow her down one bit as she sidled away from him along the counter. "No. Claims? We can't. . . . This is ridiculous. I'm still a geek. I don't . . . You can't want me. Not for a lifetime. Nobody wants me like that. No one ever has, not even family."

Her words just broke his heart. Clearly, she hadn't taken

him seriously when he told her he was playing for keeps. "Your parents did."

"They did." She nodded, as if reiterating that fact to herself. "Before they died. No one else, though."

"I do."

"You can't."

"I can. I do."

"No, it's . . . My work is enough."

"No, baby, it's not."

"I don't need people."

"You're not a damn island, Chantal. You need people to love you and for you to love. You need me. You need family, too and I've got a really good one I want to share with you. Maybe we can even talk about making one of our own. You said this would be a great place to raise children."

She looked ready to bolt, her eyes rolling. "No. You don't mean it. Don't tease me."

"Not teasing. Want you. In every way." Mat followed her movements and reached out to reel her in when she got to the swinging door.

No way was he letting her run from this, not when her eyes said she wanted what he was offering but was just terrified of taking it.

"You left me." She swallowed, looking so scared his heart squeezed in his chest. "Before."

"I won't leave again. I won't." He leaned down and kissed her, nothing overtly sexual, just a brush of his lips over hers. A promise.

She went completely still in his arms.

"I am claiming you." He kissed her again, this time allowing his tongue to trace the contours of her lips. "I *do* want you for a lifetime." Another kiss, this one with the barest nibble on her bottom lip. "I'm not playing. Not now. Not ever again."

"*Non. Vous pas* . . . you don't. . . . It's not love." The disjointed words revealed her inner confusion. Her French accent was so thick, you'd never know she'd spent close to half her life in the States.

"Ten years ago I believed that lie. I've gotten wiser since. I know love when I hold it in my arms, and you are it for me, Chantal."

She vehemently shook her head.

Words weren't working. It was time for something else. A decade ago not only had this woman given him her virginity, but she had given him a night filled with unbound passion. Mat meant to have that now too.

He swung her up in his arms.

She made the cutest squeaking sound and he smiled. He leaned down and pressed their mouths together again. Then he whispered, "Shh . . . Elle will hear you. Do you want her to come running?"

Chantal's cheeks turned bright red. "*Non*," she said in a vehement whisper.

"Me neither."

He pushed against the swinging door with his back and stepped into the hall. The sound of Elle's fingers clicking away on the computer's keys came from the living room. Making very little noise (skills a man learned as the oldest of five children never disappeared), he carried Chantal upstairs while she sent worried looks behind him. Now see, if she didn't want him, she wouldn't be so quiet. She'd be calling for Elle, or telling him to put her down, not looking to make sure Elle wasn't going to discover them heading up the stairs together.

Chantal gasped as they came into the master bedroom and Mat smiled. Maybe he had more than useless words and hopefully not nearly so ineffective lovemaking with which to convince her of his sincerity.

"You like?" he asked.

She was looking around with an expression of awe. "It's my fantasy bedroom."

"You told me about it. That night. How the only thing that could make our intimacy more perfect would be to have been in a room like this." He'd forgotten that until recently, but her description of her ideal boudoir had made an impact on his subconscious.

She'd blushed, the tendency just as endearing then as it was now, while describing a room that could have doubled for a Turkish harem. She'd spoken in detail about an oversize bed with lots of pillows and a wood canopy that had richly colored silks hanging from it—fabric that would create a barrier of sensuous walls when the ties around the four posts were undone. She'd rhapsodized over furniture made of darkly stained wood and rattan with a Middle Eastern feel and silks that matched those on the bed hanging over windows covered by metalwork. The final detail in her dream room had been a fireplace, in front of which there would be a long Roman couch.

Mat had bought the house because of the fireplace in the master bedroom. The Roman couch looked good, but it was damn comfortable for a six-foot-two scientist as well. "I didn't know it, but I created this room for you."

"No."

"Yes. Damn it, Chantal, the sheets are even silk. I slid right off them twice before I got the hang of sleeping on something so slippery. If not for you, then why?"

"You didn't know you would see me again."

Now that was one argument he could refute absolutely. "I made a call to my brother Mykola a few days before coming out here for my new job. I asked him to look into your where-abouts."

"You didn't."

"I did."

"But . . ."

"If you don't believe me, you can ask him. Only, not right now."

"Why not now?"

"Mykola is an INS agent. He's on a deep-cover assignment."

"Oh." She did that lip-biting thing. "What about Elle?"

"What do you mean?"

"Is she an INS agent too?"

"No."

"But she's more than a security consultant, or you wouldn't believe she was going to find the people threatening me."

"She's a federal agent, but I don't know whom she works for. Apparently, she's in black ops."

"That's heavy."

"Yeah."

"So, how did you end up a scientist?"

"Elle could be one too. She's got a degree and she's incredibly smart."

"But she took a different direction."

"Yes."

"How do you feel about that?"

"It used to bother me, but I realize she needs to do what makes her happy, not what our parents want."

"Your parents wanted you to be a scientist?"

"Yes. Lucky for all of us, I agreed. It could have been an emotional bloodbath otherwise. I would never have tolerated the kind of flack Elle's gotten for her choices."

"Wow."

"My brother Roman went into the military, but he's in research, not warfare. Or at least that's how my parents see it."

"You don't?"

"I don't know; he's a private man. I think he's probably worked on more than one top-secret project."

"The projects at ETRD are supposed to be top secret."

"Yep. Elle's going to make sure in the future they stay that way."

"You really are proud of her."

"I am. I wish I'd told her sooner."

"Why?"

"Her husband died four years ago. He was killed after being taken hostage by bank robbers. Since then, she's stayed away from the family for the most part. Everyone thought it was the grief, but maybe part of it was that she didn't want to deal with the disapproval for who she chooses to be."

"She's so beautiful, but she's dangerous too. Really dangerous."

"Yes."

"You look scary sometimes, but I feel safe with you."

"I'm glad. I plan to spend a lot of time with you."

Chantal's eyes filled with tears as she looked at Mat. "I want to believe you."

"Then do."

"It's not that easy."

"I'll make it that easy." With that, he kissed her. Full-on, passionate you're-mine lips devouring lips, like he'd warned her he'd do.

Her hands fluttered against him for a couple of seconds and then latched on to his shirt in a death grip while she reached up on her tiptoes to push into the kiss. Her small body pressed against his, and wild little sounds from her were muffled between their lips. They kissed like that for several long moments until she started scrabbling with the buttons on his shirt. She made a noise of frustration against his lips and then yanked at his shirt. Buttons went flying.

She was strong for a little thing.

Mat carried Chantal to the bed and laid her down, but she didn't let go of him. One hand was still holding tightly to his shirt. The other one was inside it, touching his hairy chest and rubbing against one of his nipples.

Oh, damn, that was good.

He tore his mouth from hers. "Let me lock the door."

Chantal reached up and her lips latched on to his again. He'd about given up on the door when she broke the kiss.

"Lock it." She looked so intent, so filled with desire that his knees about buckled.

He stumbled backward to lock the door, his gaze never leaving her. Once the door was secured, he rushed back to her, not caring if he was acting with less finesse than a horny teenager. He might be thirty-four, but he was damn horny and somehow he didn't think she minded knowing that. Not with the way she was undulating on the bed, her tight T-shirt riding up to expose smooth, golden skin.

He ripped his own shirt off over his head, ignoring the few buttons remaining. The khakis went next and then his boxers. He'd been barefoot since about five minutes after getting home, so no shoes or socks to worry about. Thankfully.

They might not have made it off.

Chantal was giving him a look that was three parts lust and one part niggling concern.

"Something wrong, little one?"

"I know it fits. I mean, it fit really well ten years ago." She fanned herself. "I mean, ooh la la . . . But you're not exactly petite *anywhere* on your body, are you?"

"Nope. Big feet." His toes dug into the hardwood floor. He stretched and then curled his fingers. "Big hands."

"Really big um . . ."

"I think the word you're looking for here is *penis*."

"I was going to say *cock*." Butter would not melt in her mouth.

He burst out laughing. "You were not."

She smiled. "Maybe not."

"I won't hurt you."

"This I know." Memories heated her gaze.

His knees giving up the fight, he sank onto the side of the bed. "I guess Eddie wasn't anything to be jealous about?"

"He was a lackluster lover, and no, not so big. In fact, not big at all, but I thought men did not like to hear about other lovers."

"Depends on what you say."

She smiled. "If I say no one could ever hold a candle to you, you would like that, yes?"

"Yes, but I would also have to agree. Ten years, Chantal, and no woman has ever come close to you."

# Chapter 12

"I like hearing that as well," Chantal admitted.

Could this really be happening? All of her secret fantasies come to life. Matej Chernichenko wanted her; he implied he loved her. He'd said walking away ten years ago was a mistake. Just like in her dreams—only better. And scarier. Could she believe him? Could she trust him with her heart?

If she didn't, would she be able to live with the loneliness of her life made colder by regrets of what might have been? No. She didn't want to be alone any longer. There had been only one time in her life since the death of her parents that she had not felt isolated by the connections she saw all around her. That had been when she and Matej were friends.

The one night they had spent together had been the happiest moments of her adult life, but the pain of losing him the next morning had easily rivaled the loss of her parents. A coward might fear the pain more than the loss of an opportunity to know that happiness again.

She might be a geek. She was usually too shy for her own good. She definitely understood scientific theory better than she did psychology, but she was no coward. She would take a risk on this man—the only one she had ever loved. With that decision made, an amazing happiness poured over her.

Maybe, just maybe, she would not be alone anymore.

Mat laid a hand on her stomach. "It looks so big against you."

Chantal looked down to where his spread fingers spanned her hip bone to hip bone. "What can I say? You're a giant, but I don't mind."

"I think you like it."

She did love his size. She'd never felt overwhelmed by it, just sort of awed and definitely aroused. "Maybe I do."

"That's good to hear since I'm not about to shrink."

"I'm not going to grow either." The worry tingeing her voice surprised her, but maybe she knew where it was coming from. He could have anyone, not just a shrimpy science geek.

"I like you just the way you are."

"Do you?"

"Oh, yes." He leaned forward, sharing his body heat, his big body dwarfing her, and that felt so very good. So right. "Very much."

"Elle is so tall. She looks like a cover model."

"She's my sister. Trust me when I tell you she's not what turns me on."

That made Chantal giggle. "I should hope not."

"I know not. I find petite blondes with more brains than fashion sense extremely appealing." He nuzzled the hollow of her ear.

She shivered. "You don't think I have any fashion sense?"

"I said *more* brains, not that you didn't have *any* fashion sense. You're beautiful." He kissed her softly, right there behind her ear. "Smart." He flicked his tongue out and tasted her earlobe. "So damn sweet you've got a choke hold on my heart." He nibbled, making her body shake with desire. "And exactly perfect for me."

"I'm glad."

"Me too." He continued nuzzling along her neck.

It was so hard to think, but she had to get something straight. "I promised myself after . . . that night that I would never have casual sex again." And she hadn't. She'd had bad sex, boring sex, unfulfilling sex, but she'd never again had casual sex.

Mat lifted his head so their gazes met and locked. "You didn't think you were having it then."

"No, I didn't." She'd discovered otherwise the next morning.

"I thought I was." He frowned and shook his head. "It turns out that you were right and I was wrong. There's nothing casual about how I feel about you."

"You walked away." Somehow, if this was going to work between them, Chantal was going to have to let that part of the past go.

"Because I was an idiot. Every man has to make at least one mistake in his life, or he's not human."

"Are you trying to say that was your only one?"

"No." His molten silver eyes were oh so serious. "Every day I didn't go looking for you was a mistake. That makes three thousand six hundred and twenty-two marks in my only human register."

"Depending on when the leap years fall, there are three thousand six hundred and fifty-one or fifty-two days in ten years."

"But it has been three thousand six hundred and twenty-two days since I walked away the morning after." He rattled the words off as if it was perfectly natural to know exactly how many days had gone by since that painful morning.

"Almost ten years."

"Do I get points for figuring it out before a decade passed?"

"You get points for keeping track. Lots and lots of them." Oh, wow, did he get points. Maybe everything he had claimed had been the truth. Chantal hoped so because she wasn't sure she'd survive otherwise.

"I'm glad to hear it. I need all the points I can get." His mouth was covering hers in one of the sweetest kisses imaginable before she had a chance to reply.

But no matter how gentle the pressure of his lips against hers, it ignited a passion in her hotter than magnesium fire. This man was the only one who had ever tapped into this feeling. The voracious desire screaming through her at this moment had lain dormant for ten years.

His touch had awakened it, and her memories told her that that same touch would sate it and, in fact, was the only touch that could.

Big hands skimmed off her clothing, caressing her as they did so. Heat emanated off her, her skin so sensitive that each brush of his big fingers left a trail of fiery passion in their wake. All the while his mouth claimed hers in that gentle, amazing kiss. Her own hands were all over his torso, touching the big body that had inspired numerous fantasies before and after their single night together.

When she was completely naked, he finally broke the kiss so he could sit up and look at her. She remembered this from the first time they'd made love. He'd spent what she'd considered an inordinate amount of time just looking at her then too. This time he did more than look. He trailed his fingertips over her again, the caresses methodical and thorough—as if he was memorizing her by feel as well as sight.

It was extremely erotic.

Mat rested his hand on Chantal's stomach again, like he had done earlier—only now there was no barrier between their skin. "*Vrodlývyy* . . . you are so incredibly beautiful."

Ten years ago, he'd said the same thing. And she'd told him she was a science geek. This time, she merely smiled. For him? She was beautiful. Just as for her, he was perfect among men. Others saw him as a cranky man whose brilliance barely made up for his gruff manner.

She saw the man inside. The man who would spend time secretly tutoring a struggling undergrad so he wouldn't get kicked out of the program. The man who had an almost child-like enthusiasm for his research. The man who helped when other people ignored someone in need. The man who would take on a position he didn't want because someone had to do it. The man who loved his family with an abiding loyalty worthy of envy. That man had always fascinated her.

He saw the woman inside her, the one who burned with a passion only he could ignite, the one who was more woman than scientist.

The hand the size of a dinner plate trembled against her tummy. "I want you so much."

"I can tell and I'm glad." Chantal reached out and curled her fingers around his hard-on. Her fingertips didn't quite meet, but she didn't let that scare her. He had fit ten years ago and that night she'd been a virgin. She wasn't one any longer.

Mat's body jerked at her touch and she smiled, loving the power she felt over this giant of a man. Stroking him up and down, she nearly purred with the pleasure of holding him in her hand like this. He was so hard and yet so smooth. The skin so incredibly soft. He was so very vulnerable to her touch, every movement of her hand eliciting groans and jerky move-ment from him.

She cupped his low-hanging scrotum. The skin here was soft too, but wrinkled with anticipation. His pulsing erection jumped in her hand and pearly fluid condensed on the tip. She leaned forward, her lips a mere breath from the end of his shaft. "Is it safe?"

Would she be able to stop herself from tasting if he said no?

"Yes."

She gave in to the urge to flick her tongue out and lap up a bit of that masculine cream. She had quickly discovered she didn't like the taste of other men and had not made it a habit to put her mouth on them this intimately, latex or no. Only just as in everything else, with Matej, this was different. He tasted both sweet and salty, *addictive.*

She took the head of him into her mouth, her lips closing on the other side of his corona. She had to stretch her jaw wide, but she didn't mind. She knew he wouldn't try to shove himself in farther. And he didn't. He made noises filled with need, begged her to taste him and told her how wonderful she was as she swirled her tongue around the spongy flesh in her mouth.

His hands gripped the sides of her head. "Stop, sweetheart. Please."

She released him and leaned back so she could see his face. He looked like he was in pain.

"You didn't like it?" she asked, knowing darn well he had loved it.

"I was going to come and I want to be inside you when that happens. I want you to share the pleasure."

"I was enjoying myself."

"Trust me, you can enjoy yourself just that way any time you like, but for right now, let me pleasure you so we are on a level playing field."

"Are we playing?"

"For keeps, for a lifetime—those are the stakes and I warn you now, I intend to win."

"If I don't oppose you, is it still a game?"

"It was never a game, but if you don't oppose me, then we both win."

"I like that."

"Me too."

Then Mat was doing as he'd promised, pleasuring her body until she was just as close to reaching her pinnacle as he had been. He put on a condom and entered her slowly, stretching her swollen, sensitive inner tissues until she was sure they wouldn't stretch any more. But they did and finally he was seated fully inside her.

He looked down into her eyes, his own deeply serious. "We are one."

Chantal couldn't say anything, but she nodded. She felt connected to him at a molecular level and her emotions twined with his in a knot she didn't want to try to undo. Ever.

Then he started to move, and the memories of ten years of lackluster sex got blasted from her, to be replaced with shattering delight.

She reached her climax first, her whole body bowing up, going rigid while her inner muscles convulsed. He came with a roar above her.

Afterward, Mat cuddled Chantal, telling her about a near decade of searching for something he'd only realized recently that he'd had once and lost.

She knew what he meant, only she'd known exactly what she'd lost. "I spent the last ten years comparing every other man to you. It was stupid—you weren't there—but I couldn't help myself. I had boyfriends, but they were all like Eddie. Mistakes."

"I am not a mistake."

"No. You are the one I have wanted."

"And I am the last man you will have."

"Oh, so possessive."

"Desperate."

She smiled and snuggled into his big body. "We have to go downstairs and face your sister. She had to have heard you. You shouted really loud at the last."

"She will be happy for us both."

"I hope so."

"I know it."

\* \* \*

Beau did catch a ride with Frank after their meeting at ETRD. They talked about the investigation and speculated on who might have put the bug in Frank's office.

"I thought I was going to laugh out loud when Elle accused Mr. Smith of doing it."

Frank chuckled. "I know what you mean. That lady is a match for our mysterious boss."

"Did you wonder, for a minute, if it had been him?"

"Nope. I'm not saying I'd put it past him to bug my office, or anywhere else at ETRD, for that matter, but he has full access. He'd put something in hooked to ongoing power, not something that required a battery."

"So, who do you think did it?"

"Honestly?"

"Yes."

"If the security breach on the project hadn't happened, I would have immediately assumed it was Archer Sandstone for no other reason than so that he could know what was going on."

"He has access to everything."

"Not our private meetings."

"You really think he's that jealous?"

"I'm not sure. I'm just telling you what I would have thought if I didn't know there was someone after the antigravity project."

"The thought of those plans falling into the wrong hands is enough to give me nightmares."

"You and me both."

"People could die."

"And it would be our fault. We should have had better security to begin with."

"No matter how good security is, there will always be someone willing to sell out the people who trust him if the

price is right. I don't care how good Elle is, she can't guarantee against that."

"No."

Beau and Frank shared a moment of frustration at Eddie
Danza's betrayal and the threats leveled against Chantal.
They didn't have to talk about it for Beau to know his mentor was thinking about the same stuff he was. He knew Frank
well enough to guess. Beau was pretty sure that at this point,
his boss didn't know anything more than he did. It went
without saying they were both angry at Mr. Smith for keeping them in the dark about the nature of Gil Bigsley's disappearance.

They decided to work a little of that stress off with some
racquetball at their club. Beau won the first game, Frank the
second and Beau the next two. Beau figured he might have had
a tad more frustration to work off.

Especially after the way Elle had acted after the meeting.
She was withdrawing from him, but he wasn't ready to let her
go. It might only be sex, but right now it was addictive sex.
And no way was she going to convince him she didn't want it
every bit as much as he did.

A couple of hours after leaving ETRD, Beau was once
again in the passenger seat of Frank's car. Rather than taking
him home, the older man was headed toward Mat's house.
Beau had told him he wanted to talk over some things with
Elle regarding the security breach. He also wanted to meet
the bodyguards for Mat and Chantal.

If he planned to convince her to take him home after the
Black Eagles arrived, that was his business. Though he doubted
he fooled Frank. The man knew him better than anyone else.

"Do you think this is a good idea?" the older man asked as
Beau went to get out of the car.

Beau stopped and faced his friend and mentor. "I don't know, but I do know it's something I can't ignore."

Frank nodded. "Just don't go getting yourself hurt. She's not a settling down kind of woman."

"I know."

"Okay then. See you Monday. Call me if anything comes up beforehand."

"Will do."

Beau wasn't surprised that Elle answered the door when he knocked. She was the bodyguard. What did surprise him was the look of absolute consternation on her features when she did so.

"You didn't expect me?" he asked, a little stunned.

She was a smart woman. She had to realize her brush-off at the company was only going to work for so long.

"I . . . uh . . ."

He followed her into the living room and noticed that she'd been working on that subcompact laptop of hers. It was out and open on the coffee table.

A moan sounded from the room above them, followed by a litany of French that Beau was kind of glad he couldn't understand. Considering the fact it was in Chantal Renaud's voice. A voice clearly strained by passion. The sounds were coming through the heating duct and echoed a little, but other than that, the noise could have been created in the same room.

Elle turned wild eyes on Beau. "They're making love. I mean seriously. They couldn't wait for tonight? A sister shouldn't be hearing this kind of thing."

"I doubt Mat realizes the acoustics carry like this."

"Right. And it's not like I'm going to knock on his door and tell him."

He managed to suppress his grin. Just. "Why not?"

"You're kidding, aren't you?" She sounded as close to panicked as he was sure the supercool, über-efficient spy ever got. "That's my big brother up there. With his . . . his . . ."

"Girlfriend?"

"I think she's more than that."

"After only two weeks of working together?"

"They knew each other ten years ago. At university, I think." She started pacing. "I wasn't trying to listen. I didn't even realize what I was hearing at first. Thought he'd turned a television on, or something. But then I heard them talking and I got caught up in what they were saying. Curiosity, it's one of my good-bad traits, you know?"

"I get that."

"As soon as I realized they were getting naked, I hightailed it for the kitchen."

He looked down and realized her computer was in standby. "You forgot to take your computer with you."

"I know. I just couldn't come back in here for it."

"We're in here now."

"I thought they were done. It's been going on forever!"

A loud roar sounded through the vent and Beau was surprised the rafters didn't shake. Elle looked like she was going to faint. "Get my computer," she gasped and then rushed from the room.

Laughing like a hyena the whole time, Beau grabbed the computer and her phone, which she'd dropped when the first moan had sounded. He never would have guessed his sexy, very together lover would have this side.

He found her in the kitchen, making tea, her expression hunted.

"Computer." He put it down on the small table dwarfed by the open expanse of the kitchen. "Phone." He laid the hi-tech cellular beside the laptop.

"Thank you."

"So, what have you been doing, standing in here and trying to work up the courage to retrieve your notebook?"

"Something like that." She waved her hand vaguely toward the tea things. "Want a cup?"

"Sure. So, if not worrying about how to get your computer back, what?" Then he latched on to what would really be worrying her. "Ah, you've been wondering how you're going to tell your big brother about the sound system between the living room and the master bedroom."

"Yes."

They doctored their tea and he put both mugs onto the table, one beside the computer and the other across from it. "I'll do it."

She looked over her shoulder at him, from putting the tea things away, a glimmer of relief showing in her eyes before it was doused by mistrust. "I should be relieved, but I have a feeling that if I let you, there wouldn't be one iota's diminishment of my mortification. Or his either. Though he probably deserves it, putting me through this."

Beau shrugged, unable to deny the allegation. This was just too damn fun.

Elle collapsed into one of the dinette chairs, her head landing on her hand in a classic pose.

Beau laughed out loud.

She looked up at him. "Why are you here?"

"Why, princess, you don't act glad to see me. After I rescued your computer and everything."

She sighed. "I do appreciate that."

"You really thought they'd be done?" he asked, on the verge of another belly laugh.

Oh, she had a good glare on her.

Luckily, Texans were impervious to that sort of thing.

"Don't you remember last night?" They'd taken all night long.

"It's not nighttime!" Elle retorted.

"Elle, I never would have guessed you were so puritanical."

"I'm not. It's just—"

"Your big brother."

"Exactly."

He patted her shoulder and pushed her tea in front of her. "Relax, sugar. You've faced worse."

"I have? I don't know. My job . . . it's dangerous, I guess. Can even get scary sometimes—a lot less often than you might imagine—but this? I think I'm mentally scarred for life."

"What's scarred you for life?" Mat asked from the doorway, barefoot, wearing a pair of black jeans that had been washed so many times they were faded to gray and a black T-shirt, his hair shiny wet.

Elle groaned and hid behind her mug of tea.

Mat's brows furrowed and then he sighed before giving Beau a questioning glance. "Did I know you were coming over?"

"Nope."

"Did Elle know?"

Beau shook his head. "It was a spontaneous decision."

"Related to work, or related to being at my sister's apartment for breakfast wearing nothing but a pair of jeans?"

"Both."

Elle made another pained sound and was now sharing her death glare between Beau and her brother.

Mat's scowl was directed entirely at Beau.

Beau couldn't help grinning. Who would have known hanging out with a grouchy scientist and his sexy but deadly sister could be this entertaining? "I wanted to talk some things over with Elle."

"I wouldn't mind hearing what she found out this afternoon myself."

Now, that was too good to pass up. "I think she discovered her brother is indeed human and enamored of one of his coworkers."

"My feelings for Chantal were pretty obvious this morning." Mat looked pained and then faced his sister head-on with the attitude of a man about to face a newbie ISO auditor. "If you're talking about my loud and according to Chantal unmistakable-as-to-the-cause-for shout, I'm sorry about that."

Elle just covered her face with her hands and moaned. Damn, she was cute when she was pitiful. And Beau'd bet it wasn't a look he'd get to see often, if ever again.

He laid his hand on Mat's shoulder. "I think this is where I tell you that the forced-air ducts transmit sound a lot less carrying than the aforementioned shout—from the master bedroom directly to the living room. With surround-sound quality."

"The hell it does. This house is practically soundproof the way it was built."

"Maybe room to room, but trust me, the duct system installed for the heat and central air has added a new dimension to the equation."

"*Sukin sin*," Mat bit out.

Elle let out a sort of strange-sounding laugh. "If you're using Ukrainian to protect my sensibilities, one, they've already been demolished." She shuddered. "And two, I know just as many cusswords in the mother tongue as you do."

Mat closed his eyes and appeared to be counting to ten—or maybe fifty. Eventually, he asked, "You heard us?"

# Chapter 13

Elle shook her head vehemently. "Not *that*. I mean, I left. After . . . I heard some. Oh, this is just not the kind of thing I want stuck in my head. It's worse than a badly done horror movie."

Mat looked offended. "Hey!"

Beau knew he had to hide his amusement, but it sure wasn't easy. "You chased her out of the living room. She's been hiding in the kitchen like a scared rabbit since the discovery. She even abandoned her precious computer."

Mat gave his own impression of a man trying very hard to hold in his hilarity. "Sorry about that, sis. It wasn't on purpose, I promise."

"I never thought it was, but darn it—couldn't you have waited until tonight?"

"No."

Beau understood the certainty in Mat's voice. He was, after all, another man. But Elle? She was gulping air like a drunk with a bottle of fine wine and the expression in her eyes was turning downright scary.

"Think of it this way: you wouldn't want the Black Eagles to discover the way sound carries in the house, would you?" Beau asked.

"Yes." Elle was nodding like a bobblehead on the dashboard of a car with bad shocks. "Definitely. Way better."

"What would be way better?" Chantal asked as she came into the kitchen, her hair damp.

They all froze. Elle jumped up, and the change that came over her was phenomenal. The wild-eyed baby sister who had overheard her big brother roaring out his climax became a calm, collected woman without a care in the world. In like one second. This was Beau's sugar's game face; he was sure of it.

Elle smiled serenely. "I would have preferred it if Mr. Smith had revealed the nature of Gil Bigsley's disappearance before today."

Beau was impressed. She hadn't lied, but she hadn't told the whole truth either.

"Me too." Chantal gave a sweet little secretive smile to Mat and then focused on Elle. "Did you get a chance to talk to Gil today?"

The sexy TGP agent nodded. "Mr. Smith called me on a three-way not long after we got back here."

"What did Gil say?" Beau asked.

"His story is almost identical to Chantal's except that whoever is trying to get the plans for the antigravity project threatened his elderly parents as well. He got scared and went straight to Mr. Smith. Turns out it was a smart move. Mr. Smith had him and his parents in a safe house within hours."

"I guess there are benefits to not having a family," Chantal said.

Mat hugged her from behind, wrapping his arms around her waist. "You have one now, *miy liúbyy*."

Elle's expression softened.

"What does that mean?" Beau asked, guessing it wasn't anything like another Ukrainian swearword.

"My precious," Mat interpreted for him.

"My brother is right. You have a family now, Chantal. You are not alone and you never will be again. We're a tough bunch to get rid of; trust me, I've tried."

Mat winced, but Chantal looked really moved by Elle's words. "Thank you."

Elle lightly punched her brother in the arm. "I didn't try that hard; you know I didn't. And I'm done avoiding the people I love, okay?"

"Okay."

"So, you didn't learn anything new from Gil?" Beau asked.

"I'm not sure. He thought the man he talked to had an accent, but not British. What about you, Chantal?"

"Um . . . let me think. His accent isn't British, but it's close. Not Australian. Definitely not Canadian."

"South African?" Elle asked.

Chantal's eyes widened and she nodded. "Yes. That's it. It's very subtle, but it's there."

"Was it always the same man who called?" Elle asked.

"Yes. I don't recognize the voice as someone I've met before, but it's definitely the same one."

"Gil said the same."

"So, that means what?" Chantal asked.

"I'm not sure except that it looks very much like the same person who contacted Gil threatened Chantal. The agent who investigated the initial security breach has a list of names, buyers who were supposed to participate in the auction for the plans. We can cross-reference it for a South African connection."

"You're kidding. That's great, isn't it?" Beau asked when Elle didn't look quite as enthused as he thought she should.

"It gives us a place to start, but we can't rule out the possibility that this attempted breach is unrelated to the first one.

The problem is, too many people at ETRD know more than they should about the top-secret projects."

Beau had to agree. "We have a pretty open work environment."

"If you want to prevent this sort of thing from happening again, that has to change to an extent."

"I can see that."

"Good." Elle opened her little laptop and pulled up a file. "My associate is doing additional research on the initial parties interested in the plans. Even if he does find a South African connection, we can't dismiss the other potential buyers as possible players in this case as well. The threatening man's country of origin may have nothing to do with the case at all."

She wasn't going to leave any stone unturned in this investigation and, knowing that, Beau felt a lot better about the safety of employees at ETRD. "Thank you, Elle. I'll admit, I was pretty pissed when Frank and Mr. Smith told me they were letting you come in under the guise of a security consultant, but it worked out for the best."

Elle opened her mouth to answer, but her cell phone rang. She grabbed it and answered, "Elle here."

Someone with a deep voice spoke on the other end. There wasn't enough bleed for Beau to tell exactly what was being said, though.

"Great. You've got the address for the GPS. Okay, see you then." She hung up. "That was Nitro. He and his wife are on the way here from the airport."

"Nitro? He's named after an explosive?" Beau asked.

"It's his nickname. He's an explosives expert, but that's only a small part of his training. Like I said earlier, he and Josie are the best of the best."

"How do you know them?"

"The associate who is doing the research on the possible

suspects, he worked with Nitro and his partners on a case. They made a strong and favorable impression on him. Ever since they opened their doors as security specialists, I also made it my job to know about them. They're good and they're honest. They were mercs that specialized in extractions."

"A dangerous job," Beau said.

"Yes. It pays well, though—*if* you live long enough to spend the money you earn."

"Wow," Chantal said, patently impressed.

"So, this couple will be watching over her," Mat said with satisfaction.

"They'll be protecting both of you."

Mat just shrugged, but Beau was glad Elle had made the distinction. "This cloak-and-dagger shit is over our head, buddy," Beau said.

"Not to interrupt what would no doubt be a fascinating debate on whether or not Matej needs bodyguards just as much as I, but I don't want to meet the Black Eagles for the first time with wet hair. I'm going to go make myself a little more presentable," Chantal said.

Mat kissed the side of her head. "You're always presentable, sweetheart. A little wet hair can't detract from your beauty."

Chantal didn't even roll her eyes at this blatant flattery. She smiled, like she thought Mat could walk on water if he tried hard enough. "I'm still going to dry my hair."

She led Mat from the kitchen, both of them smiling all goofy-like.

Beau couldn't imagine a woman looking at him like that, especially not Elle. She didn't do adoration, though he had a feeling Kyle had seen a side to her that she hid from most of the world.

Elle had returned to her computer, but she looked up when

the other two were gone. "So, you're glad that I'm on the case now?"

"You bet, sugar."

"But you were angry before, when you knew I was coming in . . . only you were fine with pretending not to know who and what I am."

"Not really. I thought all the subterfuge stank to high heaven, but I'm not the one who calls the final shots at ETRD."

"No, that would be the mysterious, irritating Mr. Smith."

Beau sat down across from Elle and took a sip of his now lukewarm tea. "I'm not sure why you're so angry with him. He wasn't any more untruthful than you were. It's not like you came to management and just told them the government wanted to inventory our projects and determine how effective our security is."

"First of all, if I had done so, Frank would have denied access just like he did when the request came through other channels." Elle sat tall, all evidence of her earlier confusion wiped so completely, it might not ever have been there. If he wasn't sure of his own memories, he'd wonder if this woman was capable of freaking out at overhearing her brother's *amore,* like she'd done. "Second of all, I didn't come to assess your security; I came to improve it. Trust me, I will."

"Good. It obviously needs it."

"Yes, it does."

"So, you think our government has the right to know what private enterprise is doing in its research and development departments, to spy on its own people when that information isn't forthcoming?" He wasn't trying to start an argument with her, though that could be fun, but he really wanted to know.

"I think someone has to watch out for our nation's safety."

Her clear gray eyes shone with certainty. "And yes, some-times that means spying on our own people."

The tea wasn't half bad almost cold. It was some kind of pomegranate something. "How does that make us any different from a totalitarian regime?"

"My job doesn't necessitate the subjugation of U.S. citizens, or stealing from them. The difference between an agency like mine overseen by a democratic government and a totalitarian regime is what we do with the information when we get it. We are charged with protecting the interests of our nation's scientists, as well as their safety. We do not dictate what they research or even what they do with the results of that research."

"But you try to keep it from falling into dangerous hands."

"Yes, to the extent that we can do so without compromising a citizen's constitutional rights."

"You really believe in what you're doing, don't you?"

"Yes."

"Even if it requires you to make trade-offs with your personal integrity."

Elle's game face was giving nothing away. "I guess it depends on how you define that."

"You've spent your life lying to your family. Your brother doesn't even know the name of your agency."

"That's need-to-know information and he doesn't."

"Doesn't it bother you? They love you. You're so close." A lot closer than he was with his parents. "And yet there's this big chunk of your life you can't share with them."

"I'm aware of that, but it doesn't change who I am. What I do. My parents and *baba* aren't going to approve of me being a black-ops federal agent any more than they approve of me being a security consultant. Where I work isn't an issue for them because it's not in the field they believe I should have pursued."

"Mat is proud of you."

"More than I believed he was, yes."

"Elle, he thinks you rock."

That made her smile. "Don't tell him you said so. He'll feel like he has to refute it."

Beau laughed and shook his head. "Little sisters can be such a pain."

"Mat's said that many times. I'm not sure what the problem is. We're a lot easier to have around than big brothers."

"I'm sure my sister would agree, but Mat and I know better."

"Because you've had a big brother to compare to."

"You know I haven't."

"Well, I've got a little sister, and believe me, she's a lot easier to deal with than my brothers."

"Sure, you say that now, sugar, but you just wait. Little sisters are a time bomb waiting to happen."

Elle laughed out loud. "You are insane."

"Nah, just experienced. Tanya was easy as pie until she started dating. It's all been downhill since."

"You are so full of it. You love what she's doing with her life."

"I love her. Just like your parents love you. Doesn't matter what you choose to do with your life."

"That's not how you sounded a few minutes ago."

He wasn't her family, but then neither was he a judgmental asshole. "I met you knowing you were lying to me from the start. I didn't like it. The dishonesty didn't match the woman I perceived you to be, but then that's part of the cover, isn't it?"

"I'm not sure what you are accusing me of."

"I'm not accusing you of anything, sugar."

"That's not what it sounds like."

"I'm just saying, you must cultivate a trustworthy demeanor for your job."

"I am trustworthy."

"Depends on your definition, I guess."

"Don't throw my words back at me."

"Why not? They're true, aren't they? You and me, we define personal integrity and trustworthiness differently."

"Do we?"

"Yeah, I think we do."

"You spent just as much time lying to me as I did withholding all of who I am."

"If I'd had a choice, I wouldn't have."

"You think that's not true for me too? You think I like keeping my real job from my parents, refusing to tell my brother the name of the agency I work for? I made promises when I hired on at TGP and I keep those promises, even when it's hard. That's part of my definition of personal integrity."

"Point taken."

"I don't lie unless I have to, but yes—sometimes it is necessary. That doesn't mean I can't be trusted."

"You mean I can trust you to have my back, but the bad guys had better be on their toes."

Her lips quirked at that, but she nodded. "Exactly."

"You lied to me about why you were here."

"No, I didn't tell you the entire truth of why I took the assignment at ETRD. I did not withhold information that could cause you harm."

"You don't think so?"

"I know so."

"You don't think spying on my company for the government harms me?"

"Not with the motivation behind doing so that is part of my agency's charter."

"You're pretty amazing, Elle."

"In a good or bad way?"

"I'm leaning toward good."

"Should I be flattered?"

"You tell me. Does my opinion of you matter?"

She looked past him, her gray eyes filled with a distant expression. "It shouldn't."

"But?"

"It does."

"I don't think I could do what you do." But if someone was going to do it, Beau was glad it was somebody like Elle.

"I don't think so either." She stood up and walked toward the front of the house.

He followed, not sure how he felt about her easy agreement. "What's going on?"

"Nitro and Josie are here."

"Did they knock?" He hadn't heard anything, but he'd been concentrating on her.

"No. I heard the car coming up the street. I assume it's them. Regardless, it doesn't hurt for me to check it out."

"You're giving me a hard-on here, sugar."

Her fluid movement forward checked for a bare second, then continued. "Not going there."

"Maybe not right now. Unlike your brother, I'm not into exhibitionism."

"He didn't know I could hear."

"But later? We are so going there, over and over again," he said, ignoring her defense of Mat.

Elle muttered something, but the only word he caught was *arrogant*. He was getting to her. He let a satisfied smile curve his lips.

She checked out the window by the door without turning on the hall light. "It's them." She turned and headed back toward the kitchen.

"Aren't you going to let them in?"

"I told them to park in the garage. They'll come in through the kitchen."

"Say something else in that no-nonsense, superspy voice. I might just come in my jeans."

"That's definitely more than I wanted to know," Mat said from the top of the stairs.

"Nonexhibitionist. Right," Elle grumbled.

"At least I'm not roaring out my orgasm loud enough to shake the rafters."

"I knew they heard." Chantal's voice sounded both exasperated and embarrassed.

"I could have stubbed my toe," Mat said.

"I wouldn't mind stubbing my toe like that—as long as Elle was in the room too," Beau said.

Mat and Elle let out identical sounds of exasperation.

Beau caught Chantal's gaze as she came down the stairs with Mat. "Isn't that cute? Matching sister and brother growls," he said.

Chantal giggled. "That's not the only thing they have in common. Did you notice how clean Elle's apartment was?"

"Yep. And they've both got that tall-gene thing going."

Chantal stopped at the bottom of the stairs. "I like it."

"So do I."

"They're both really smart too. According to Mat, it's a family trait."

Beau nodded. "Princess is pretty loud when she stubs her toe too."

Elle made a sound of pure frustration and slammed into the kitchen.

"You'd better watch yourself there, cowboy," Mat said. "She threw me earlier. Didn't break anything because I'm her beloved brother. You, she might put out of commission for a while."

"I may be from Texas, but I've never been a cowboy. As for the other, I'm up for any kind of wrestling Elle would care to engage in." Literally. He might have been teasing Elle about his arousal, but that didn't mean it wasn't real. He was as hard as a rock.

"See that, Josette? I'm not the only guy who likes to wrestle with his woman." The man speaking looked like he would be as comfortable in a loincloth as he was in the dark camouflage pants he was wearing. Big, with Native American features, he had long black hair pulled back in a ponytail.

The woman who came through the door after him was taller than Chantal, but only by a couple of inches. She kind of looked like Sandra Bullock, right down to the mischievous glimmer in her green eyes. However, she moved with the same fluid grace as Elle. Her dark tank top and snug jeans showed off muscle every bit as toned and developed as Elle's too.

"I bet Elle can take him down just as nicely as I do you." The look she gave her husband said she'd be happy to prove it right now.

Oh, man, she was a live wire. Beau bet those two had fun tying it up.

"Beau's not trained," Elle said dismissively. She'd followed Josette Black Eagle out of the kitchen. They all stood at the bottom of the stairs at the back of the hall. "I bet it would take me less than ten seconds to have him begging for mercy."

Mat snickered, giving Beau a knowing look.

It was a good thing Beau's masculine ego was nice and healthy. Man alive, his princess could be vicious when she was riled.

"I'll take that bet, sugar. Plenty of defensive linemen made that same mistaken assumption. You might have me begging for something, but it won't be mercy." He winked at her.

"You're welcome to test that out tonight when you drive me home, though. Because, like I told you, I'm not looking to have an audience."

"Sounds kind of like Hotwire, doesn't he?" Nitro asked his wife, sounding amused.

She nodded and let him pull her in so she leaned against him. One of her arms went around his waist and she smiled at Beau. "Where are you from?"

"Texas, ma'am."

"Ma'am? Oh, I don't think so. You can call me Josie. Hotwire is from Georgia. You've both got that honeyed drawl thing going, though."

"Now, there's a world of difference between a Georgian accent and a Texas drawl. You just ask your friend."

She looked up at her dark-eyed husband. "Oh, they do sound alike and it isn't just the accent." She grinned at Beau. "If you say so, I'll take your word for it."

"I so do." He might have lived away from Texas long enough that his drawl had gotten less pronounced, but he didn't sound like some Georgia cracker. No, sir.

"Seems to me the South produces men who like to tease the women in their lives, though, no matter what kind of drawl they have," Josie said.

"It's not just Southern men," Chantal muttered with a significant look at Mat.

Beau grinned at Josie. "Could be, ma'am. Excuse me, *Josie*. I only know I'm just a tad addicted to that fiery spark in Elle's eyes."

Josie looked at Elle and shook her head in obvious sympathy. "He's cruising, isn't he?"

"Yes." Elle was giving him the death glare again.

He turned up the wattage on his grin, not at all worried.

Elle liked him, even if she didn't want to admit it. After all, she cared what he thought of her. It'd be a sure bet that there weren't a lot of people in her life that that was true of.

Yep, he was going to take that gorgeous woman home with him tonight and show her just how much he appreciated all her attributes.

# Chapter 14

Elle wasn't sure if she wanted to kiss or kill the over-confident but too-sexy-for-her-own-good Texan. "We can meet in the kitchen or upstairs in Mat's office. I think Josie and Nitro should stay out of the rooms at the front of the house except to patrol."

Nitro nodded. "Once we set up surveillance in them, we won't have to do that either."

"Let's meet upstairs. I'd like to get a feel for the house," Josie added.

Mat's office boasted only a single desk chair, so they gathered on the floor in a circle. Somehow, Elle found herself beside Beau, their legs touching. She didn't bother trying to move. He'd just follow her and make it blatant too. Besides, Nitro was on her other side and she didn't exactly want to scoot closer to him.

He clearly had a soft spot for his wife, but all his other edges were good and sharp. Perfect for guarding Elle's brother and Chantal. Just not someone Elle wanted to end up snug against. Which is what would happen because Beau wasn't about to give her an inch.

The man was on a roll, flirting and teasing her with clear intent.

Ignoring her body's reaction to the Texas-born scientist, Elle apprised Nitro and Josie of the current situation. Her brother and Chantal told the bodyguards their schedules. Beau wasn't silent by any means. He asked questions that showed he was personally concerned about Mat and Chantal's safety.

Nitro's dark eyes met Elle's. "Do you have a recommendation for a base of operations?"

"The attic, or the empty guest bedroom. I think the attic is good because if someone drops in on Mat, your stuff won't be anywhere it might accidentally be seen."

"Is there a bed up there, or are we roughing it?" Josie didn't sound like she'd mind the latter option.

"You could take the bed from the other guest bedroom," Chantal offered, with pink-tinged cheeks. "No one else is using it."

Mat nodded, looking very happy with that fact.

Nitro ran through their plan for Mat and Chantal's protection. It was beyond the standard, but similar to what Elle herself would have done. She approved.

"Our best option for figuring out who is making the threats is to have Chantal pretend to get them what they want," Elle said. She'd been thinking about it all day and nothing else made as much sense.

Mat grabbed Chantal, scooting her right into his arms. "You are not using her as bait."

The petite blonde didn't seem to mind the overt protectiveness, but she was giving Elle a look of resigned fear. She was too smart not to have realized this was the direction the investigation was bound to take.

"Calm down, big brother. I'm not going to do anything that puts Chantal at risk."

"Damn right you're not."

Elle had to force herself not to roll her eyes. "If you could notch it back just a little, I think we can get some productive planning done here."

"Don't talk to me like that, little sister. I know this is your job, but we're talking about the woman I love. I don't care if it is easier, she's not going to be put at risk. I won't lose her again."

Chantal petted Mat, soothing the beast. "You will not lose me. The past is behind us, *cher*."

Elle so wanted that story, but later. "I understand, Matej. I really do. I won't put her at risk, but I do need her to play a part."

"What part?" Chantal asked.

"The frightened but cooperative stooge." She put up her hand before her brother could level another protest. "Only on the phone." She looked at Chantal. "Speaking of which, we need to forward your apartment phone to this one."

"I don't have a landline in my apartment. He's only called on my cell phone; he's never contacted me at ETRD."

"Why don't you have a landline?" Mat asked.

"Two bills for redundant uses. Seemed like a waste of resources, and living in Southern California is expensive. I'm not paid as much as you are, Dr. Chernichenko," Chantal said, with a teasing smile.

Elle liked seeing her show the humor. She might be wound tight by all this, but she wasn't buckling under it.

"Cell phone numbers aren't listed," Beau said.

"They're not hard to find if you know whom to go to, or have a good hacker working for you," Nitro answered.

Elle took some notes on her computer. "That will make it easier."

"For what? For Chantal to get more of those nasty phone calls?"

Her brother was one breath away from getting on her nerves. She understood his instincts to protect. She did, but right now he was just being argumentative. It was one of the ways he relieved stress and Elle got that, but she was losing patience. "Listen, we can end this a lot faster if we can lure the perps into showing themselves. The best way to do that is to coordinate a drop. Chantal can help us do that."

"She won't be making the drop, though. I can do a blond wig," Josie said, with a grin.

Although technically the Black Eagles had not been hired to help with the investigation, Elle had not doubted for a minute that they would. Not after everything Alan had told her about the ex-mercenaries.

It was nice to know she was right. "Thanks. I really appreciate your willingness to help."

"No problem. We like a challenge," Nitro said.

"What about you, Chantal, can you play the part?" Elle asked.

"I'll do my best."

"Thanks. That's all anyone can ask."

"I'll be there with you. From now on. No matter when they call." Mat kissed her temple and then her lips as if he couldn't help himself.

Mama was going to throw such a party.

Elle and Beau helped Josie and Nitro set up their command center, but the bodyguards opted to use the guest bedroom for sleeping, as it would put them closer to Mat and Chantal if a problem arose. Elle offered to buy groceries for them before she took off, but Mat had stocked up recently, so it wasn't necessary.

"You going to let me drive to my place?" Beau asked when Elle finally felt it was okay to go.

He looked so delighted by the prospect, she found she didn't want to say no. She handed him the keys. "Don't think this means you're getting your way about everything."

"Don't worry; I expect you to make your wishes known, princess. Making love wouldn't be a lot of fun otherwise."

"I didn't say we were going to make love."

"You'd rather go back to your lonely apartment and lose sleep wishing you'd said yes?"

"Maybe I'd rather go back to my apartment and simply sleep."

"You really think that's going to happen?"

No, she didn't. For the second time that day, she opted for silence over false denial.

Not that it did her any good. When they got to his condo, he turned the car off and got out, the keys in his hand. She climbed out of the passenger side and closed the door. Without a word, he used the remote to lock the car as he walked toward the condo. She heard the unmistakable snick and saw the blinking light go on that said he'd armed the alarm as well.

Her heels clicked on the paved pathway as she followed him. "I didn't say I was staying."

"You didn't say you weren't." He stopped at his door, unlocked it and then ushered her inside.

She let him, which was as good an answer as any.

Once inside, he surprised her by leading her into the living room instead of the bedroom. It made it easier to say what needed saying, though, so she was grateful.

Ignoring his silent offer for her to be seated, she faced him squarely. "Last night was a mistake. One I don't intend to repeat."

His jaw went taut, but other than that, he gave no indication he'd heard her. "Would you like a drink, princess? I thought we could order out later for dinner."

"You're not deaf. Don't pretend you didn't hear what I just said." She winced at the harshness of her own words. She didn't enjoy sounding like a harpy.

"My hearing is just fine. I'm not pretending anything or ignoring you. I'm being civil. It's called hospitality. They teach that sort of thing where I come from. Now, it's your turn. You answer, 'Yes, thank you' or 'No, thank you.' Or even, 'What do you have?'"

"I should leave."

"No."

"Beau—"

"We obviously need to talk, sugar. We might as well be comfortable while we do it. I'm thirsty. Are you?"

She sighed. She agreed they needed to talk, if for no other reason than so there wouldn't be awkwardness between them while she worked on her case at ETRD. But that didn't mean she had to like it. "What do you have?"

"Wine, whiskey, juice, water, milk. I can also make you a hot drink. I've got some Kahlúa left over from Christmas. Frank's wife loves the stuff."

"A glass of wine would be nice, thank you." She could do polite.

"Wine it is. Have a seat. I'll be right back."

She relaxed onto the suede sofa and looked around Beau's domain. It was peaceful but showed hints of where he came from. With wrought-iron accents, the room was done in hues of brown ranging from the dark chocolate sofa to the tan walls. A large painting of a desert sunset hung over the gas fireplace. She'd be willing to bet it was of the Texas, rather than California, desert. The wood and wrought-iron coffee table rested in the center of a Native American rug made with the browns of the room and some of the colors found in the sunset painting.

Beau wasn't the neat freak she and her brother were. A couple of scientific journals sat on the coffee table, one of them open to an article about hydrogen power. A T-shirt hung over the back of one of the armchairs, and a newspaper from a couple of days ago had been folded messily and left on the floor to the right of the sofa. She liked it. The room felt lived in and warm.

"Your wine, princess."

She took the glass, not in the least surprised when he opted to share the sofa with her rather than take one of the two armchairs flanking it. He minimized the distance between them, his thigh brushing hers. Unlike at Mat's house, she did try to move away, but Beau managed to eat up any distance she created without seeming to move at all.

The man might not be trained, but he was good all the same.

The only surprise she felt was at herself. She'd left herself wide open for his maneuver. *She* should have sat in a chair. So, why hadn't she? She was a better tactician than this.

What the action said about her subconscious desires didn't bear contemplation. Not if she wanted to get through this discussion with any level of equanimity.

"Gee, do you think you could get any closer?" Wedged between him and the arm of the couch, she fervently wished his nearness was not having the effect it was on her libido.

The look of hungry desire in his brown gaze coupled with the way his six-foot, six-inch frame dwarfed hers sent a thrill of pleasure right up her spine. She wasn't used to feeling like the prey and would never have guessed she might actually like it.

Like it? Her panties were growing damp and she was vibrating with the need to melt into the hard body so close to her own. Yeah, she *liked* it. Darn it.

The expression in his eyes said he was more than aware of the effect he was having on her. "I could, but you said something about not making love again tonight. I thought we should talk about that before I start touching you."

"No touching. That's the point." Great. She sounded like

a breathless teenager, not a trained professional laying down parameters she had no intention of crossing.

He brushed her hair away from her eyes with gentle fingers. "No. The point is that you're running scared and I want to know why."

"I'm not scared."

"Right."

Indignation was much better than the unwanted lust. "Just because I realized it was a mistake to have sex with you doesn't mean I'm afraid of something."

"Why was it a mistake?"

"I'm on assignment."

"You trying to tell me you've never had sex with someone while on a case? I don't believe it."

Why did he have to make it sound like she probably had way more sex than she did? She wasn't about to disabuse him of his notions, though. He could think what he liked as long as he didn't latch on to the fact that his accusation of fear hit closer to home than she wanted it to. "It won't advance the investigation."

"So, we shouldn't do it? Wanting each other and sharing mind-bending pleasure isn't enough reason?" Aggression poured off him.

His anger helped her to maintain her cool facade. "I don't want to compromise my investigation."

"You think sex with me will do that?"

"Yes."

He leaned in so their faces were almost as close as their touching thighs. "You *are* afraid."

"I'm not."

"Yes, you are. You're frightened of being so preoccupied with *my body*, you'll make a mistake on *your case*."

"I didn't say that. You are so flippin' arrogant."

"You didn't have to say it. There's no other explanation."

"Maybe I don't want you." *Liar!* her body screamed.

"You do. Too much. That's your problem."

Feeling hunted, Elle leaned away from Beau and took a fortifying sip of wine. It didn't help the feelings roiling through her. "Fine. I want you too much. Is your ego satisfied?"

But she wasn't admitting to fear. Special Agent Elle Gray *caused* fear; she didn't feel it.

"My ego's having no problems, sugar. And I won't be satisfied until we've worked out this difference of opinion."

"There's nothing to work out. I am not having sex with you."

"Now, see here, that's where we disagree. There's a major problem with your outlook, sugar. You're not going to stop wanting me. In fact, if you don't sate your desire, it's just going to grow. That's the way it works."

"So you say."

"So I know."

"I can control my desire."

"Can you?"

She wanted to say yes, to shout it and mean it, but she couldn't. Not with her body aching to close the meager distance between them and do some sating.

"Something you need to think about: I've got no reason to pretend I don't want you more than my next breath," he said.

"In other words, you're not going to try to make this easy for me?"

"Oh, I'll make it easy for you." He cupped the back of her head, his hand massaging her nape. "I'll make it easy for you to find satisfaction. I'll make it easy for you to come over and over again. The one thing I won't make it easy for you to do is walk away from this thing between us."

Elle had to clear her throat before she could get any recognizable sounds to come out. "You play dirty."

"I'm not playing. I want you, princess. I have no intention of spending the next few weeks sexually frustrated while I get to know my fist better than ever before."

"Your frustrations aren't my problem."

"But yours are."

She glared at him.

"You're worried about being preoccupied by me, right?" he asked.

Worried wasn't afraid. "Yes."

"So, let's say you were a chocolate addict."

"Why?"

"For the sake of argument."

"Okay."

"Now, let's say you've got a piece of chocolate that's going to follow you around, spending lots of time with you, even when you aren't staring right at it. You with me here, princess?"

"Yes."

"You tell yourself you can't have that chocolate and you're going to spend all your time thinking about it and fighting the temptation to eat it, aren't you? Because it's always going to be there. It's not going away."

She knew where this was going, but the trouble was, he had a point. "It's a possibility."

"You're going to be way more distracted by *me* if I'm not in your bed than if you're working out your sexual frustrations when the need arises."

"If you'd behave, I wouldn't be sexually frustrated."

"You really believe that?"

"I . . ." She couldn't make herself continue with the lie.

"The thing about that chocolate is that even if it never gets unwrapped and lets off the scent of all its chocolaty goodness, you've eaten chocolate before. You're gonna know you want it."

"You're not chocolate, Beau."

"Nah, I'm way more addictive."

She rolled her eyes in answer, though the truth was, he so was.

"I'm not saying I'll behave. Like I said, I've got no reason to ignore what I want. Even so, do you honestly expect that if I *were* to ignore you, play Mr. Professional and Disinterested when I was around you, you wouldn't want me anyway? You've tasted me, sugar, and that's not something you're likely to forget."

"We could try it."

"Bullshit."

"Beau—"

"Don't. You're not a hypocrite, Elle. You may have to tell lies for a living, but you don't lie to yourself. Don't start now."

"It's not a good idea."

"And the alternative, having all the distraction and none of the pleasure, is a good one? I don't think so."

"It's not that simple."

"Do you think I'm a suspect?"

"No."

"So, if I'm not one of the bad guys, or a person of interest you are trying to get information from, I'm not worth going to bed with?"

"Don't put words in my mouth."

"Then don't put such unpalatable thoughts in my head."

"I didn't mean to imply that." But she was the one who had said sex with him wouldn't advance the investigation. She'd been shoring up her defenses, not trying to undermine how amazing she had found the night before.

"Then stop thinking sex has to have an ulterior motive or it's not worth engaging in."

"I didn't have any motives but mutual pleasure last night. Can you say the same?"

"Absolutely. Hell, do you think I wanted to share myself intimately with a woman I knew was lying to me?"

"Then why did you?"

"Because I couldn't help myself, damn it."

"What about now?"

"What do you mean, what about now? You know damn well that I want you."

"I meant do you still see me as untrustworthy?"

Something softened in his dark gaze, and he shook his head in the negative. "You've made me see your role in my company, in my life for now, differently. I want *you*, sugar, and I *will* have you."

"You trust me?" She didn't know why it mattered, but it did.

"Yes. Now all you have to do is trust yourself."

"I do."

"Prove it."

"By having sex with you?"

"Yes."

"That's a pretty unique variation on the high school guy's line that if his girlfriend loves him, she'll have sex with him."

"This isn't about me. It's about you."

She laughed. "Right. So, it doesn't matter to you either way."

"Hell yes, it does. I'm just saying I'm not conflicted about it."

"I don't want lovemaking to get in the way of the investigation. I have to have distance, to keep my professional perspective."

"That is so much cow pucky."

"What?"

"Your brother and the woman he loves are at risk because of this investigation. No way are you operating from a professional distance."

"I know how to keep my personal and professional life separated."

"Have you ever had to before?"

"Of course."

"Really? You've been on a case where someone you loved was at risk?"

"No. This is a unique situation."

"And when Kyle died, you accepted the fact you'd been on the job and it wasn't your fault you weren't there?"

"That was different!"

"No, honey, that was your professional life running smack-dab into your personal one. The only distance you maintained was between yourself and your family afterward."

"How did we go from talking about sex to my actions after Kyle's death?"

"You claimed a professional distance that a woman who cares about her family as much as you do yours isn't going to be able to maintain. You love your family. No matter how much you've been avoiding them since Kyle's death, that hasn't changed. In this case, there is no separation between the personal and professional for you. You're just going to have to live with that, sugar."

Deep inside herself, Elle knew that Beau was right. "That doesn't mean I have to compound the problem by having an intimate relationship with you. In fact, it's the biggest reason why I shouldn't."

"That's the quandary for you, isn't it?"

"What?"

"It's not just sex. Oh, it's not the romance of the century. We're not in love. Neither of us is offering a commitment, but it's not just physical release either."

"I . . ." She didn't know what to say. She felt his conversational volleys were more like live hand grenades that kept going off around her.

He massaged the tight muscles at the base of her neck while giving her a wry smile. "It isn't for me either, sugar."

"It's not?"

"Do you really have to ask that after last night?"

"From listening to you talk, a woman might get the impression that sex is like that every time for you."

"I'm a good lover for sure, princess. You ain't no slouch either. But together? We're explosive. Last night was pure damn exceptional."

# Chapter 15

Elle tried to ignore the heat curling through her belly from Beau's words. "So, if it's not commitment, romance and all that stuff, then it *is* just sex. *Exceptional* sex, but still sex."

"You think? Feels bigger to me."

"I don't want it to be bigger."

"Trust me, I don't either." He sat back against the couch, giving her the space she'd thought she'd wanted. "I've been burned twice by bigger and I'm not getting singed again."

The loss of his in-her-face presence made her feel bereft, and wasn't that just idiotic. "Then you should agree that sex between us isn't a good idea."

So should she. Really.

"Nah, hiding from it will only make it worse. At least if we give in to the desire between us, we can work it out of our systems."

"You think that's possible?"

"We've got at least a couple of months for your security analysis and implementation, isn't that right?"

"Yes."

"Sugar, even for us, that should be enough time."

Beau looked like he actually believed that. Elle wasn't going to tell him she had her doubts because that would be admitting things she had no desire to.

"Tell me about the times you got burned," she said instead.

Taking a sip of his wine, he let the silence around them build. When she was sure he was going to ignore her request, he said, "I fell in love for the first time when I was in college. She was beautiful, ultrafeminine, but she had this thing for sports. I thought that we had so much in common, that she was perfect for me. I was besotted. I asked her to marry me."

"She said yes?"

"She did, but then I decided not to put my name in for the NFL draft. I already told you how my parents reacted to that. They were really disappointed in me. My dad was calling me every other day with new arguments about what a mess I was making of my life. My mom cried every time we talked. You'd think I'd told them I was signing on to be a drug runner or something. I needed my fiancée's support more than ever."

"And she didn't give it to you?"

"She pretended to. I figured out later that she was pretending to support my decision in hopes of being able to influence me to change it. She waited to make her move until my dad stopped calling all the time and my mom told me maybe I shouldn't come home for the next break. I felt like I was losing my family. At the time, even my little sister thought I was being a dolt. My granny was the only one who truly supported the decision all the way, but she was sick."

"That would have been really hard."

"It was. My fiancée told me that maybe I should consider going for the draft, that I could play for a couple of years and make my parents happy and then go back to school. It sounded rational to me. She even pulled out the guilt card about my grandmother. She said that if I was playing professionally, I'd have enough money to make sure her final days were the best I could give her."

"She sounds persuasive."

"Manipulative, and yes, she was. I almost fell for it, but I was hesitating. She didn't know how close I was getting to declaring for the draft. It's a good thing too. If she'd known, I wouldn't have found out the truth about her until later, until I'd become someone I didn't want to be to keep someone who wanted *what* I was, not me."

"What happened?"

"She was hedging her bets, but I didn't know it. She was two-timing me with a teammate. I walked in on them. Ironically, I had come by her apartment to let her know I'd decided to declare for the draft."

"Ouch." Reading the bones of it was nothing like hearing the remembered pain of betrayal in Beau's whiskey-smooth voice.

"That's one word for it."

"What about the second time you got burned?" That hadn't been in his file.

"She was another scientist at ETRD. Only it turns out she wanted her brains and training to earn her money and fame, not necessarily help her make the world a better place. She moved to a commercial-product development lab after dumping my ass for being too much of an idealist."

"I'm sorry."

"That's life. At least I didn't ask her to marry me. Anyway, I learned my lesson about trying to share my life with someone who doesn't share my outlook on it. I won't make that mistake again." He turned his full-wattage, prime-grade, Texas-stud grin on Elle. "Sex, on the other hand, is something else."

He'd said he trusted her, but his words implied that he thought they looked at life from opposing viewpoints. Like her family, he didn't see the value in what she'd chosen to dedicate her life to. And maybe he still believed they defined things like personal integrity differently. "Was it as explosive with the women you loved?"

"Sex has never been as wild for me as it is with you."

Which was presumably why he wasn't willing to let it end. Not because he had any kind of emotional attachment to her, thank goodness. Nevertheless, she said, "Something this big is bound to impact our emotions."

Shaking his head, he laughed. "Do you always overthink your physical impulses like this?"

"What if it's more than that?"

"Like what? Love? You and I have both played and lost at that game. Badly enough that neither of us is going to be tempted to go there. This is pleasure I'm talking about, princess. The kind of pleasure we'd be idiots to ignore." He winked at her. "And neither of us is any kind of stupid."

He made it sound so simple.

And logical.

And risk-free.

So, why did she feel like she was on the edge of an abyss and making love was the step that would take her over?

"No. Not stupid." Only, Elle hoped she was smart enough not to confuse physical pleasure with an emotional connection, or allow it to lead to one.

Regardless, Beau was right about one thing: without his cooperation, she had no chance of ignoring the sexual tension between them. Maybe he was right about the other too—that she wasn't going to be able to ignore the craving for him even if he was an angel of innocence in how he treated her. She wasn't sure if she wanted to thank him or drop-kick him for being so stubborn. Her body had no such qualms. It was practically vibrating with anticipation.

"So," he drawled all husky and slow. "You're okay with me doing this?"

"This" was curling his warm hands over her shoulders and tugging her toward him for a kiss. The brush of his lips against hers dissolved the last of her mental resistance. She didn't want to spend the following weeks fighting this attraction and doubted she would be successful even if she did.

Elle had never responded so quickly and completely to another man. Not even Kyle. There was just something about the chemistry between her and Beau. Every kiss was like a rocket blast inside her, sending her pulse and pleasure into the stratosphere. Every touch transmitted itself to nerve endings she hadn't even known she had.

Her toes curled, the tips of her ears tingled and the intimate flesh between her legs grew even more damp and swollen. He hadn't touched her breasts, but they felt sensitized and her nipples were achingly hard inside her bra. She wanted skin against skin.

Now.

He seemed to want the same thing because the wineglass was taken from her hand a second before he started removing the clothes from her body. She returned the favor, kissing him back with violent passion. He might be a scientist, but she wasn't afraid to let him feel her deepest desires or the strength of her need.

With other lovers, including Kyle, Elle had always held part of herself back, afraid to overwhelm or even hurt an unwary partner. Instinctively, she knew Beau could take everything she might dish out and serve it back to her with more bliss than she'd ever known. He could more than handle her intensity; he would revel in it.

They were both fully naked within moments.

She flipped him on his back and attacked his chest with

her mouth. He tasted so good, and the sculpted muscles felt incredible against her tongue. So hard. So male. So different from her, despite the excellent shape her body was in. His nipples were stiff little nubs, silently begging for attention. His whole body shuddered when she gently nipped one. She laved it with her tongue, soothing any sting, then sensually worried it with her teeth again before moving to the other nipple to do the same thing. She bit down and sucked up a mark right beside his left aureole. He shouted something nasty and oh so sexy in that wonderful Texas drawl, his strong fingers gripping her hips and tugging her toward him as he pushed his pelvis upward.

Hot, masculine flesh rubbed against her throbbing labia, spreading the silky wetness and teasing her clitoris. So good, but not enough.

She lunged for his lips, kissing him so hard their teeth clicked. He just moaned, kissed her back with equal fervor.

"Want you." She mashed their mouths together again, unable to stop the kiss long enough to get the whole thought out at once. Then she pulled back just far enough to get words out. "In me."

He tilted his head so her lips had to make do with his jaw. Make do she did, nibbling, licking and kissing the stubbled flesh with abandon.

He groaned, long and loud, then cursed when she started sucking the underside of his chin. "Condom. Wallet."

Then he moved his head so their mouths were once again in alignment. Their tongues dueled while she reached around on the floor for his jeans. She found them, not letting go of his lips. He tasted so good. Because of her training, she was good at searching blind and she found the wallet quickly. She was pretty sure she dumped other stuff out of it getting to the condom, but she didn't care.

Once she had the foil packet in her hand, she broke the kiss to tear it open with her teeth.

"You are so damn sexy like this," he growled.

"Don't talk, or I'm not going to get the glove on you before I start riding."

His cock jumped against her at the words, but he didn't say a thing.

She managed to roll the condom over his erection without breaking the latex or losing control, but it wasn't easy. Beau had the perfect penis. Big, thick and so hard it bowed toward his stomach. He'd been circumcised and there was no extra skin, just a smooth, deliciously shaped rod her mouth watered to taste.

But her vaginal walls were spasming with desire, and she knew if she didn't get him inside her soon, she was going to lose her mind.

Elle lowered herself over the hard shaft, taking him in faster than was comfortable, but there was pleasure in the burn and stretch of her tender flesh. Her body adjusted quickly to accommodate him, though, and soon all she felt was intense delight at the sensations zinging through her. She'd felt empty and now she experienced a fullness that only he had ever given her.

He might be on the bottom, but Beau was far from a passive lover. He started a rhythm from below that she followed, because it felt so good. Perfect even.

"That's right," he praised. "Faster. Come on. I want to see you!"

She went faster and faster. He matched her movements until they were both covered in a sheen of sweat and breathing like marathon runners sprinting in the last stretch.

His roar as he came only echoed at the fringes of her consciousness as she had one of the most intense, heart-pounding orgasms of her life. Her fingers convulsively kneaded his chest as every muscle in her body tensed and then released. Her arms felt like rubber and she had to lock her elbows or she would have collapsed on top of him.

She would have liked nothing better, but there was the condom to consider. And the aftermath of sex that wanted to mean more than either of them would allow. Although she may have given in to the inevitability of sating their desires together, she wasn't going to make the mistake of wallowing in the afterglow. Nor did she have any intention of falling asleep in his bed.

That would carry a whole host of intimate connotations she refused to deal with. She'd never slept in a man's bed since Kyle. Beau was on a short list of men she'd allowed to sleep in her bed since then too. She wasn't going to make that mistake again either.

No more cozily domestic breakfasts the morning after.

She let herself stay where she was until they were both breathing pretty normally, and then she climbed off of him. "Shower, I think."

"Sounds good, sugar."

He led her to the bathroom and shared her shower without asking if she minded. She found she didn't, especially when it led to another climax that had her knees collapsing under her and her body feeling like a puddle of goo. Melted or not, though, she was still determined to go back to her temporary housing.

Beau swiped at the water droplets on his chest with a towel. "I'll order in some dinner. Any preferences?"

"Curry okay with you?"

"Indian or Thai?"

"Either."

"My favorite is Thai, and there's a restaurant nearby that

delivers, so it'll get here soon. Now that we've satisfied our sexual cravings for the time being, my stomach is reminding me that the last time I ate was breakfast."

"It's been a busy day."

"It has. What do you want to eat?"

"Yellow curry with chicken, if they have it. No onions."

"Got it." Feeling more settled in his bones than he had in a long while, not to mention physically replete, he went to make the order.

Dinner was relaxed. They shared their curries. He'd ordered the restaurant's special pumpkin curry and Elle said she'd found her new favorite. When they were done eating, she helped him clean up and put away the leftovers. Then she disappeared into the living room.

He found her on the sofa, putting on her shoes.

"Where are you going?"

"I've got work to do tonight."

"You can do it here."

She flicked him a glance. "It's better if I go back to my apartment."

She was fighting the intimacy. He should have expected this. And while part of him wanted her to stay, he was glad she was going. Glad that he hadn't let himself start to see this as something more than what it was.

Sex.

Mind-blowing sex, but not life altering. He wouldn't let it be, and obviously, neither would she.

It took Elle about six months after Kyle's death to stop reaching for him in bed at night and another six to get used to waking up alone in the morning. She'd adjusted, though, and no longer expected a warm body upon waking, or someone else around to chat with while she got ready for her day.

So, why the heck did her small corporate apartment feel so

vacant this morning? Despite her own things hanging in the closet, it felt like no one was living there. Maybe that was the problem. She was staying in the space, but not filling it with life. Not like Beau's condo, where his presence could be felt in every room she'd visited.

Alone in the big bed and somehow made subconsciously aware of the fact, she'd woken before the alarm had gone off. She'd been unable to go back to sleep and had gotten up and dressed to go work out. Unoccupied by anyone else, even the cleaning crew, the ground-floor facility available for those staying in the apartments had echoed with the sounds of her training program. Her lunges. Her falls. Her kicks and extensions. Her breathing. But nothing else.

She usually liked working out by herself, but this morning it had been unsatisfying. Afterward, she'd taken a swim and then returned to her apartment to shower and dress.

As the warm water cascaded over her naked body, memories of her shower with Beau made her regret leaving his place the night before. A silent breakfast of high-fiber cereal and fruit juice while she checked her e-mail left her feeling lonelier than she had since adjusting in a practical way to the loss of her husband.

She would always miss Kyle—she accepted that—but she didn't have to ache for him. And she hadn't. Not for a couple of years. Not with the painful inner stinging she'd known right after his death.

She didn't feel that stinging now, but something didn't feel right. The apartment felt antiseptic in its cleanliness, sterile in its sameness to every other corporate apartment in the building and empty.

Really, really empty.

It hadn't felt empty before she'd let Beau spend the night and woke up to a pretty pleasant morning after. She enjoyed his company. Too much if she was going to start pining for the man after a single sleepover.

It was a good thing she'd come back here last night. It really was. How much worse would these feelings of withdrawal be when she finished her investigation and it was time to leave if she made it a habit of staying with him or vice versa?

She didn't want to get back to D.C. and have this same sense of aloneness in her home. She'd had all she could take of that sensation after Kyle's death.

Beau hummed along with his MP3 player as he checked over the results on the latest fix they'd tried for the problem with the antigravity project. The results weren't promising, but he wasn't discouraged. They were further along on the project than anyone else in the country, or out of it.

Eventually, they would find the solution for the excess discharge. It was just a matter of time and effort. Not giving up.

Beau's innate stubbornness served him well in his job as a research scientist. It didn't do too badly for him in his interpersonal relationships either. Making love with Elle the evening before had been incredible.

He wondered if she'd be up for a nooner. He'd never had one. Not even when he'd been dating a fellow scientist here at ETRD. But, man, Elle put his libido in overdrive. He hadn't been this perpetually horny since first discovering what it felt like to shoot jism with an orgasm.

The woman was just too damn sexy.

Speaking of sexy, here she came. Walking with Dr. Archer Sandstone. Talk about the perfect way to ruin a nice view, not to mention Beau's mood. What was up with the two of them being together?

Beau couldn't hear what they were saying because of the music playing through his earbuds, but he could see by the set of Elle's shoulders and the snarky expression on Archer's face that it wasn't a pleasant conversation.

The other project manager wore his thinning brown hair long, and he dressed like a flower child from the sixties. Never mind the fact that he'd been a baby at the end of that decade, not a teen influenced by the upheaval of the world around him. The small silver peace sign hanging from the leather cord around his neck couldn't have been less fitting. A more uptight man would be hard to find. Besides which, Archer spent most of his working hours stirring up discord.

No doubt that was exactly what the weasel was trying to do now with Elle.

With grim acceptance that he wasn't going to be able to avoid talking to the other man, Beau turned off his music. He tugged the buds from his ears and tucked them in the pocket of his lab coat. "Morning," he said as the two approached.

Elle gave him a stiff smile and he wanted to know if that was because she was trying to back off again or the result of her less than charming company.

Archer just sneered. "Well, if it isn't the resident whiz kid. How did the tests go on the electrostatic discharge stabilizer?"

"It's not the fix we're looking for, but we'll find one."

Archer's expression said he doubted it.

"Was there something you needed?" Beau asked.

"I wanted to know if Frank had mentioned anything I need to know about in your morning meeting."

Well, hell . . . here they went again.

Frank and Beau started each day with a quick planning session, but this was the first time in a couple of months that Archer had come by to ask what had been said. He used to make a pest of himself about it until Beau had told him flat out that if Frank had something to tell him, he'd do it. And if Beau did, he'd find him, but to stop coming by his lab wasting time asking about it every morning.

Archer had been livid and complained to Frank, who, in one of his brutally honest moments, had informed the PM that while Beau was Frank's second in command, Archer was not Beau's. If Archer wanted to have a daily morning meeting, he should do it with his own team and stop taking up Beau's time.

Archer had called in sick that afternoon, but when he came back to work the next day, he'd seemed resigned to the status quo.

Beau wasn't going to get into a big to-do over it this morning, so he simply said, "No."

Archer's eyes narrowed and his mouth pursed like he'd been sucking really sour lemons. "Naturally. I should have known."

"Then why come by and ask?"

"I wanted to check on the results of the test too."

"Are you always so curious about other teams' projects, Dr. Sandstone?" Elle asked, her tone neutral.

"I'm usually too busy, but none of us can afford to ignore Beau's projects. He's Frank's Golden Boy, or didn't you know?"

"I'm aware he's Frank's second in command, yes. However, I was led to believe that each project manager was responsible for his own team's projects, not anyone else's."

Beau gave his fellow scientist an exasperated frown. "Archer *isn't* responsible for the antigravity experiment."

"I should have been. If I were, it would be further along."

"Are you more qualified than Dr. Ruston for a project of this type?" Elle asked, sounding just this side of sycophantic.

Archer visibly preened. "Well, he has a PhD in quantum physics and mine is in chemistry, but I'm the older scientist. I have more experience. Anyone can tell you that counts for a lot in the world outside academia."

"You're older than me by eight years, Archer, but you've only had your PhD two years longer, and you didn't start working at ETRD until a couple of years ago, whereas I've been here since interning during my doctoral program." It was an old argument, and even as he made it, Beau was frustrated with himself for letting Archer pull him to his ongoing contentiousness.

"Be that as it may, the project should have been mine." With that, Archer stormed from the lab.

# Chapter 16

"Asshole," Beau muttered. Then he frowned at Elle. "What was that sycophantic BS about?"

"Just doing my job."

"Your job is to wind up the current drama monger?"

"If that's what it takes to get him to reveal his inner thoughts and motivations."

"Because he's a suspect?"

"Yes."

"So, I guess I should be glad you don't count me as one."

She grinned, eyes shining silver with mischief. "I already know what motivates you and it isn't petty office politics. It's a lot sweatier."

Oh, thank you, ma'am. She was not going to try backing away again today. "You ever had a nooner, sugar?"

Her laugh sent heat straight to his groin. "Yes, are you offering one?"

"Yep, I sure am." He stepped closer to her, invading her personal space and inhaling her scent. "I, myself, have never had the pleasure. Wanted to try something new."

She laid her hand against his chest, rubbed just slightly with her thumb. "Is that your excuse for middle-of-the-day sex?"

"Does it sound convincing?"

She gave him a sloe-eyed look that curled his toes. "Very."

"Good. Do we have to wait until noon, though?"

"Yes!" She shook her head, laughing. And wasn't that sound sweet. "You are such a horn dog."

"You think?"

"Yep," she imitated his drawl. "I so do."

"I don't think about sex all the time."

"Right."

"I don't."

"Prove it."

"So, what were you and Archer talking about when you came in? Neither of you looked happy." There, definitely a topic designed to keep his unruly sexual thoughts under control.

She frowned and stepped back as if mention of the other man was enough to cool her ardor too. "He doesn't think ETRD needs a security upgrade. That man likes to complain, and he managed to lodge about a dozen complaints with me just between his office door and here."

Beau rolled his eyes. "Sounds like Archer."

"He asked a lot of questions about what I was doing specifically to check current security levels and beef them up."

"And you didn't tell him a thing, which is why he looked so sour."

"Right. I don't think anyone besides you and Frank needs to know every aspect of security here. Especially regarding the new measures."

Beau wasn't sure he agreed. "We can't keep our employees in the dark about things that concern them, not even Archer."

"Don't worry, they'll be apprised of all security measures that affect them directly. But some measures won't affect them directly—unless they breach security with unethical or criminal behavior."

Interesting. "Give me an example of something you don't think they need to know."

She did a quick check around the lab, confirming other members of his team were far enough away not to overhear. She hadn't done so when they'd been talking about their nooner and he counted that as progress.

"I intend to fit all computers with new firewalls. Everyone will know about them, but what they won't be told—though they could certainly speculate to be the case—is that if an attempt is made to enter a computer's database through a backdoor method, that will trigger an alarm. The hacker will be back-traced."

"You mean if Archer tries to hack into my system, he'll be caught."

"Exactly."

"I thought we already had something like that."

"Nope."

"Oh."

"Another example is that the facility will be swept randomly for listening and other spycentric devices."

"If we'd been doing that, we would have found the bug in Frank's office sooner."

"Exactly."

"It's pretty pathetic that we need to keep such a close eye on the people who work for a company dedicated to the betterment of the human condition."

Elle just shrugged. "Archer Sandstone works here."

"Yes, he does." Beau sighed.

She squeezed his arm. "Don't let it depress you. A few bad apples might require security measures that wouldn't otherwise be necessary, but they don't really have the power to spoil the whole barrel. Not when it comes to people."

"That sounds like something my granny would have said."

"From what you've told me, it sounds like she was a wise woman."

"She was. I've never been real sure how my daddy turned out the way he did, having her for a mom. They were so different."

This time Elle stepped into his personal space, meeting his gaze with a direct look. "When was the last time you talked to your parents?"

"When my sister went into the Peace Corps."

"Have they tried calling since then?"

"Once. They left a message. I ignored it."

"Still angry?"

"Yeah."

"You've never tried calling them since?"

"No." He'd thought about it, but being disowned by his parents once in his lifetime had been enough. He wasn't giving them another chance to reject him.

"What about your sister?"

"We talk whenever we can, e-mail a few times a week and send each other care packages."

"What does she say about your parents?"

"We agreed not to talk about them after they initially disowned me."

"Do you think maybe they've changed their tune since losing you?"

"They didn't lose me; they threw me away."

Elle nodded, but she said, "It's possible they regret that."

"Maybe."

"You might consider talking to your sister about it."

What was going on here? "You want me reunited with my parents?"

"It couldn't hurt."

"Why?"

"Because everyone needs family in his or her life."

"Frank and his wife are my family."

"So? There's enough of you to extend to your parents too."

Beau looked away from her but was drawn back to that staid rainwater gaze. "Why does it matter to you, Elle?"

"I like you, Beau. No matter how you deny it to yourself, you're hurting from the estrangement with your parents. Maybe that can't be fixed, but then again, maybe it can. If it can, I think it should be. What's the use making the world a better place if we don't share it with people we love?"

"A lesson you learned coming back to California?"

"Yes."


Chantal grinned as Mat growled at the techie. Some things didn't change. But when the other man gave her a pleading look, she had to admit that that at least was different. Either her intervention on Friday was showing its effects, or the fact that in the two hours they had been at work, Mat hadn't let her out of his sight was.

Lucky for the technician, Chantal's cell phone rang just then. Mat was at her side before the second ring sounded. She checked the ID and the breath froze in her chest. It said blocked call, just like all the other times she'd been contacted by the man demanding she procure the antigravity project's plans.

She pressed the call button. "Hello?"

"Ms. Renaud." She knew that voice. It was unmistakable, the subtle South African accent apparent in even that short greeting.

With one look at her no doubt stricken face, Mat had his own cell phone out and was dialing. The techie took the chance to escape Mat's wrath, disappearing from the lab with speed.

"Why are you calling me at work?" she asked, not having to fake the nervousness in her tone. "Don't you know how dangerous that is for me?"

Elle had told her to play scared and to keep the guy on the phone as long as possible. Well, frightened was easy—she was. The other, she could only hope she could do.

"It is a little reminder what you have to lose if you do not cooperate with us. You do enjoy your job at Environmental Technology Research and Design, don't you? You are pleased with your *life*?"

His emphasis on the word *life* sent chills skittering down her spine. "What do you want from me?"

"You know the answer to that. We want the plans for the antigravity plane. Give them to us, and you will never hear from us again."

Like she would believe him. If she had allowed her fear to get the better of her and had gone along, she was sure they would have no compunction about using her actions as leverage for getting her to get other delicate information for them in the future. Sheesh, did people really fall for that line?

"You've gone silent, Ms. Renaud. Is this a bad time?"

"No. There was someone in the lab with me, but they've left," she lied. Sort of. The tech had left, but Mat was still there.

He laid his big hand in the center of her back, confirming that she was not alone and giving her courage.

"Good," the man said.

"I told you before, I don't work on that project." Elle had told her not to give in too easily or her cooperation might be considered suspect.

"That's not what Eddie Danza said."

"You know where Eddie is?" she asked. "You've been talking to him?"

"Don't concern yourself with your previous lover. I'm sure you miss him, but you'll be missing a lot more if you don't have the plans for us by this Friday."

"Who is 'us'?" She'd asked every phone call. "Who are you?"

"Does that really matter? You need only know that we are willing to do whatever it takes to achieve our objective."

"But—"

"Do you understand, Ms. Renaud? We will do *anything*."

"I understand."

"So . . ."

Elle came into the lab, moving quickly and silently.

"Despite what Eddie told you, I'm not an official team member on the project."

"But you can get access to the plane's plans."

Elle stopped right beside Chantal, indicating she should tilt her phone so that Elle could hear as well.

"It's not a plane."

"So, you have seen it." Eagerness had crept into the man's voice.

"Yes."

"And you *can* get the plans."

"I don't know."

"I suggest you figure it out, Ms. Renaud. You have until Friday."

"That's only a few days. What if I can't get access by then?"

"You're an intelligent woman. I'm sure you can be equally resourceful given the proper motivation."

"You mean your threats."

"Crudely put, but yes."

"If I don't help you, you're threatening to destroy my reputation with lies, but what difference will that make if I get caught trying to steal technology secrets from my company?"

"I suggest you don't get caught."

"What if I can get the plans? How am I supposed to let you know I have them, much less get them to you?"

"I will call with instructions on Friday evening. Have the plans in your possession then." Dead air told Chantal the connection had been cut.

Elle said something low into her own phone and then disconnected her call before looking around the lab. "Meet me in my office in ten."

Chantal nodded, her throat too tight to speak.

Elle waited in her temporary office for the others to arrive. She'd been assigned the space on Friday for the duration of her consult, though she'd spent very little time in it so far. She'd made sure it was secure, however, and had rechecked just now for good measure.

Beau arrived first. He leaned against her desk. "Now this could work for a nooner, but from the expression on your beautiful face, I'd say that's not why you asked me to meet you here."

"You'd be right. Chantal was contacted by the perps."

Beau tensed. "I thought they didn't call her at work."

"They hadn't to this point, but they're stepping up the psychological warfare."

Mat and Chantal arrived just then, and Elle checked the hall with the mini spy cam she'd installed outside her door. A couple of people were walking down the corridor, but neither seemed interested in Elle's office.

"Shut the door," Elle said.

Mat did as she said.

She hit the button on her Bluetooth and gave a voice command to dial Josie's phone.

"Josie here."

"It's clear."

"Got it."

A few seconds later, Josie joined them, locking the door

behind her. "Daniel is still installing surveillance equipment in Chantal's apartment. I'll update him after the meeting."

Elle kept the video cam up as a small window on her computer screen, so she could watch for anyone trying the old-fashioned type of spying: listening at doors. It was an activity she wouldn't put past Archer Sandstone, though she had yet to decide if the man was a security risk or merely a nuisance.

Elle smiled reassuringly at the woman she was convinced would become her sister-in-law. "Chantal, can you try to repeat the conversation you had with the perp as close to verbatim as possible?"

Elle was impressed with Chantal's memory. If her recollection of the portion of the call Elle had not overheard was as accurate as the short bit she had, Chantal had indeed repeated both sides of the phone call verbatim.

"What do you think?" Chantal asked when she was done.

"I think his mention of Eddie Danza cinches the fact that this attempt to get the plans for the antigravity experiment is connected to the first one. That's not bad news for us either. My associate discovered two buyers on the initial list with links to South Africa. One of them was representing a group of known smugglers with their base of operations two hours outside of Cape Town."

"Smugglers are looking for the antigravity technology?" Beau asked in obvious shock.

"It looks that way."

"But . . ." He shook his head as if trying to clear it. "*The hell.*"

"You've got to admit, having the technology would give them an edge over the competition."

"They are not using my project to transport illicit goods."

"No, they aren't. They'd probably kill themselves just trying to get liftoff for the first trip."

"And how many innocents?"

"Exactly."

"You run into this kind of shit often in your job, princess?"

"More often than any regular citizen would be comfortable knowing about."

"I hear that," Josie said in a flat tone.

That woman had seen more than her share of the underbelly of humanity, and Elle had nothing but admiration for her upbeat attitude and ready smile in spite of it all.

"So, we think it's the smugglers?" Mat asked.

"Chances are, but we aren't ignoring other possibilities. I'm not leaving any long shots out there to turn around and bite me in the ass," Elle replied.

"Nah, that's my job, sugar," Beau said.

Laughter erupted and Elle thought she should have been irritated by Beau's blatancy, but she must be getting used to it. Because she found herself laughing right along with everyone else.

"But what about the Friday deadline?" Chantal asked. "What are we going to do?"

"Give him what he wants," Elle replied.

Beau's body jerked, his hands fisting at his sides, but he said nothing.

"Not the actual plans. I trust you can come up with something that looks good, but wouldn't put people or the project at risk," Elle said to him.

He nodded.

"And I'll make delivery," Josie said. "I need to go wig shopping. I wouldn't mind finding an Ulta store around here too. You got one of those around here?"

"What's that?" Chantal asked.

"One of my favorite stores," Elle admitted. "They carry every brand of cosmetics from the cheap to the trendy and ultraexpensive."

"They've got more than makeup, though," Josie said with the enthusiasm of a woman who had discovered her feminine side as an adult. "They've got nail polish, hair stuff, everything."

"Uh . . . smugglers trying to steal my top project's plans?" Beau said. "Anybody remember that?"

Elle ignored him, checking the website's store locater for an Ulta. "There's one in Cerritos. Is that far from here?"

"About twenty-five minutes," Chantal offered timidly while Mat and Beau scowled.

Elle gave them both the "get-over-it" glare. "Lighten up. I'm not going to ignore my case, but Chantal could use a chance to relax. Besides, I'm sure she's going to love Ulta."

"Because she's so into makeup and all that frippery crap," Mat said dismissively.

"Are you saying I'm not feminine?" Chantal asked, incensed. "I'll have you know, I'm French. That sort of thing is in my basic genetic makeup."

"Great, we'll go tomorrow while Beau is working on replicating the plans with a couple of significant changes," Elle said.

"What about your job here, assessing the security?" Beau demanded.

"Just because I won't be here doesn't mean I won't be working. I do most of my preliminary work in my head."

"And your head is going to be focused on ETRD while Chantal and Josie are exploring the delights of this beauty mecca. Right."

"You're just cranky because I won't be around tomorrow for a nooner."

Mat sputtered, trying to say something, but not quite getting it out. He had no problem skewering both her and Beau with his scowl, though.

She just rolled her eyes and gave Beau a significant look. "Big brothers—they are definitely harder to deal with."

"Are you seriously going shopping?" Beau asked.

"I can't live and breathe my case. I give my job my all, but I need balance. If I don't take breaks, I miss things because I'm too close."

Beau nodded like he understood.

Elle fixed her attention on Chantal. "I'm hoping you can supply me with some names, anyone who Eddie was friends with or associated with. Frank drew a complete blank when I asked him."

"I'm not sure. I thought he was like me. Alone. Maybe shy sometimes. But now I think he never cared about anyone enough to want to be a friend," Chantal said.

"So, you can't think of anyone he might have spent time with?" Elle asked.

"Well, he and Archer Sandstone talked sometimes, which was odd, considering the fact that Archer likes to dress like a nonconformist, but he's more aware of role distinctions than anyone else I know. They'd have lunch together off-site sometimes, but you know, I always got the impression Archer was pumping Eddie for information. He's really jealous of your role as Frank's confidant, Beau."

Beau frowned. "I know."

"No one else?" Elle asked, mentally noting the need to investigate the relationship between Sandstone and Eddie further.

"Eddie and the other guards would get together for a drink after work sometimes, but nothing personal that I noticed. His boss gave him a ride home a couple of times when Eddie was too drunk to drive on his own."

"He was living with you?" Mat asked, trying to sound nonchalant about it and failing miserably.

Chantal nodded. "Or I was living with him. Anyway, I moved out right after I found out he'd stolen information from ETRD."

"Did he tell you?" Elle asked, surprised that the guard might have done so.

"No. He was walked off the job. I went to Frank to ask him what was going on and he told me what Eddie had done. I didn't understand why ETRD didn't press charges, but I was just glad they weren't tarring me with the same brush. It hurt enough that I'd been dumb enough to believe he cared about me, but his activities could have ruined my whole life too. Mr. Smith was the one who told me I wasn't being blamed. I didn't even know anyone knew Eddie and I were a couple."

"Mr. Smith is like your mother—he knows everything you've been up to," Beau said with a kind of angry amusement.

"I guess. I only know I'm grateful neither he nor Frank thought I was part of Eddie's scheme."

"If you had been, you would have told him the plans weren't viable yet," Beau said.

"Oh."

"I think your innate goodness shined through too, sweetheart," Mat said.

Elle had to bite back a smile. Her brother sappy—it was cute. In a nauseating way.

Beau waited until everyone else had gone, then smiled at his sugar. "It close enough to noon yet, you think?"

"You have a one-track mind."

"I've been accused. Though usually by people frustrated because I'm concentrating on my latest experiment and not on them."

"People or *women*?"

"Women mostly, but even Frank's been known to grumble about it a time or two."

"It takes dedication to get where you are in the field. And

I don't mean your position as Frank's right hand. I'm talking about how far you've taken your projects, the breakthroughs you've made. Those kinds of results don't come from a mind that easily multitasks."

"You saying we all have our strengths and that's a good thing, princess?"

She looked a little embarrassed. "I guess that's what I'm saying."

"Is that why you didn't pursue your talent for science, because you're a damn fine multitasker?"

"Yes. I'm a firm believer in living up to your strengths, not your weaknesses."

"That's not a bad motto to adopt."

"Thanks." She gave him a commiserating smile. "It's hard when you have divergent talents and you have to make a choice between them."

"You can only go with where your passion lies at that point."

"If you're you or me, yeah. Others have a different standard for making the choice, and it can wreak havoc in relationships when that happens."

"You're talking about my parents again."

"You said your father is a banker, didn't you?"

"Yes. He manages the bank where my mother is a loan officer."

"It's not really so surprising that their first consideration is fiscal security, is it?"

"My chosen profession isn't exactly one that leaves me living out of cardboard boxes." But the truth was, Elle made sense. He'd always assumed his parents were upset because he'd given up his chance at fame and fortune. But maybe it had more to do with them thinking he didn't give enough credence to the money angle. To being financially solvent on a bigger scale—their definition of fiscal responsibility.

Weird, but definitely possible.

"No, but maybe they needed time to see that."

"And my sister?"

"She's not exactly amassing a healthy IRA in the Peace Corps."

"But she's investing in the future of the world, not just herself."

"Absolutely. That counts for something to both you and I, but maybe it's lower on the priority scale for your parents. That doesn't mean it's not on their list at all. I find it hard to believe that both of their children grew up with such strong social consciousness without any positive input in that direction from them."

"They said I took the recycling thing too far, but they always did the basics. They also both do pro bono financial advising for the minority workers in the area where I grew up."

"So, they put being financially stable first and donated time and resources that were left over to making the world a better place. You and your sister flipped that set of priorities and I bet that scared your parents."

"I'm not going to get my nooner, am I?"

Elle laughed and stood. "Is that your charming way of changing the subject?"

"Could be." Beau had a lot to think about. Maybe some stuff he needed to talk over with his sister.

# Chapter 17

Elle came around her desk, moving with the grace that had caught Beau by the balls from the minute he'd watched her climb out of her Lamborghini Spider for the first time. "Lucky for you, I'm caught up on my e-mail and don't have anything pressing right this second. I talked to both The Old Man and Frank this morning already, and I've got things in place to let me know if status changes on anything of importance."

"Cool."

Elle rubbed up against Beau. "No, I'd say hot. Maybe even molten."

"Damn, princess, you take me zero to sixty in a heartbeat."

She gripped his hard cock through his slacks. "Oh, yeah . . . though I'd say you're going better than sixty here, sexy."

He pushed into her hand. "You keep doing that and I'm going to spring a leak."

A soft laugh accompanied her moving away. "Keep that thought." Then she locked the door.

When she turned back to face him, her eyes were silver with passion.

He leaned back against her desk and put his hands out. "Come here, sugar."

She obeyed him with an added layer of sensuousness over her usual graceful movements that had him moaning.

"You are the sexiest woman I have ever had the pleasure of sharing my body with, princess."

She laid her hands in his and let him reel her in the rest of the way. "The feeling is mutual."

"I'm all that to you, huh?" he asked as her body came into contact with his.

"Do you honestly think I would be doing this with you— against my better judgment, I might add—if you weren't?" Oh, her voice was husky with desire and not a little exasperation.

"No man has ever turned you on as much as me, huh?" he asked while inhaling the scent of her hair. There was a trace of coconut and something more exotic.

Everything about this woman appealed to his senses.

She didn't answer, but the way she melted into him said it all.

"Not even Kyle?" Oh, shit. Where had that come from?

He expected her to go all stiff and find an excuse to put him off, but she didn't.

Her whole body shuddered against his and she said, "Not even Kyle," in a lost voice that he was damn sure she wished she could have held back as much as he did the initial question.

He cupped her face and tilted it so her lips were right where he needed them to be. Then he kissed her—gently, reverently, letting her know how much the admission meant to him. What followed were long minutes of the most intensely pleasurable and *tender* kissing he'd ever experienced.

They undressed each other with more care and time consumption than any nooner should allow for. He tasted her skin as he uncovered it, reveling in the satin-smooth beauty. She returned the favor, making soft little noises of need unlike any he had heard from her yet.

When they were finally in position to come together, her lying on the top of the desk, her legs draped over his arms, him standing between her thighs, his gaze fixed like super-epoxy on her nude form, it was nowhere near an office quickie.

He rubbed his naked dick against the silky wet flesh between her legs. "Are you on b.c.?"

"Birth control?"

"Yes."

"I am."

"I'm clean."

She stared at him and he waited. She knew the unspoken question between them.

Her hands moved from their grip on the edge of the desk to his forearms and she curled her fingers around them, connecting them that tiny bit more. "I'm clean too."

"I don't want to use a glove." Would she trust him enough? He trusted her—even though she'd come into his life under false pretenses, he knew she would never lie about this kind of thing.

"No."

Disappointment crashed through him, but he understood. They hadn't known each other long enough for this level of trust. His was pure instinct and illogical to boot.

"I don't want to either," she clarified.

Oh, oh . . . yes. Thank you and hallelujah. "I want to feel your flesh around me."

"Need it," she said simply.

"Yes."

"Yes."

Beau pushed into her, going slow so that he could experience every centimeter of new sensation.

Elle reveled in it just as much, her eyes going unfocused in her passion, her breath quickening. "Feels so good."

"Better than good."

"Yes."

Once he was completely inside her, he stopped to take in every nuance of the feeling. Her inner muscles massaged him and he was so hard he could feel his own heartbeat in his cock.

"We fit," she said.

"Perfectly."

She nodded. "Need you to move."

"I will. Don't want it to end too soon."

"Please . . ."

He leaned forward so that his pelvis would rub against her clit when he moved just right. Then he set about finding out exactly what that would take. It was slow; it was deep; it was intense.

He hadn't gone bare inside a woman since college and he'd regretted doing so with his fiancée when he found out she'd been cheating. He knew he would never regret this.

It was too right.

No matter how temporary.

They climbed toward the pinnacle of pleasure together, both their bodies tensing as the sensation spiraled higher and higher.

"Come for me, sugar. I want to feel it around me while I'm still hard."

Her eyes fluttered, shut, and then just like that her body convulsed, squeezing his cock so tight it temporarily held back his climax. He kept moving, driving her toward a second orgasm. He knew she could give it to him. He leaned forward and took her mouth with gentle dominance, claiming the interior with his tongue and molding their lips together seamlessly.

She squirmed under him and he knew she was going to explode a second time. He increased the swivel on his hip on the downward thrust and then they were coming together, their mouths muffling each other's cries.

Perfect.

They kept kissing until a dinging sound impinged on his consciousness and Elle went stiff under him.

Beau stood carefully, pulling out with regret. "What's that?"

"One of those things I was telling you about earlier."

His brain still wasn't working all that great. "What things?"

"A reminder to get back to work." She stood up and moved around her desk, opening a drawer while looking at the monitor on her mininotebook. "That particular sound is someone going into Frank's office when he's not there."

"There's an alarm on Frank's office?"

"As of this morning, there is. And he remembered to set it when he left for lunch. Good man."

"He may have come back and forgotten to turn it off too."

"Nope. That's not Frank feeling up his bookcase."

Beau came around the desk to see what she was talking about. A small window on the monitor showed Frank's office, and in it, searching under the shelf where Elle had found the listening device, was Archer Sandstone.

"The little creep," Beau said.

Archer was frowning, but then he smirked and pulled something from his pocket. Elle handed Beau a wipe from the pack she kept in her drawer while they both watched Sandstone implicate himself beyond redemption. He was installing another bug, but this one he put under Frank's desk somewhere.

"Are you going to catch him red-handed?" Beau asked her.

"Nope. I've got him on video." Elle began dressing with efficient movements that were nevertheless arousing.

He glared down at his semierect dick. "Down, boy."

"Is J.T. giving you trouble?"

He laughed. "More like me seeing you is giving John Thomas ideas."

"Save that thought for later; we've got work to do."

They finished dressing and Elle wrinkled her nose. "I need to keep Febreze in my drawer too, I think. It smells like sex in here."

"I'm surprised you had the wipes. What are they for?"

"You never know when you're going to want clean hands."

"You really do share your brother's penchant for cleanliness, don't you?"

"I don't get cranky when people leave notes on my desk."

"I'll remember that."

"So, do you want to be with me when I tell Frank about Archer breaking into his office and planting another bug?"

"Definitely. How did he get in, anyway? Frank always locks his office. I'm the only other one with a key."

"You and security."

"Security?"

"Yep. For such a high-tech facility, certain areas of your security are dangerously low-tech: keyed locks without a biometric component to which security and janitorial staff have masters."

"How the hell are we supposed to have our offices clean if they can't get in?"

"There are ways around the kind of unlimited access they have right now."

"You really are good at your job, aren't you? Both of them."

"So they say."

"You impress the hell out of me, princess. You surely do."

Elle went still and stared at him. "I . . ."

"The polite response to a heartfelt compliment is 'thank you.' "

"I may not be from Texas, but I do know that."

"There's my sugar."

"Thank you."

He grinned. "You're welcome. Frank probably won't be back for another twenty minutes. You want to grab something to eat in the cafeteria?"

"Sounds good." Elle moved her mouse and clicked a couple of times. "Just let me check my e-mail."

Beau waited quietly while she did so.

She made a sound of satisfaction.

"What's up?"

"Alan e-mailed me. He's got information that two men with known links to the smugglers in South Africa are here in the States."

"You think they're here in California?"

"It would make sense. He's tracking it, but that could be impossible to find out, depending on where they're staying and how they're paying for things."

"If they're part of a known smuggling ring, what are they doing here?"

"Neither of them has a rap sheet yet. Could be that they were let in in hopes of catching them red-handed, or that customs simply didn't flag them on arrival. If another agency is responsible for them being let in, Alan will find out."

"Alan?"

"My associate."

"I figured that out. Up until this conversation, though, you've been careful not to use his name."

Elle looked at him with too serious eyes. "You know who and what I am. If I can trust you with that, I can trust you with the first name of one of my associates."

"You didn't have a choice about me knowing you're a TGP agent."

She shrugged. "Doesn't matter. I don't mind you knowing."

Well, hell. What did that mean? It was something he was going to have to think on in regard to his casual-sex partner. "Let's go get something to eat."

Elle's expression flickered with relief as if she didn't want to delve any further into her admission and what it meant either. "Let's. I'm starving."

"Worked up an appetite, huh?"

"While sating another one? Yes."

He was laughing when they exited her office together.

Frank was clearly angry when Elle showed him the video of Archer, but just as obviously unsurprised. They were meeting in her office because she wasn't sure she wanted to remove the listening device from Frank's. She'd made Beau take out the garbage and find her some air freshener before she'd called Frank and requested the meeting.

"I'm going to fire his ass," Frank said.

"Good idea, but you might want to wait on that until after Friday," Elle said.

"Why?"

She and Beau told Frank about their meeting earlier with Chantal and the others.

"Why didn't you call me into the meeting?" Frank asked.

"Beau is my official liaison, so frequently having him in my office isn't suspect. You, on the other hand, are another matter. I would have arranged to meet in your office if it wasn't compromised."

"Why is it compromised? You disarmed the bug?"

"Archer Sandstone is watching you and your office. I'm hoping Sandstone isn't aware that you are here right now."

"I see. Little bastard."

Elle agreed completely with the sentiment.

Beau shifted in his chair to face Frank a little more. "I was going to come by after lunch and tell you all about it any way."

"Why not meet me for lunch?" Frank asked.

Beau blushed.

Elle laughed. She couldn't help herself. She didn't think she'd ever see that particular phenomenon.

Frank shook his head and put his hand up in a stopping motion. "Never mind. I don't want to know what put that look on your face," he said to Beau. "So you think there's someone on the inside?" he asked Elle.

"I doubt it, considering how they are coercing Chantal's cooperation, but I wouldn't bet her life on it."

"And you think that's what we'd be doing."

"If it *is* the smugglers we're dealing with? Definitely. They don't have a lot of finesse and they've made mistakes I'd fire them for if they were my men, but they're also known to be ruthless. It's a very good thing Mr. Smith got Gil Bigsley out of the picture when he did."

"So, why wait to fire Archer?" Frank asked.

"If they do have an inside man, he's the best candidate for the role right now."

"No." Beau sounded absolutely sure. "If it was Archer, he'd have gotten them the plans himself."

"Unless he didn't want to be held responsible when they build the ship and death and mayhem result," Elle countered.

"Nah, just because they're criminals doesn't mean they're stupid. Archer wouldn't risk not telling them the antigravity prototype failed. He's too much of a coward."

"So, you think his bugging Frank's office is totally unrelated?"

"Yes," both Frank and Beau said at once.

"You're serious?"

Beau sighed. "Unfortunately, yes."

"But why?"

"He's jealous of my knowledge. He wants to know what's
going on. His behavior this morning makes sense to me now.
He'd lost his little bug and he really did want me to tell him
what Frank and I talked about in our morning meeting. I bet
I can even pinpoint when he planted the first listening device."

"So, you want to fire him?"

Frank's expression was pure cold determination. "Yes."

"Can we do that?" Beau asked.

"He bugged my office, we damn well can."

"We videotaped him doing it. Is that legal?"

Elle answered for Frank, "The building is posted for video
surveillance."

"But we've never had it in any offices." Beau said.

"You could have. The posting is in general enough terms
to cover doing so without announcing it to the general popu-
lation of employees. In fact, that's one of the things I'm going
to suggest for improving security," Elle said.

"Cameras in our offices?" Beau asked.

"No, but in all the labs and the halls outside your offices."

"We've got hall surveillance," Beau said.

"With far too many nonmonitored areas."

Frank steepled his fingers under his chin. "Although I do
not believe that Archer is using the information he gleans
from spying on my office to feed anyone else at the moment,
once he's fired, that could change."

"But he doesn't know about the continued threat to security on my project," Beau said. "We didn't talk about that until after Elle removed the bug and took out its battery."

"However, there's a very good possibility he knows that Elle is an agent for The Goddard Project."

Elle's insides twisted. Of course he would. Frank hadn't known his office was being monitored. He, Mr. Smith and Beau probably had discussed her role as a federal agent more than once. The Old Man was not going to be pleased.

Elle herself was extremely unhappy about it. One of her quirks was that she read things like employment manuals cover to cover. And since she had a photographic memory, she recalled everything they said. The manual for TGP stated that if an agent's cover was blown to a potentially hostile party, said agent lost field-assignment privileges.

It had happened the first year she worked for TGP. The agent in question had transferred to the FBI since not all agents for the Bureau work undercover.

Well, crap.

Frank and Beau were watching her silently as these thoughts processed in her mind.

"I'll apprise my boss of the possible breach in my cover," Elle said.

"Do you want me to wait to fire Archer until you have done so?" Frank asked.

"That's not my decision to make." No matter what Beau said, they weren't a totalitarian government and she had no authority to dictate policy or behavior to a private company.

Frank nodded. "I'll call Mr. Smith. You call your boss and we'll discuss what they both have to say before I take any action."

"I appreciate that. Thank you."

Feeling like she was free-falling into that abyss she'd sensed the evening before when she'd agreed to make love with Beau again, Elle stood. "You're welcome to make the call in here. I'll go back to my apartment and use my cell."

She started packing up her computer.

"You're coming back, aren't you?" Beau asked, looking concerned.

"Yes."

"But you're taking your computer."

"I never leave my computer unsecured."

"Are you going to be okay?"

"Of course." Then she took a deep breath. "I'm actually not sure The Old Man will want me to return. My guess is that he'll allow me to finish out this assignment because he didn't attempt to take me off of it when my cover was blown to you and Frank, but I won't know until I talk to him."

"What good would taking you off the case do?"

"I don't know, but it is a possibility."

"That's stupid."

"I'm an undercover federal agent, Beau. I no longer *have* a cover."

Beau cursed.

"Go, make your call, Elle," Frank said.

She nodded.

"Phone me after you've spoken to him," Frank said.

"I'll call your cell." So he could leave his office to talk if he'd gone back to it after his own call to his boss.

"I *will* see you later?" Beau asked.

"Yes."

"Regardless?"

"Yes." And why his insistence on that point made her feel just a tiny bit better, she wasn't going to question.

Beau didn't say anything after Elle left. He just waited in silence while Frank called Mr. Smith. Their conversation was not a long one, but Frank looked very upset when it was over.

"What's the matter?" Beau asked immediately.

"Mr. Smith said that TGP policy is to take an agent whose cover has been blown to a potentially hostile source off of active field duty."

"Elle's going to get fired because that little creep was bugging your office?"

"Not fired. Reassigned."

Same damn thing. "That's bullshit."

"I agree."

"Why the hell did Mr. Smith tell us about her if that could happen?"

"He trusts us. We aren't potentially hostile witnesses."

"It was still a huge risk he had no right taking on her behalf."

"Mr. Smith doesn't see it that way."

"Bastard."

"He's still your boss, Beau."

"But for how long is in question."

"You won't leave ETRD over this?" Frank asked, alarmed.

"I don't know, Frank. Elle loves her job, but she's going to lose it because of Mr. Smith's little games."

"He has his reasons for doing things."

"They're not good enough when they impact other people's lives like this."

"He didn't expect this outcome."

"He's smarter than the average man. He should have known it was a possibility."

"I think we all made the mistake of trusting everyone who works for ETRD too deeply."

"Damn right, including trusting Mr. Smith."

"He suggested I wait until after the issue with Chantal has

been dealt with to fire Archer, to minimize the risk to both Elle's investigation and our employee."

"That's not going to save Elle's job, though."

"No, it isn't. Keeping Archer on won't either, though. Even if I could stand to do so. Mr. Smith informs me that working for us or not, Archer would be considered a potentially hostile party."

Beau nodded. A man who would bug his own boss's office isn't someone who could be trusted to keep his knowledge of Elle and TGP to himself. "We don't know for a fact that Archer overheard the conversations regarding Elle being a federal agent."

"His behavior implies he makes it a habit of listening in on our morning meetings. We discussed Elle Gray and The Goddard Project during at least two different ones."

# Chapter 18

Elle returned to ETRD an hour and a half later. Beau had a request in to security to let him know as soon as she entered the building again.

He was on his way to her office a second after learning she'd scanned in at the main security station. She met him halfway between there and his lab.

She stopped and turned without a word, leading him to her office.

Once inside, he put his hands on her shoulders, stopping her from moving away. "Mr. Smith said you could lose your job over this. Are you going to?"

She nodded. "I can go into research and development or transfer to another agency, but I'm out of the field for TGP." She took a deep breath and let it out. "After this assignment."

He turned her around and just hugged her. She let him and that told him more about her state of mind than anything else.

"You call Frank?" he asked.

"Yes. I told him to meet me here."

"You were coming to get me." And damn if it didn't feel good knowing that.

She nodded against him but didn't say anything.

"You going to be okay? Maybe we should put off this meeting with Frank for a while."

"No. I need to know his plans for Sandstone."

"I'm sorry about this, sugar."

"It's not your fault."

"No, but Mr. Smith knew the risks and he blew your cover to Frank and I regardless."

Elle just nodded again.

"I'm really pissed about that, sugar."

"Me too."

A knock sounded on the door and then the knob turned.

Elle sighed and pushed away from Beau just as the door opened.

"Beau, you're already here," Frank said as he came into the room. "I was going to ask Elle if she minded you being in on this meeting."

"Clearly, I don't." Elle was all business, not a glimmer of her usual charm showing. "What did Mr. Smith say?"

"About Archer Sandstone?"

"Yes. I'm not particularly interested in his opinion on other matters."

Frank cleared his throat. "Uh . . . right. I can't say that I blame you. Anyway, he instructed me to wait on firing Archer until the current attempt to procure the antigravity plans has been dealt with."

"Good."

"He thought you might be able to come up with something that will mess up Archer's bug without letting him know we've found the second one already."

"Do you want it to fail completely, or merely have intermittent transmission problems?"

"Could I control the intermittency?"

"Absolutely."

"That sounds like the best alternative, then. Hopefully by the time he risks trying to fix or replace it, the smugglers will have been apprehended."

"If they are indeed responsible."

"What's to stop them from coming after the experiment again?" Beau asked. "I mean, even if you arrest those in the U.S. now, there's still a whole organization who think they want the plans, not to mention the other buyers who didn't get their chance at the plans before."

"I've been thinking about that," Elle said, her expression not happy.

"And?"

"I considered having Chantal come clean with them on the nonviability of the experiment, but there's no reason for them to believe her."

"Right."

"Don't you think she should try it anyway?" Frank asked.

Elle's eyes glinted as cold as steel. "I think the men threatening her deserve to be brought to justice."

"I agree," Beau said.

"Good." Elle smiled. "However, once that has happened, I think a press release with the results of the initial tests, including the dangerous levels of electromagnetic discharge, should be circulated."

"One of the reasons we've kept the project under wraps is so that our version of antigravity won't get the bad rep nuclear power has because of safety issues. When we fix the discharge issue, it could languish as a new technology if public perception of it has already taken that direction," Beau said.

"It's your choice, of course, but given the circumstance and the risk of the plans getting stolen at some point, I would say that some possible public concern would be the lesser of two evils. Not ideal, but doable," Elle said.

Frank adjusted his stance in his chair. "There was resistance to the automobile at first too, Beau, but now it's one of our base technologies."

"This whole situation makes me madder than hell."

Elle gave Beau a look of commiseration. "I hear you, but I really think it's the right path to take."

Beau nodded. "You're right. If we'd done the press release to begin with, neither Gil nor Chantal would have been put in danger."

"You didn't know someone else was going to come after the plans," Elle said.

"We should have guessed it would happen," Beau said.

"When you're an honest person, it's hard to foresee the dishonest actions of others," she said.

"You do it, and you're one of the most honest people I know," Beau said.

Elle looked shocked, then smiled. "Thanks, but it's my job." The smile slipped. "At least for the next few weeks."

"I'm very sorry about that, Elle."

"Thank you, Frank, but you aren't responsible for Sandstone's behavior." The words were gracious, but Beau could feel the difference between Elle's reaction to him and her response to Frank.

"The man is an idiot," Beau growled.

Frank rubbed his temples, a sure sign a headache was coming on. "I agree."

"You can bring stalking charges against him for this," Elle mentioned.

"Good." Frank looked ready to tear someone a new asshole and Beau thought his mentor just might be planning to use the legal system to do it to Archer.

"You'll have to look into what other charges can be brought against him," Beau suggested.

"Don't make it a vendetta. You'll just end up using energy that would better be applied to making the world a better place." Elle smiled. "Remember, that's what you all do around here."

"And people like you make it possible," Beau said, believing it fully as he finally accepted how much Elle's current career had cost her life.

"Like I said, it's my job. And I'm going to make sure I don't mess up this final case, so if you'll both excuse me, I've got a bug interrupter to put together. I'll install it tonight, after everyone is gone."

"Sounds good." Frank stood. "I think I've got some pressing things that will keep me mostly out of my office for the rest of the day."

After he left, Beau asked, "Will I see you tonight, princess?"

"I'll have to work so I can take time off tomorrow to go shopping with Josie and Chantal."

"Can I help with anything?" He just wanted to be with her but didn't want to sound lame saying so.

"I . . ." She didn't say anything more, looking lost again.

He bit the bullet. "I don't think you need to be alone tonight."

"I'm a big girl. I can handle disappointments in my life."

"Losing the career you passionately enjoy is more than a mere disappointment. It's okay to lean on someone else once in a while."

"I thought your doctorate was in physics, not psychology." She was smiling a little wistfully when she said it, so he didn't take offense.

"You learn all sorts of stuff at school, don't you remember?"

"I remember learning that I didn't want to spend my life in a lab."

"Then don't."

"I'm not sure I'm ready to leave TGP."

"You don't have to make that decision tonight."

"That's good, because I don't want to." She looked down at her hands. "I love being an agent."

"I know."

"I never wanted to work for a different agency, even though I couldn't tell my family about TGP. I believe in what I do."

"And you're damn good at it." He waited a beat of silence. "Are you going to tell Mat?"

"I don't know. I'm so used to hiding everything to do with my job, but now I don't have to do that. I've already been outed."

"You don't have to tell him about TGP in order to tell him the result of Archer knowing about your career there."

"You're right." She met his eyes, hers not quite so dispirited. "It's going to feel good to tell him, you know?"

"I can guess."

Elle waited to tell her brother until she and Beau were over at Mat's house after work.

Mat surged to his feet, his fury a palpable force in the kitchen. "That son of a bitch!"

Chantal laid her hand on Mat's back. "Calm down, *cher*. Your sister needs your support right now, not the roaring grizzly bear. *N'est pas?*"

"I can't believe your agency is pulling you from active duty just because one creep made your cover." Josie was shaking her head.

Elle laughed, surprised she could feel amused after finding out her career at TGP was irrevocably changed and maybe gone for good. "I'm not a soldier, but I know what you mean. It's policy. I'm sure they had a good reason for making it."

"But this is the government, and even if the implementation of a policy doesn't make sense, it has to be done," Nitro said sarcastically.

Mat was sitting down again, but he was still plenty mad. "You can't tell me your boss doesn't have any latitude."

"There's no question that Archer Sandstone falls under the potential hostile-party determination," Elle said.

Josie frowned. "But that doesn't mean he could blow your cover in the future. I mean, what are the chances?"

"It's not like your boss couldn't bury the fact that Archer knows about you," Mat said.

"I'd never ask him to do that. I wouldn't let him if he offered to either, and I think he knows that."

"Personal integrity." Beau said it like it was a code for something.

And in a way it was, because both he and Elle knew exactly what he meant by that. "Right," Elle said.

"So, this is your last active case for the agency?" Josie asked.

"Yes."

Chantal reached out and hugged Elle. "I, for one, am glad you're on it."

"Thanks." Elle patted the back of the smaller woman somewhat awkwardly, but she really appreciated the sentiment.

"So, anything new with the case?" Nitro asked Elle.

"Josie told you about the meeting earlier today?"

"Yeah, I know about the Friday deadline."

"My associate had a break in locating the two men currently Stateside known to associate with the smuggling ring out of South Africa."

"Yes?" Nitro asked.

"They're in Southern California, staying in a hotel about forty-five minutes from here."

"Do you want me to set up surveillance?" Nitro asked.

"If you don't mind."

"Whatever the job takes—you should know that."

Elle nodded. "Mat, I'll need you to stay at ETRD and in contact with Beau while Josie and Nitro are both out of range."

"I'm not a little kid. I don't need a babysitter."

"No, you are my brother, and if you won't do this little thing, then I'll skip the shopping trip and keep an eye on your stubborn ass myself."

"I'm going to tell Baba you swore at me."

"Have you told her about Chantal yet?" Elle asked with obvious threat.

Mat glared, but everyone else in the kitchen cracked up.

"Little sisters are definitely the harder species to handle," Beau piped up.

"I wouldn't know," Josie said, with a smile. "I was an only child."

"Me too," Chantal said, "but if I had to hazard a guess, I'd say big brothers with stubborn streaks are the bigger challenge."

"You coached her," Beau accused Elle.

She shook her head. "I didn't. I swear. She just has enough brains to recognize the truth."

Elle didn't say anything when Beau made no move to pick up his bike after they returned to ETRD for her to install the interrupter for the listening device in Frank's office.

"You need clothes for tomorrow, or can I just take you by your apartment in the morning?" he asked as he pulled out of the parking lot.

She'd let him drive again. The man was getting seriously spoiled, but for some reason, that didn't bother her. "You're really taking my not being alone tonight as a personal mission statement, aren't you?"

"Yes." She loved his honesty.

"We can go by the apartment in the morning." If they went now, she'd feel like she had to make a bid for independence and tell him she'd be fine on her own.

Only she didn't want to be alone, but not because of what

had happened with her job. She'd slept terribly the night before and missed Beau's presence in the morning. She should be running fast and furiously in the other direction, but she couldn't make herself do it.

She wanted to spend the night with him.

She couldn't pretend otherwise. Not to him. Or to herself. She had let him make love to her without a condom. No other man had done that except Kyle. She'd even admitted to Beau that she wanted him with a deeper intensity than she'd wanted the man she'd loved and lost.

She'd fallen over the edge into the abyss, and all she could hope for now was not to land at the bottom and shatter.

Again.

It was time to have a talk with Mama.

It was surprisingly comfortable working on the new security plan for ETRD while Beau muttered at the printout of test results he was going over. Companionable.

Elle liked it.

She'd never done this kind of thing with Kyle. She'd wanted to talk about her cases with him, but since there were so many things she wasn't supposed to say, they had agreed she wouldn't say anything at all. That had led to the mutual bargain to leave the job at the office and concentrate on one another when they got home. That had been good, but sometimes it had also been really difficult.

And there had been nights when she'd laid in bed and questioned how well Kyle could know her if he knew nothing about how she spent her hours away from him. And vice versa. She'd loved him so much, but she'd wondered if she knew him. Really.

They'd known each other when they got married. They both were university students when they met, and their lives had meshed easily. It was when they graduated and began to pursue their chosen careers that life had begun to change them both. If he had lived, Elle wondered if they would be two total strangers living in the same house by now or if they would have made changes so their marriage could thrive.

She hoped they would have been smart enough to do the latter.

Her phone rang and she looked at the caller ID. It was Alan Hyatt, the other TGP agent who had had the initial case that linked to the antigravity plans. He'd transferred to a research-only position afterward because he hadn't wanted to be separated from his new love, an actress filming out of Vancouver, British Columbia. Elle was glad The Old Man had okayed the position.

They'd needed somebody on staff doing the backup research for a while now. Alan had already been invaluable on this investigation, and she knew he'd help the other TGP agents in the future as well.

A future she might not share with them in any capacity.

She flipped open the phone. "Hey, Alan, hold on a second."

"No problem."

She touched Beau on the knee. He hadn't even looked up when the phone rang.

He gave her a slightly unfocused gaze from gorgeous brown eyes. "Yeah?"

"Will it bother you if I take this call in here? I can go in the other room to talk," she offered.

"No problem." He waved his hand vaguely and went back to his printouts.

She grinned and put the phone back to her ear. "Hey."

"How you doing, Elle?"

"I'm okay."

"The Old Man told me about the reassignment of our position after this case."

Elle sighed. "I'll figure it out."

"It sucks."

"Yes."

"You sure you're going to be okay?"

"What is this, life with Jillian making you soft?"

"You're a friend, Elle. A prickly, private-to-the-point-of-paranoia one, but a friend nonetheless."

"Thanks. I didn't mean to . . . I . . ." She sighed. "I appreciate your concern—I really do."

"No problem. If you need to talk, I've got an ear."

"I don't know that I want to stay with TGP," she heard herself saying.

"You're not going to be happy in a lab, and I don't see The Old Man approving a second research position, even if you wanted it, which I doubt."

"I've got the education for the lab."

"But you'd be miserable. It's not your thing and you're intelligent enough to recognize that."

"My family lives here."

"In Southern Cali?"

"Yes."

"You thinking about staying out here?"

"I sort of am." She hadn't realized she was, but that thought had been in the back of her mind since The Old Man had confirmed TGP's policy regarding her blown cover.

"You've still got your security consulting business. You're good at it."

"I am. I enjoy it, but I'm not sure it's enough."

"Don't sell it short. There's a lot you can do without government red tape holding you back."

"You make it sound like I'd be a mercenary."

"More like a hired gun, just not the kind that shoots."

"I can do that very well, thank you."

"Yep, but as good as you are with weapons—and we both

agree you're deadly—you're a genius with securing a client's interests. It's a gift."

"You really think so?"

"I know so." He said something away from the phone. Probably talking to Jillian. Elle had met the redheaded actress at the wedding. She liked the other woman. A lot. "You'd make a great information source as well."

"In other words, you'd make sure I kept my finger in the pie."

"Something like that."

"You are a good friend, Alan."

"Just remember that. No matter where you work."

"Thank you."

They hung up before she realized he must have called simply to make sure she was okay, because they hadn't talked about the case at all.

She put her phone down only to realize she had Beau's undivided attention.

She smiled. This not being alone thing wasn't so bad at all.

"You're thinking of staying here?" Was that hope in his gaze? It certainly wasn't indifference.

"I don't know. Maybe."

"I'd like that."

Then, before she had a chance to respond to that amazing statement, he was swinging her up in a fireman's hold and carrying her off to his bedroom. Their lovemaking was strangely silent and very intense.

But she thought she heard him whisper, "I really would," before she drifted off to sleep.

The shopping trip was fun. Both Josie and Chantal treated Elle's knowledge of the beauty industry like it was something awe inspiring. Elle ended up insisting they do a little clothes shopping too and, man, the outfits the two shorter women bought were so going to leave their men breathless and want-ing.

Elle bought herself some butter-soft black leather pants to wear riding on Beau's motorcycle. She'd brought her favorite leather jacket with her, so she figured she was good to go.

Now, she just had to remind him of his promise.

They were on the way home, in Josie's rental SUV, because Elle's car didn't have a backseat for the third person, when the former mercenary asked, "So, have you considered what you're going to do about being taken out of the field?"

"I'm probably going to leave the agency." She hadn't planned to say it but realized there was no use going around the subject. She loved being an agent for TGP, but she had no desire to take a position in the R&D lab.

Like Alan had said, it just wasn't her.

"And do what?" Chantal asked.

"I've still got my security consulting business."

"Would you consider moving the headquarters here? I know Mat would be really happy if you were living in California again."

Elle smiled. She knew that, but hearing Chantal say it made her feel good. Man, she really had been away from her family too long. "I've thought about it."

"You have?" Chantal asked with unmasked delight. "That's wonderful!"

"We've considered having a second base of operations," Josie said casually.

"Really?"

"Yes. The guys were talking about how much they admire your agency when the call came to help you on this case. Do you think you might consider a partnership? I think you'd bring a skill set that is invaluable to the company and it wouldn't hurt for you to have backup, especially once you're no longer moonlighting as a government agent."

"I always thought the moonlighting was the other way around."

"Well, now you know differently."

Incredibly, Elle laughed. It should hurt, but she appreciated the irony and Josie's offer made her feel really good. "I think I might be interested in talking to you all, once this case is over."

"Fantastic." Josie grabbed her phone, and seconds later she was telling Nitro that Elle was considering the offer.

The enthusiasm warmed Elle. There was a small part of her that couldn't help feeling the sting of rejection from being sidelined at her agency. Knowing there were others out there in her line of work, people she admired hugely, who were truly interested in having her on their team soothed some of that sting.

"Ask him if he finished the install of surveillance," Elle said.

Josie listened to Nitro talk and then nodded. "He'll tell you all about it when we get back, but he's got it covered."

"Perfect."

Josie told her husband she loved him before she disconnected the call, and Elle smiled. "Between you and Nitro and my brother and Chantal, I'm surrounded by lovebirds."

"What do you call you and Beau? Crows?"

"We're not in love."

"Aren't you?"

Elle didn't have an answer for that. Because she wasn't at all sure anymore that the feelings she had for Beau were anything less than full-out, soul-deep love. And wasn't that just more terrifying than jumping out of an airplane with a ten-year-old parachute.

Luckily for her sanity, between the case and contemplation of where her career was going, over the next few days, Elle didn't have time to dwell on the love thing ad nauseam. Not that she didn't think about it at all, but she had some success with redirecting her thoughts, and for that she was grateful.

There was just too much coming at her at once and she still hadn't had that chat with Mama.

# Chapter 19

Friday came and everyone was on edge. Beau had created a set of fake plans that looked nearly identical to the originals. The difference was these didn't work at all, and because of that, there was no dangerous electromagnetic discharge. Elle had taken pictures of them and put the images on a thumb drive for Josie to pass off as the plans.

Nitro's surveillance showed that the two smugglers hadn't left the hotel all morning, and Chantal's phone did not ring. Of course, the smugglers had told her to have the plans ready tonight. Nitro was in place to follow them when they did leave to meet Josie masquerading as Chantal.

Elle would be following Josie as backup. Chantal was to be sequestered in ETRD until the trap had closed on the smugglers. Mat had insisted on staying with her, and Elle hadn't put up even a token resistance. He would be safer in the secured building.

Not that he was technically at risk, but still.

It was a good plan. Elle knew it. However, she kept going over it again and again in her mind. That wasn't unusual, but she wanted a break from thinking about it. Maybe it was time for that call with her mother.

She dialed the cell phone and Mama picked up on the second ring. "Hello? Elle?"

"Yes, Mama, it's me."

"Are you coming for dinner this weekend? Maybe bring that nice Dr. Ruston with you."

Elle huffed out a laugh. Some things never changed and she was glad. "That's kind of why I'm calling."

"I remember this tone of voice," her mother said, an edge of joy lacing her words. "You had it when you told me you were in love with Kyle. Such a nice boy. He should not have died so young, but life isn't so black-and-white, is it? Bad things happen and we have to survive. Baba has always said this. She should know. Life wasn't always kind to my mother."

Mama's words buzzed in Elle's head like a droning bee as Elle sucked in a shocked breath. She felt like she'd been sucker punched, and that didn't happen often. But how could her mom know she loved Beau when she herself was just coming to terms with the possibility?

"I'm scared, Mama," she blurted over a well-known story about her *baba*'s life as a young woman.

"Ah, yes. I thought you might be."

"It's hard."

"Because Kyle died."

"He's gone, Mama. He left me alone."

"It was his time, *miy amúr,* but that doesn't mean you have to spend the rest of your life by yourself. It is time for you to live again—to come back to your family."

Was the woman psychic? "I'm thinking of moving back to California."

"Good. Where you live now is filled with crooks and people who lie for a living. You come home." Her mother's opinion of politicians hadn't improved any over the last few years.

"What if Beau doesn't love me?" What if he *did,* but ended up leaving—through death, or simply them growing apart, as Elle had come to realize she and Kyle had been doing before he was killed.

Her mother tutted in disbelief. "Of course he loves you. I saw the way he looked at you."

"I think that was lust."

"What do you think comes first for a man? You think they start off considering what a wonderful wife and mother a woman would be? No, they think how well the woman would warm their bed. Your father was the same."

"Ew! Mama, I didn't need to hear that."

"What, you thought we never had sex? We had five children, Elle. You girls nowadays, so squeamish about life."

"You're my mother. I don't want to think of you having sex."

"No one said you had to think about it." Mama made a sound of disgust. "I'm just giving you advice. Like my own mother gave me."

Picturing her *baba* talking about sex to Mama was not a pretty mental landscape. "Okay, okay . . . just . . . stop. . . ."

"Bah, never mind that. Elle, daughter, loving is scary. It's a risk. What if you love someone and they die like Kyle? Or stop loving you? Or move away three thousand miles and take your heart with them?" Elle had a feeling her mother wasn't talking about romantic love with that last one. "That's the risk you take loving, but it's a bigger risk to hide from it. Loneliness can be like a living death. I've seen it with elderly neighbors; their children never come to see them. Or young people so wrapped up in work, they forget the heart wasn't meant to be ignored like that until they wake up one day and realize they have no one to call their own."

Elle thought that last comment might have been aimed at her as well. "I've missed you all. I don't want to go away again."

"We've missed you as well, *miy amúr*. More than you can know. I am glad your heart came out of hiding before it was too late to spend time with the people you love."

Like her *baba,* who was old and would not live forever. "I was grieving."

"Yes, and maybe you needed some distance. A little independence to become the woman you wanted to be and not the woman we expected."

"I . . ."

"I'm not blind to your feelings, daughter. I never have been. Maybe I should have been more accepting, but we all must follow our own paths in life."

"Yes, Mama."

"I'm proud of you, Elle. Whatever you think. Your papa and Baba are too."

"Thank you." Damn, she could feel tears clogging her throat, but Elle never cried. "I think I love Beau," she admitted in a shakier voice than she'd used in a long time. "But we've known each other such a short while."

"I knew your father two days before I knew he was the one. He is still the one, my precious girl."

Elle smiled at that. Yes, her parents were still very much in love. "Beau likes the family."

"Of course. We are likable."

"He even likes Mat."

"Why should he not? He's my son, isn't he?"

Elle laughed, but then she sobered. "I don't know if Beau wants more—I mean anything lasting."

"You will not know until you ask."

So much for her mother expecting her to be a traditional, demure woman. "And if he says no?"

"If he is worth fighting for, you fight. If not, you let me fix you up with Mrs. Niedleson's son. He's a heart surgeon and has the sweetest little boy."

"Mama!"

"What? I'm only saying Beau, as handsome, smart and kind as he might be, isn't the only fish in the sea."

"He's the only fish I want."

"Then reel him in, *miy amúr*. What are you waiting for?"

A brief knock sounded on Elle's office door and then Beau walked in.

"I need to go, Mama."

"Okay. Come for dinner on Sunday. Baba will cook."

"We'll be there." She was speaking for Beau too, but the worst he could do would be say no. And then her mother would call Mrs. Niedleson. Oy.

Was Elle *sure* she wanted to move back to California?

She put her phone down on the desk.

"How's your mom doing?" Beau asked, with a smile.

"Good. She wants us to come for dinner on Sunday."

He rubbed his belly. "Yum."

"Is that a yes?"

"Definitely."

"Good."

"Are you nervous about tonight?" Leaning against her desk, he rearranged the things on top.

"Nervous? No. Obsessing over every little detail? Unfortunately, yes."

"That's what makes you so good." He grimaced. "I'm on pins and needles myself."

"We've got it covered. Sound surveillance of their room confirms they believe Chantal is cooperating, but they've made mention of a backup plan—they called it their insurance—that I wish they'd elucidate on."

"Too bad you can't dictate the conversation of those you spy on."

"Isn't it?"

"I'll be glad when this is over."

"Me too. I want to know Chantal is safe."

"Definitely, but I can't wait to see the back of Archer Sandstone either."

"He's got a rude awakening come Monday morning."

"Frank is positively gleeful about it. Archer really made him mad with the bug in his office."

"Is he still going to press charges for stalking?"

"Yes."

"Good. That kind of behavior can spiral downward pretty quickly and get dangerous."

Beau's gorgeous brown eyes turned serious. "So can emotions."

"Come again."

"It's not just sex."

*Oh, man.* Was she ready for this? "Is this the right venue for this discussion?"

"Does it matter where we talk about it?"

"I can't help wondering why you didn't bring it up last night . . . in bed."

He shrugged. "We were busy and then you were asleep. Talking to you about serious stuff when you are naked isn't something that's going to be feasible for a while—maybe ever."

"I see. So I can look forward to a lifetime of personal discussions in the workplace?" She was asking so much with that one question.

His expression told her he recognized that fact. "Yes."

"I . . ."

Her phone buzzed. It was Mat. She stared between Beau and the phone, torn for the first time ever between personal issues and doing her job.

Beau smiled. "Get it. We'll finish this later."

"We will." She grabbed the cell.

The perps had called early. They'd given Chantal instructions on where to drop the plans. They didn't want a face-to-face meet, which was good for the Josie-Chantal switch.

This time, Chantal had been prepared with a way to record the call. With the recording of the phone call and video footage of the two men picking up the thumb drive with the false plans on it, they'd be dead to rights on charges of piracy and blackmail.

Josie, wearing the blond wig and looking eerily like Chantal, made the drop and then fell back to position. She and Elle watched for the pickup. It came an hour later. Only one of the smugglers showed, though.

"Nitro, where's Perp Two?"

"Still in the car."

Elle got the video of Perp One picking up the thumb drive and making a quick call. She wanted to take him down so badly, but that wasn't the way TGP worked. Unless they had no choice, they left the collar for someone else.

Elle called Whit. "I've got the video."

"The FBI is set to move in once they return to the hotel."

"Perp One and Two leaving the parking lot," Nitro announced over the headset.

"They're on the move," Elle told Whit.

"Good."

She disconnected the call. "Nitro?" she asked.

All she got was static. "Let's get back to the car," she said to Josie. "You want to connect with Nitro on the cell?"

"I'm already on it."

They met back at the Spider. Josie pulled off the wig as she listened to whatever Nitro was saying on the phone.

She turned to Elle. "They're not headed to the hotel."

"Where are they?"

Josie relayed the coordinates and Elle executed a perfect U-turn, accelerating the powerful V10 engine. She continued to follow the directions from Nitro until Josie verified she had the SUV in her sights through the small field binoculars she was using.

"I can see Daniel too. He has a car between him and the perps and he's hanging back," Josie said.

"Good."

They took another couple of turns and Elle started suspecting their direction. "I think we're headed to ETRD."

Josie was still keeping visual contact with the smugglers via the binoculars. "That doesn't make any sense."

"No, it doesn't. They think they already have the plans, why risk exposure at the facility?" Maybe they were going after Chantal to eliminate the link back to them.

Elle called Mat with her handless Bluetooth.

"What's up, sis? Did the drop go as planned?"

"Yes, but the smugglers didn't go directly back to their hotel like I expected. They could be headed toward a small airport north of ETRD, but they're definitely headed in your direction. Keep Chantal inside the building; your office would be even better. If she gets any visitors, instruct security not to allow them access to the building and don't let her go to the lobby for anything."

"You've got it," her brother growled, and the phone went dead in her ear.

She then called security herself to tell them not to allow any visitors at all into the building for the next thirty minutes. The head of security balked and said she didn't have the authority to make that kind of call.

"I assure you, I do. Call Frank and verify it if you need to, but if I find out you let anyone in when I arrive at the facility, I'll stick my Gabriella Rochas so far up your ass that you'll be walking funny for the next month. Do we understand each other?" she said in a voice that could have frozen anything in range.

"Uh . . . yeah . . . I'll just put a hold on visitor passes while I track down Frank."

"Good idea. Now, tell me who has checked in as a visitor in the last hour." They couldn't be sure the two smugglers were working alone.

The list was short and on the face of it innocuous. Nevertheless, she instructed him to text the names to her and she forwarded the text to Alan with instructions to do quick-and-dirty background checks on the four names.

She got a call from Whit saying the FBI agents who had been waiting to do the pickup of the perps at the hotel were on their way.

Groggy and his vision blurry, Beau shook his head to clear it, immediately regretting the action when it sent spiking pain behind his left eye. Damn, that felt like a migraine. He'd only ever had one once before, when he'd been injured on the football field and given a narcotic for the pain that didn't agree with him.

He hadn't been shooting up painkillers in the lab, though.

But he couldn't be in the lab unless this sensation of being in a chair very different from his lab stool was another aspect to the headache. His lids cracked open only to make him wince in pain again at the light. He didn't shut his eyes again, though.

Because he wasn't in his lab.

He wasn't in ETRD at all. He was buckled into a plush leather airplane seat next to the window on what looked like a private jet. The tinted windows didn't entirely block the California sunshine, but no doubt blocked view of him from the outside. His hands were tied with a plastic tie in front of him, but his feet were free.

The sound of small planes droned intermittently from outside.

How the hell had he gotten here?

He thought about it while trying to unbuckle his seat belt with his constricted hands.

One of the components he needed for a test hadn't come in. No one had answered the phone when he'd called the supplier about it. He'd had that problem with this supplier before, but he needed the component. So, he'd gone to the warehouse.

Or, rather, he'd meant to.

When he had come out to his bike, a man had been dealing with an engine problem on his sleek-looking sedan. Beau remembered commenting that it was the new cars that seemed to have problems sometimes, not the old clunkers. The man had laughed as his friend had come around the car to Beau's side.

He hadn't been laughing. He'd looked damn scary, Beau had thought just as he'd felt a small prick and the world had gone black.

Well, day-um six ways from Sunday. He'd been kidnapped.

Elle was not going to be happy about this.

Elle voice-dialed Beau's phone for the second time, but it went to voice mail. Again.

She called the security office at ETRD again. "Is Dr. Ruston in the building?"

"I'm not sure. Let me check." It was a younger voice than the head of security. The other man was probably avoiding her at this point.

"He checked out twenty-seven minutes ago."

"To go where?"

"He didn't say, Ms. Gray."

A really bad feeling settled in the pit of Elle's stomach. She relayed the news to Josie, who relayed it to Nitro.

"Do you think something has happened to him?" Josie asked.

"He could be on the road and not answering his phone. He rides a motorcycle," Elle said.

Just then she got a call from Alan. She connected, putting him on speakerphone and signaling to Josie to do the same with Nitro. "Hey, guy. Any news on the visitors to ETRD?"

"Nothing worth pursuing yet. Listen, I did some checking on a hunch. You know me and my hunches."

"And your propensity to double-check research. It's one of the things I like about you."

Alan laughed. "Good. But I don't think you're going to like this."

"What?"

"A private jet registered to a subsidiary company of one known to associate with the South African smugglers flew into a municipal airport outside of Vancouver yesterday."

"And?"

"They left early this morning with a flight plan for a small airport in Eastern Oregon, one that doesn't have their flight plans accessible on any computer database."

"In other words, they could be in California right now."

"Exactly."

"The perps' getaway plans."

"Maybe. But maybe there's more to it."

"Is that what your gut is telling you?"

"Yes."

"Mine too," she admitted. "Chantal is safe, so far."

"What about Beau?"

"He hasn't been in this at all."

"But he's the lead scientist on the project."

"So?" Was Alan seeing something she wasn't?

"Now that they have what they believe are the plans, why not take the scientist?"

Beau? No. This was not happening.

"If they were going to take him, why not just start off that way?" Josie asked.

Things had started clicking into place as soon as Alan mentioned Beau, and Elle had an answer to Josie's question, or at least a suspicion. "Because he doesn't have the plans in his brain, or at least most scientists wouldn't. Beau probably does, but that's just him. They no doubt guessed that it would be harder to coerce him into sharing the plans than Gil Bigsley or Chantal."

"Right," Alan said. "Their first objective was to get the plans, but now we know what they were talking about when they mentioned their insurance."

Josie swore. Very effectively. "They weren't talking about a backup plan, but a second part to the original objective."

"Get the plans and the scientist most likely to be able to bring them to fruition," Nitro said.

"Exactly," Elle and Alan said simultaneously.

"Josie, call Frank and see if he knows where Beau went. Alan, call The Old Man and get the plane's takeoff delayed," Elle instructed.

"I'd love to," Alan said, "but we don't know what airport they're flying out of."

"Oh yes, we do," Elle replied as the smuggler's SUV didn't slow down for the turnoff to ETRD. She named the airport another fifteen minutes away.

Alan clicked off without saying good-bye.

"Frank said Beau went after something he needed for a test he was supposed to conduct today," Josie said.

Elle had to force herself not to increase her speed and over-take the primary perpetrators' car. "Have security verify if his bike is still in the lot."

A few seconds passed and then Josie said, "It's still there. His cell phone was on the ground beside it."

Elle did her own swearing, viciously in Ukrainian, but it didn't make her feel any better.

"Frank's hyperventilating at the other end of the phone."

"Tell him to chill, that we're on it." Nothing was going to happen to Beau. Elle wouldn't let it.

This time, she was on the scene and she was going to stop the bastards from taking the man she loved out of the country, or hurting him.

"They're turning in to the airfield," Josie said. "Good call, Elle."

Elle just grunted and got a chuckle from Josie. "You sound like Daniel on a case."

"And you're better?"

"Not really."

Josie's positive attitude helped keep Elle's fear at bay. This was Elle's job, what she did best. Take down the bad guys. She'd done it in person more often than most TGP agents, and she had no doubts in her personal abilities.

She allowed her need for speed to take over and pulled into the parking area for the airfield only moments behind the perps and right behind Nitro.

"Going back to headsets," Josie said as they both stepped out of the car.

"Don't worry, Elle, we're taking these bastards out," Nitro said in her ear. He sounded deadly and she appreciated that.

Josie said, "We're not going to let Beau get hurt."

"We can't stop a bullet no matter how much our will might want to," Elle felt compelled to say.

"We'll shoot first, if that's what it takes," Nitro said.

"I think I like private security rules of engagement over the TGP handbook in this instance," Elle said as she checked her gun.

Her phone rang in her other ear on the Bluetooth headset. It had about fifty feet of range and she'd left it in the car. The ring tone was The Old Man's, but she ignored it. He'd either gotten the takeoff delayed or he hadn't, but she didn't want to talk to him right now.

He would tell her to wait for the FBI to get there to go in. And there was no way on this green earth that was happening.

Elle felt like she was going to puke as the engines started warming up on the idling plane Perp One and Two were headed toward. Then cold calculation took over and she measured the distance between herself and the plane.

"Nitro and Josie, you take the men on the ground. I'm boarding the plane."

"You have no way of knowing how many men are on board," Nitro said.

"It doesn't matter. They aren't taking Beau."

"Josie and I will be right behind you," Nitro said, instead of arguing further.

Elle smiled grimly. They *were* good backup.

When the door at the top of the ramp opened, they all started moving as one smooth, extremely fast machine.

Elle trusted her partners to take out Perp One and Two while she took a running leap at the stairs. She landed exactly where she'd expected. She grabbed the handrails and used them to leverage a full-body flip, sending her sailing into the body of the man standing on the top step.

He'd been trying to get his gun from its shoulder holster, but she heard a sharp crack as her designer boots connected with the arm crossing his chest. She landed on top of him and used a quick forward thrust with the heel of her hand against his nose to further incapacitate him. Then she was up and assessing her situation in a split second.

Another man to her right went down under a damn fine tackle from her beloved former football hero.

"Good job. How many more?" she asked.

"I don't know. One, maybe two, but they'd be in the cockpit."

The plane started to move. The pilot must have seen something. Elle ran for the door as she heard clattering on the stairs outside the plane. Then both Nitro and Josie were there as well, securing the two downed men.

Grabbing her gun from the thigh holster, Elle ran to the front of the plane. She kicked the cockpit door in and immediately put her gun to the head of the pilot. "Stop the plane."

There was no copilot, or maybe one of the other men was supposed to be, but he wasn't in the cabin.

The pilot hesitated and Elle coldcocked him in the temple. Then she lunged forward and cut the plane's engines.

"Nicely done," Nitro said from the doorway.

"I agree, but damn I've got a headache." Beau was smiling, but there was no mistaking the grayed-out pain in his face.

"At least you're alive," Elle said with fervent gratitude.

"Yeah, thanks to you, sugar."

"You had a pretty nice tackle back there."

"And that's about all I could handle. *One* tackle."

She grinned. He was a fighter, but he wasn't an arrogant macho jerk who had to insist he didn't need a woman's help. "I love that about you, you know?"

"What that exactly?"

"That you can admit you needed my help."

"I need a lot more from you, sugar. Come home with me and you can tell me what else you love."

Her throat constricted for some odd reason, but she nodded. "Good plan," she choked out.

They didn't get to go home right away.

It was a messier collar than Elle was used to, but not every job went according to plan. The FBI arrived eventually—

after the local authorities. The Feds weren't happy she'd gone for the perps without them, but she didn't care. Beau was safe and that was all that mattered.

She wasn't trying to save her career at TGP or make a new one with the Feds. She was done working for the government. That part of her life was over, but she had a lot to look forward to, and the knowledge that the job she loved was lost to her didn't hurt anymore.

It was all about priorities, she told herself.

The FBI agents perked up when Elle turned over the video and voice-recording evidence. The questioning went on for longer than she wanted, but it could have been worse.

Which is what she told Mat when he came out of the building the FBI had used to question them and started complaining about her and the others being detained for so long.

Finally, they all got to head back to Mat's place.

# Chapter 20

As Beau and Elle left the parking lot, Beau flipped his phone out and dialed. "Hey, Mat. Look, we'll come over for a debriefing tomorrow, but tonight your sister and I have some things to work out."

Her brother said something, probably some tease for her, but she didn't hear it.

"Yeah. See you then." Beau flipped the phone shut.

Elle didn't bother to protest. She was coming down from the adrenaline rush and wanted nothing more than to snuggle up on Beau's big chocolate-brown sofa and drink a glass of his wine.

He suggested she take a hot shower to relax when they got there, and though she felt like she should be taking care of him, she went with it—after getting a promise from him to take something for his headache, which thankfully had gotten better during the questioning, not worse.

When she got out of the shower, there was a man's robe hanging on the back of the door and she slid into it. Entering the living room a few seconds later, she saw that Beau had a fire going in the grate and two glasses of wine already sitting on the coffee table.

He'd stripped to his boxers and looked frankly edible. "I

can see why you think talking is at risk when we get naked," she said.

"We're not naked. Yet."

"Getting that way has me preoccupied." She curled into the corner of the couch and took a sip of her wine. "But I do think we need to talk."

Instead of sitting beside her, Beau came around to kneel in front of her. "You saved my life, princess."

"It could have gone differently." She shuddered at the thought. "It did for Kyle."

"Kyle's death wasn't your fault. You weren't there, but you were *here* and I'm grateful for that. If you hadn't been on the case, I would have ended up in South Africa, and probably dead when I refused to build the antigravity ship for them."

"You stick by what you believe in. I love that about you."

"You were going to tell me what else you love, remember?"

She swallowed around a suddenly dry throat. "I love you, Beau." Oh, man, she'd said it. She really had. And she meant it.

"Thank God. And I do mean that." He leaned forward and kissed her until they were both breathing hard. "I love you too. So much. I don't want you to leave, but if you go, I'm following you."

"I'm staying."

"Here."

"With you."

"Kids?"

"I want them, but maybe not right now."

"Me too."

"Your family?"

"I'll talk to my sister. And then maybe my parents."

"Your job?"

"I don't know. I'm pretty pissed at Mr. Smith."

"But you believe in what you do. Don't let Archer Sandstone's actions take that from you."

"I'll think about it."

"Besides, I've still got the security measures to work out. And you're my liaison."

"You're going to finish the project?"

"I always finish a project once I start." It was an interesting conversation to have with their mouths only a breath away from each other.

"How about this project?" And then he was kissing her and she felt the final walls around her heart crumble into dust. Mama was right: loving someone was a risk, but Elle was good at taking risks.

She would have been a lousy government agent otherwise.

She might not be a field agent any longer, but that didn't mean she was going to start balking at the hard stuff.

Especially when the potential for good was so strong. She had a whole life shared with the most amazing man she'd ever known ahead of her. Not to mention a ride on his superfast motorcycle.

Definitely worth it.

# Epilogue

The family dinner at Mama and Papa Chernichenko's that Sunday was more of a party than anything else. Elle had insisted on bringing a couple of extra guests besides her and Mat's lovers. Frank and his wife hit it off immediately with the rest of the family, and Elle could tell that made Beau very happy.

Mat introduced Chantal as his fiancée, and Elle told the family she'd agreed to marry Beau and was moving back to California. Her parents and Baba were ecstatic, and the two older women started in immediately on planning not one, but two weddings.

The next day, Archer Sandstone was fired and served with a restraining order as well as charged with stalking and a list of other criminal activities Frank's lawyer had come up with. Beau was ecstatic, and since he was in such a good mood, he called his sister and asked her about their parents for the first time in years.

He discovered his mother and father regretted their actions more than a little and wanted to hear from him. When he called, his banker father, who never showed emotion, cried and begged for forgiveness. For the former football star turned scientist, it was a surreal moment, but he agreed to take Elle to meet them sometime before the wedding.

"Happy now?" he asked Elle as he got off the phone.

Lying across their bed, she was dressed in little more than girl boxers and a tiny tank top. "The question is, are *you* happy?"

"Sugar, as long as I have you, I'll always be happy."

She grinned and then pounced, landing on top of him spread-eagle on the bed. "Good answer, but I hope you can have a relationship with your parents too."

"I will and we all have you to thank for it. I never would have called them otherwise."

"Baba would have talked you into it eventually or called them for you."

He didn't doubt his beautiful, über-smart, ultraproficient fiancée. Her *baba* was a scary woman sometimes.

"Just as long as she never talks you out of loving me."

"Never happen. I love you too much to ever let you go!"

"I believe you." Elle would never lie to him, no matter how their relationship had started.

"Love you."

"I love you. Now let me show you just how much."

And he did.

Whit dialed a number for a man he hadn't ever expected to speak to again.

"This is Mr. Smith," the man answered.

"Hello, Jonathan."

"Whit."

"You cost me one of my best agents."

"That was unintentional."

"I believe you, but I'm still pissed."

"They make a good couple."

"Beau and Elle? They do."

"I knew they would."

"You were matchmaking?"

"I find that the older I get, the more important certain things become and the less others."

"I'm finding the same thing."

"Maybe we should pool our knowledge."

Whit considered the possibility with an unexpected smile as he and his old mentor/nemesis discussed other less personal issues.

Like this book? You'll love

DARING THE MOON

by Sherrill Quinn,
out this month from Brava. . . .

"Look, Ms. Gibson . . . Taite." He sat next to her, angling his body so that their knees touched. When she shifted slightly, pulling back from him, he wasn't surprised. What did surprise him was the sense of hurt he felt at the movement. But it was no more than he deserved. "I know I've been . . . less than hospitable," he went on. "I'd like to apologize."

She did look at him then, her gaze solemn. She sighed and rubbed her fingers across her forehead. "Mr. Merrick—"

"Ryder. Please." He stretched his arm along the back of the sofa and leaned in toward her, just slightly, to gauge her reaction. She stayed put, though her pupils dilated and her lips parted.

After a moment, she broke his gaze and looked down at the book, one hand coming up to push a thick strand of hair behind her ear. "Ryder." Her voice was huskier than it had been.

His name on her lips sizzled like lightning through him. He wanted nothing more than to take her in his arms and protect her from the big bad wolf she was so afraid of.

But then who would protect her from *him*?

Meeting his gaze once more, she said, "I understand, really

I do. We've descended upon you without notice and, from what I understand, against your wishes. And then we tell you this incredible story. . . ." She sighed and played with her hair, twirling a strand around and around her index finger.

"Still, it's no excuse for my poor behavior." He took her hand in his, and they both went still. He heard her breath catch and felt the thrumming of her pulse under his fingers. Rubbing his thumb over the back of her hand, he tried to remember what he'd been about to say.

She leaned forward, her gaze fastened on his mouth, and all thought fled his mind like water sliding down a drain. He couldn't ignore his need any longer. He had to get a taste of her. Setting his lips on hers, gently, Ryder sipped at her sweetness, taking her sigh into his mouth and returning his own.

When she moaned, he pulled her fully into his arms and leaned back, drawing her over top of him. Dimly he heard the thud of the book as it fell to the floor and the flutter of paper as the tablet followed it, but his entire focus remained on the woman in his embrace.

Ryder slid his tongue over her bottom lip, then sucked on it, eliciting another moan from her. He nipped her lightly and then slanted his mouth over hers once more.

Her softness settled over his erection and, when she shimmied against him, he groaned and moved his hands to her hips to hold her in place. God, she felt so good, so right. Forcing himself to slow down, he moved his lips to her jaw, then down her throat to the curve where her neck met her shoulder. Sliding his mouth over her skin, he rested his lips against the pulse pounding there.

*Well*, he thought with self-deprecating humor, *this sort of behavior is certainly what one should expect from a host.* But then the heat and smell of her drew his mind back to more carnal thoughts.

Life thrummed beneath his tongue. Lust roared through him, tightening his body all over, drawing his beast closer to the surface. With a low growl, he twisted, sliding her under him, rocking his erection against the cleft of her body.

"Ryder." Her voice was a rasp in his ear, her hands gripping his shoulders with fierceness.

He took her mouth again, nipping and licking and sucking until she cried out and clasped his head, holding his face to hers. Her tongue twisted around his, surging into his mouth when he retreated. He sucked on it, drawing her deeper, making them both groan.

Her nipples pressed like diamonds against his chest, branding him through their layers of clothing. His entire body was taut, something dark and primal inside him urging him to strip her naked and mount her then and there. Make her his. Savage possessiveness surged through his blood. His hands tightened, holding her still, and he crushed his mouth to hers, needing—demanding—a response.

Taite was springtime in his hands—fresh and light, bringing him such a sense of renewal he felt it deep in his bones. She was everything he wasn't—soft, giving. Not wanting to scare her with his passion, to lose her before they'd even begun, he tempered his response, gentled his touch.

Drawing slowly back, he rested his forehead against hers. "I've wanted to do that from the moment you walked through my front door. What you do to me . . ."

"Is no more than what you do to me." She rolled her forehead back and forth on his, then turned her face to one side. "I can't do this."

"Can't do what?" When she pushed at his shoulders, trying to lever him off her, he settled his weight more completely on top of her. "Can't do what?" he asked again.

She made a vague gesture with her hand, indicating him,

then her. "This." She pushed at him again, frowning when he wouldn't budge. "I've got enough trouble without adding to it."

Somehow, hearing her put his own feelings into words irritated him. "So, you think I'm trouble?"

Giving him a look that suggested he was not only trouble but also a bit on the slow side, she shoved against his chest. This time he moved, sitting in the place where she'd been.

She bent over and retrieved the book and tablet. He heard her deep breath as she sat up, saw the trembling in her hands. Her arousal was a sweet musk in his nostrils, and he started to reach for her.

One slender hand came up, palm outward, warding him off. "Don't." She fisted her hand and let it fall to her thigh. "Just . . . don't. Not now."

Ryder sat back and ran his hand through his hair. She was right. Of course she was right. He had to share what knowledge he could and then send them on their way. No matter how much he wanted to lose himself in her sweet warmth, it wasn't meant to be.

And don't miss Karen Kelley's

MY FAVORITE PHANTOM,

out this month from Brava. . . .

Hell, he knew the real reason he didn't want her in the house: he had a weakness for women. Always had. His siblings had teased him unmercifully, calling him Don Juan—more so now that he was teaching that other class.

Kaci hadn't looked as if she would be that hard to resist, though. Not when she wore baggy clothes and that cap. He snorted. It hadn't been that long since he'd gone on a date. Okay, he was safe. No worries.

"I just wanted to let you know I'll be coming in and out of the house as I bring my equipment in," a voice spoke behind him, softer than before but still with a slight edge.

"Good. The sooner you can rid me of my problem, the better." He set his soda can on the table and stood, turning around to face her.

His mouth dropped open. No, no, no! What happened to the baggy clothes and the baseball cap pulled down low, and she hadn't looked like this and . . . Damn it!

He waved his arm in front of him. "You changed." Where were her other clothes? The ones that made her safe. Hell, the ones that made *him* safe.

She wore short shorts that showed off long, wrap-around-his-waist-and-pull-him-in-closer legs, and a little blue tank top that stretched across her full breasts. And no more base-ball cap. Now her long, beautiful blond hair tumbled over her shoulders.

She glanced down, then shrugged. "I'm cold-natured in the mornings. By afternoon, I get hot. I'll start getting my equipment." She turned and left the patio.

His glanced dropped to her sweet little ass. His mouth started to water.

*By afternoon she got hot?* Was that what she'd said? That was the understatement of the year. He wasn't sure what was going to be worse, the ghost or keeping his hands off the sexy exterminator.

Damn, he hadn't bargained for this. It seemed the hole he was getting precariously closer to falling inside just kept getting deeper and deeper.

Damn, she'd had a really nice twist in her walk, though.

No, he would not seduce Kaci. She was off limits—at least until she got rid of the ghost. But his mouth was already starting to water.

When his cell phone rang, he pulled it out of his pocket and flipped it open. He glanced at the number. His older brother. Great. He frowned. Things just got better and better.

"Hello."

"Hey, Peyton. How's it going? Has your ghost exterminator arrived?"

Peyton heard the unmistakable laughter in his brother's voice. Why had he even told Joe about his ghost? "Yeah, she's here."

"She?" The humor immediately vanished.

"Yeah."

"Get rid of her. You know how you are with women. It'll be the same as the last town."

He shook his head. "The last town, as you like to refer to it, was nothing more than a young woman who was infatuated with her professor. Nothing happened. I only left because I wanted to teach this other class as well as my history class and the dean offered me that opportunity. Have a little faith. Besides, I do have a ghost, and she can get rid of it."

"She stalked you." His sigh came over the phone lines. "A woman to you is like someone on a diet crashing into a candy store. You know you can't change. At least tell me she's ugly."

Okay, he could do that. "She's ugly." He wasn't lying or anything. Just telling Joe what he'd asked to be told. "I can't get rid of her until the ghost is gone."

"Please, just be careful."

"I'm always careful." Joe was acting as though he had a disease or something. Hell, maybe he did, but he really enjoyed a woman's company.

"If you need anything, I'm only a phone call away."

"Yeah, thanks, bro." He closed the phone, then slipped it into his pocket as he walked toward the front door.

Man, he should've told Joe not to tell his other brother or his sister. If they got wind there was a woman living with him, even if it was business, he'd never hear the last of it.

Could he help it if he loved women? It wouldn't matter if Kaci had been old or young. There was just something about women that he loved. All women.

The baggy sweats and cap had made her safer, though. Sort of.

But he would stay on guard around her. Just as soon as he helped her carry in the rest of her things. A slow grin curved his lips. She was damned sexy.

For just a moment, he closed his eyes and lost himself in the fantasy of her body pressed against his. Her naked body. His hands caressing her.

He quickly shook off the image.

Damn it, he was not going to sleep with her.

He wasn't.

Be sure to catch

INSTANT ATTRACTION,

the first in a new series from Jill Shalvis,
coming next month from Brava . . .

She'd been working for Wilder Adventures for a week now, the best week in recent memory. Up until right this second when a shadowy outline of a man appeared in her room. Like the newly brave woman she was, she threw the covers over her head and hoped he hadn't seen her.

"Hey," he said, blowing that hope all to hell.

His voice was low and husky, sounding just as surprised as she, and with a deep breath, she lurched upright to a seated position on the bed and reached out for her handy-dandy baseball bat before remembering she hadn't brought it with her. Instead, her hands connected with her glasses and they went flying.

Which might just have been a blessing in disguise, because now she wouldn't be able to witness her own death.

But then the tall shadow bent and scooped up her glasses and . . .

Handed them to her.

A considerate bad guy?

She jammed the frames on her face and focused in the dim light coming from the living room lamp. He stood at the foot of the bed frowning right back at her, hands on his hips.

Huh.

He didn't look like an ax murderer, which was good, very good, but at over six feet of impressive, rangy, solid-looking muscle, he didn't exactly look like a harmless Tooth Fairy either.

"Why are you in my bed?" he asked warily, as if maybe he'd put her there but couldn't quite remember.

He had a black duffel bag slung over a shoulder. Light brown hair stuck out from the edges of his knit ski cap to curl around his neck. Sharp green eyes were leveled on hers, steady and calm but irritated as he opened his denim jacket.

If he was an ax murderer, he was quite possibly the most attractive one she'd ever seen, which didn't do a thing for her frustration level. She'd been finally sleeping.

*Sleeping!*

He could have no idea what a welcome miracle that had been, dammit.

"Earth to Goldilocks." He waved a gloved hand until she dragged her gaze back up to his face. "Yeah, hi, My bed. Want to tell me why you're in it?"

"Your bed? But I've been sleeping here for a week." Granted, she'd had a hard time of it lately but she definitely would have noticed *him* in bed with her. Just thinking about it now had her glasses fogging up.

"Who told you to sleep here?"

"My boss, Stone Wilder. Well, technically, Annie. She's the chef here and—" She broke off when he reached toward her, clutching the comforter to her chin as if the down feathers could protect her, really wishing for that handy-dandy bat.

But instead of killing her, he hit the switch to the lamp on the nightstand and more fully illuminated the room as he dropped his duffel bag.

While Katie tried to slow her heart rate, he pulled off his

jacket and gloves and tossed them territorially to the chest at the foot of the bed.

His clothes seemed normal enough. Beneath the jacket he wore a fleece-lined sweater opened over a long-sleeved brown Henley, half untucked over faded Levi's. So even good-looking possible ax murderers knew how to layer in the Sierras. His jeans were loose and low on his hips, baggy over unlaced Sorels, the entire ensemble revealing that he was in prime condition.

"My name is Katie Kramer," she told him, hoping he'd return the favor. "Wilder Adventure's new office temp." She paused, but he didn't even attempt to fill the awkward silence. "So that leaves you . . ."

"What happened to Riley?"

"Who?"

"The current office manager."

"I think she's on maternity leave."

"That must be news to his wife."

She met his cool gaze. "Okay, obviously, I'm new. I don't know all the details since I've only been here a week."

"Here, being my cabin, of course."

"Stone told me that the person who used to live here had left."

"Ah." His eyes were the deepest, most solid green she'd ever seen as they regarded her. "I did leave. I also just came back."

She winced, clutching the covers a little tighter to her chest. "So this cabin . . . does it belong to an ax murderer?"

That tugged a rusty-sounding laugh from him. "Haven't sunk that low. Yet." Pulling off his cap, he shoved his fingers through his hair. With those sleepy-lidded eyes, disheveled hair, and at least two days' growth on his jaw, he looked big and bad and edgy—and quite disturbingly sexy with it. "I need sleep," he said, and dropped his long, tough self to the chair by the bed, as if so weary he could no longer stand. He set first one and then the other booted foot on the mattress, grimacing as if he was hurting, though she didn't see any reason for that on his body as he settled back, lightly linking his hands together low on his flat abs. Then he let out a long, shuddering sigh.

She stared at more than six feet of raw power and testosterone in disbelief. "You still haven't said who you are."

"Too Exhausted To Go Away."

She did some more staring at him. Staring and glaring, but he didn't appear to care. "Hello?" she said after a full moment of stunned silence. "You can't just—"

"Can. And am." And with that, he closed his eyes. "Night, Goldilocks."